WHAT WOULD SCOT
WITHOUT DEAR M

The Inspector and Mrs. Jeffries: Whe own office, Mrs. Jeffries must scour scription for murder.

Mrs. Jeffries Dusts for Clues: One case is solved and another is opened when the inspector finds a missing brooch—pinned to a dead woman's gown.

The Ghost and Mrs. Jeffries: When the murder of Mrs. Hodges is foreseen at a spooky séance, Mrs. Jeffries must look into the past for clues.

Mrs. Jeffries Takes Stock: A businessman has been murdered—and the smart money's on Mrs. Jeffries to catch the killer.

Mrs. Jeffries on the Ball: A festive Jubilee celebration turns into a fatal affair—and Mrs. Jeffries must find the guilty party.

Mrs. Jeffries on the Trail: Mrs. Jeffries must sniff out a flower peddler's killer.

Mrs. Jeffries Plays the Cook: Mrs. Jeffries finds herself doing double duty: cooking for the inspector's household and trying to cook a killer's goose.

Mrs. Jeffries and the Missing Alibi: When Inspector Witherspoon is the main suspect in a murder, only Mrs. Jeffries can save him.

Mrs. Jeffries Stands Corrected: When a local publican is murdered and Inspector Witherspoon botches the investigation, trouble starts to brew for Mrs. Jeffries.

Mrs. Jeffries Takes the Stage: After a theater critic is murdered, Mrs. Jeffries uncovers the victim's secret shocking past.

Mrs. Jeffries Questions the Answer: To find the disagreeable Hannah Cameron's killer, Mrs. Jeffries must tread lightly—or it could be a matter of life and death.

Mrs. Jeffries Reveals Her Art: A missing model and a killer have Mrs. Jeffries working double time before someone else becomes the next subject.

Mrs. Jeffries Takes the Cake: A dead body, two dessert plates, and a gun. Mrs. Jeffries will have to do some serious snooping around to dish up more clues.

Mrs. Jeffries Rocks the Boat: A murdered woman had recently traveled by boat from Australia. Now Mrs. Jeffries must solve the case—and it's sink or swim.

Mrs. Jeffries Weeds the Plot: Three attempts have been made on Annabeth Gentry's life. Is it because her bloodhound dug up the body of a murdered thief?

Mrs. Jeffries Pinches the Post: Mrs. Jeffries and her staff must root through the sins of a ruthless man's past to catch his killer.

Mrs. Jeffries Pleads Her Case: The inspector is determined to prove a suicide was murder, and with Mrs. Jeffries on his side, he may well succeed.

Mrs. Jeffries Sweeps the Chimney: A vicar has been found murdered and Inspector Witherspoon's only prayer is to seek the divinations of Mrs. Jeffries.

Mrs. Jeffries Stalks the Hunter: When love turns deadly, who better to get to the heart of the matter than Inspector Witherspoon's indomitable companion, Mrs. Jeffries?

Mrs. Jeffries and the Silent Knight: The yuletide murder of an elderly man is complicated by several suspects—none of whom were in the Christmas spirit.

Mrs. Jeffries Appeals the Verdict: Mrs. Jeffries and her belowstairs cohorts have their work cut out for them if they want to save an innocent man from the gallows.

Mrs. Jeffries and the Best Laid Plans: Everyone banker Lawrence Boyd met became his enemy. It will take Mrs. Jeffries' shrewd eye to find who killed him.

Mrs. Jeffries and the Feast of St. Stephen: 'Tis the season for sleuthing when a wealthy man is murdered and Mrs. Jeffries must solve the case in time for Christmas.

Mrs. Jeffries Holds the Trump: A medical magnate is found floating down the river. Now Mrs. Jeffries will have to dive into the mystery.

Mrs. Jeffries in the Nick of Time: Mrs. Jeffries lends her downstairs common sense to this upstairs murder mystery.

Mrs. Jeffries and the Yuletide Weddings: Wedding bells will make this season all the more jolly. Until one humbug sings a carol of murder.

Mrs. Jeffries Speaks Her Mind: Everyone doubts an eccentric old woman who suspects she's going to be murdered—until the prediction comes true.

Mrs. Jeffries Forges Ahead: A free-spirited bride is poisoned, and it's up to Mrs. Jeffries to discover who wanted to make the modern young woman into a postmortem.

Mrs. Jeffries and the Mistletoe Mix-Up: There's murder going on under the mistletoe as Mrs. Jeffries and Inspector Witherspoon hurry to solve the case.

Mrs. Jeffries Defends Her Own: When an unwelcome visitor from her past needs help, Mrs. Jeffries steps into the fray to stop a terrible miscarriage of justice.

Mrs. Jeffries Turns the Tide: When Mrs. Jeffries doubts a suspect's guilt, she must turn the tide of the investigation to save an innocent man.

Mrs. Jeffries and the Merry Gentlemen: When a successful stockbroker is murdered just days before Christmas, Mrs. Jeffries won't rest until justice is served for the holidays.

Mrs. Jeffries and the One Who Got Away: When a woman is found strangled clutching an old newspaper clipping, only Mrs. Jeffries can get to the bottom of the story.

Mrs. Jeffries Wins the Prize: Inspector Witherspoon and Mrs. Jeffries weed out a killer after a body is found in a gentlewoman's conservatory.

Mrs. Jeffries Rights a Wrong: Mrs. Jeffries and Inspector Witherspoon must determine who had the motive to put a duplicitous businessman in the red.

Mrs. Jeffries and the Three Wise Women: As Christmas approaches, Luty, Ruth, and Mrs. Goodge turn up the heat on a murderer to stop the crime from becoming a cold case.

Berkley Prime Crime titles by Emily Brightwell

THE INSPECTOR AND MRS. JEFFRIES
MRS. JEFFRIES DUSTS FOR CLUES
THE GHOST AND MRS. JEFFRIES
MRS. JEFFRIES TAKES STOCK
MRS. JEFFRIES ON THE BALL
MRS. JEFFRIES ON THE TRAIL
MRS. JEFFRIES PLAYS THE COOK
MRS. JEFFRIES AND THE MISSING ALIBI
MRS. JEFFRIES STANDS CORRECTED
MRS. JEFFRIES TAKES THE STAGE
MRS. JEFFRIES QUESTIONS THE ANSWER
MRS. JEFFRIES REVEALS HER ART
MRS. JEFFRIES TAKES THE CAKE
MRS. JEFFRIES ROCKS THE BOAT
MRS. JEFFRIES WEEDS THE PLOT
MRS. JEFFRIES PINCHES THE POST
MRS. JEFFRIES PLEADS HER CASE
MRS. JEFFRIES SWEEPS THE CHIMNEY
MRS. JEFFRIES STALKS THE HUNTER
MRS. JEFFRIES AND THE SILENT KNIGHT
MRS. JEFFRIES APPEALS THE VERDICT
MRS. JEFFRIES AND THE BEST LAID PLANS
MRS. JEFFRIES AND THE FEAST OF ST. STEPHEN
MRS. JEFFRIES HOLDS THE TRUMP
MRS. JEFFRIES IN THE NICK OF TIME
MRS. JEFFRIES AND THE YULETIDE WEDDINGS
MRS. JEFFRIES SPEAKS HER MIND
MRS. JEFFRIES FORGES AHEAD
MRS. JEFFRIES AND THE MISTLETOE MIX-UP
MRS. JEFFRIES DEFENDS HER OWN
MRS. JEFFRIES TURNS THE TIDE
MRS. JEFFRIES AND THE MERRY GENTLEMEN
MRS. JEFFRIES AND THE ONE WHO GOT AWAY
MRS. JEFFRIES WINS THE PRIZE
MRS. JEFFRIES RIGHTS A WRONG
MRS. JEFFRIES AND THE THREE WISE WOMEN
MRS. JEFFRIES DELIVERS THE GOODS

Anthologies

MRS. JEFFRIES LEARNS THE TRADE
MRS. JEFFRIES TAKES A SECOND LOOK
MRS. JEFFRIES TAKES TEA AT THREE
MRS. JEFFRIES SALLIES FORTH
MRS. JEFFRIES PLEADS THE FIFTH
MRS. JEFFRIES SERVES AT SIX

MRS. JEFFRIES DELIVERS THE GOODS

Emily Brightwell

BERKLEY PRIME CRIME
NEW YORK

BERKLEY PRIME CRIME
Published by Berkley
An imprint of Penguin Random House LLC
1745 Broadway, New York, NY 10019

Library of Congress Cataloging-in-Publication Data

Names: Brightwell, Emily, author.
Title: Mrs. Jeffries delivers the goods / Emily Brightwell.
Description: First edition. | New York, NY : Berkley Prime Crime, an imprint of Penguin Random House LLC, 2019.
Identifiers: LCCN 2018043300 | ISBN 9780451492227 (paperback) | ISBN 9780451492234 (ebook)
Subjects: | BISAC: FICTION / Mystery & Detective / Historical. | FICTION / Mystery & Detective / Women Sleuths. | GSAFD: Mystery fiction.
Classification: LCC PS3552.R46443 M6485 2019 | DDC 813/.54—dc23
LC record available at https://lccn.loc.gov/2018043300

First Edition: March 2019

Printed in the United States of America
1 3 5 7 9 10 8 6 4 2

Cover art by M. Fredrickson
Cover design by Steve Meditz

In memory of my sister,
Linda Ruth Lanham Domholt.
Much loved and much missed.

CHAPTER 1

Despite his gout acting up, Stephen Bremmer was looking forward to tonight's festivities. He had big plans for all of them. It was going to be wonderful, absolutely wonderful. That stupid cow was going to pay for her veiled insults, but before that, he'd have the pleasure of skewering James Pierce and his tarted-up little soiree, the Lighterman's Ball indeed! He snorted as his hansom cab stopped opposite the hotel.

He stepped out, paid the driver, and surveyed his surroundings. Across the busy street, he could see the electric lights of the hotel over the top of an omnibus. Hansoms and carriages discharging passengers wearing traveling clothes and evening dress lined both sides of the street. The omnibus moved on and Bremmer started to cross but he stopped, almost tripping as he spotted a face he'd not seen for eight years.

He narrowed his eyes as he focused on the slim figure but he'd not been mistaken. It was definitely she. The years had been more than kind; she was even more beautiful than he'd remembered. He smiled, enjoying the fact that he could watch her without her knowing. Judging by the sparkling diamond hair pins and the elegant red velvet cloak she wore, she'd obviously done well. She stood back from the entrance and waited as a large mob of people in varying states of evening dress poured into the hotel. Then she entered. Bremmer wasn't about to miss this show, so he hurried across the road and into the hotel lobby.

He followed the crowd into what was the hotel dining room and then eased off to one side so he could see what might happen if she ran into any of their old acquaintances. He saw her hand her cloak to a maid and then she weaved her way through the throng of people, where he lost sight of her. He surveyed the huge room, hoping that the ones who'd be most upset by Elise Newcomb's sudden reappearance would catch a glimpse of her. But he didn't see any of them. Oh well, he told himself, the night was still young and he knew something wonderfully scandalous was going to happen. He'd make sure of it.

He started to the front of the ballroom, his gaze critical and looking for something amiss or out of place. But the hotel had done a proper job. The tables, draped in white linen and topped with pots of greenery, had been pushed toward the walls, creating a dance floor in the center. Along the length of the room stood a buffet table already covered with silverware, plates, serviettes, platters, and metal tray frames. Beneath patterned gold and green wallpaper, the rich, dark wood had been polished to a high gloss, and overhead, a line of crystal chandeliers sparkled with light.

A quartet of musicians dressed in black evening clothes stood tuning their instruments on a raised platform that had been installed at the far end of the room. Two large, oval tables with enormous green and white floral centerpieces were across the aisle from the musicians. He saw her then. She was standing at the table, partially hidden by a centerpiece. He frowned and increased his pace, hoping to see what she was doing, but a waiter loaded down with half a dozen heavy overcoats and shawls stumbled in front of him and he jerked back to keep from being run over. "Watch where you're going," he yelled.

Bremmer pushed past three old women dressed from head to toe in black. "You don't know nuffink about it, 'e's way too old to be carryin' on like that," one of the ladies snapped. He winced at her accent. Ye gods, these people mangled the English language worse than the colonials. Thank goodness, he was at one of the top tables and too far away to smell them. He craned his neck and saw that she'd disappeared. He scanned the crowded room and caught a glimpse of her as she moved past the buffet toward the front of the hotel. Damn, he hoped she wasn't going to leave. That wouldn't be any fun. He'd wanted to have a bit of sport with her, let her know that he remembered the old days. But once again, she'd merged into the crowd.

He reached the spot she'd vacated and bent close to read the place cards. What had she been looking for? Surely she hadn't thought she'd be sitting here? He scanned the names and saw that hers was missing. That didn't surprise him, but he was annoyed to see who was sitting next to him. He didn't want to sit between Louise Mannion and his wife; neither of those two was much fun. Well, he'd see about that. He reached for his place card.

"Excuse me, Mr. Tibbet?" a whiny, nasal female voice said.

He turned and a tall, thin woman in a chambermaid's uniform pointed at him. "Eh, you there, Mr. Tibbet. You'd best get yerself into the office. Mr. Stargill is havin' a fit 'cause you was supposed to be 'ere at half five to check the electrics."

Surprised, he stared at her. "Were you addressing me?"

"You're the only one here, aren't ya? You're Mr. Tibbet, I saw you last week when you was 'ere. Now, get on with you. Mr. Stargill is already in a bad mood and this lot 'ere"—she jerked her chin toward the dining room—"is makin' 'im right nervous. The Wrexleys are goin' to 'ave a fit if this do doesn't go right. Ever since that incident last year, business 'asn't been very good."

"Goodness, Stephen, I wasn't aware you were an expert on electricals." Louise Mannion's blue silk dress rustled as she stepped closer. She was a blue-eyed blonde with a slim figure, porcelain skin, and perfect features. "But I'm not surprised. You seem very well informed on a number of subjects." She cocked her head to one side and gave him a dazzling smile.

"You mean you're not Mr. Tibbet?" The chambermaid squinted, stepped close, and examined his face. "Oh, sorry, my mistake. You've a bit more flesh on you than he does." She turned and hurried off toward the kitchen.

"Just a moment, now . . . ," Bremmer called after her. "How dare you accost me? What is this world coming to when a serving woman can speak to her betters in such a manner? What sort of establishment is this? I'm wearing formal evening clothes, couldn't she see that? Such behavior is totally unacceptable. I shall speak to the manager and get her sacked."

"Get who sacked?" James Pierce, a tall, well-muscled man with curly light brown hair and hazel eyes gave Louise a quick smile.

"No one, James," Louise intervened quickly. "A staff member here mistook Stephen for the fellow in charge of the lighting and he was having a little joke about her. Come on, James, let's take our seats. The toast is due in ten minutes." Laughing, she grabbed his hand and pulled him around the table to their places. "Oh good, Mr. Parr's here on time." She smiled brightly at the middle-aged man who'd taken his seat at the far end of the table. "Let's hope the others are as prompt." She glanced at Bremmer as James pulled out her chair. "Didn't Anne come with you?"

"I came in a hansom, she used the carriage tonight. She promised she'd be here on time. James did make a point today of telling us how important this evening is to Pierce and Son." He yanked out his chair. "There she is."

Bremmer sat down next to Louise and surveyed the crowded room. He almost laughed aloud when he saw her standing just inside the entry. He cast a quick look at Louise. She was talking to Pierce, but he was paying no attention to her. His attention was fixed on Elise Newcomb.

Louise poked his arm. "James, I asked you a question. Have you heard a word I've said?"

"I'm sorry," he muttered as he suddenly pushed back his chair. He banged the table so hard as he leapt up that the centerpiece swayed.

Bremmer snickered as James Pierce charged toward the front of the room, dodging around clusters of young women chatting in the aisle, ignoring the waves and well-wishes of his staff and friends until he'd reached his goal. Pierce, a huge smile on his handsome, arrogant face, grabbed Elise Newcomb's hands in his and pulled her close. Bremmer looked at Louise. But to her credit, the only sign of agitation he could see on her perfect features was a slight narrowing of her eyes. That wouldn't do at all. "Well, well, well, looks like James' first love has decided to return," he said, hoping to goad her into saying something embarrassing.

Anne Bromley Bremmer, a chubby woman with graying blonde hair, deep-set brown eyes, and a sharp nose, took her seat next to her husband. She ignored him; her attention, like everyone else's at both the two tables, was on the front of the room. "Good Lord, I thought she was dead."

Louise mumbled something.

"Sorry, I didn't catch what you said." Bremmer cocked his ear toward her.

"I said he's making a spectacle of himself," she muttered.

"She's got half the men in the room staring at her." Anne smirked at Louise.

"Indeed, my dear. Isn't it convenient that she's back. It's more than a year since James lost his wife. There won't be any gossip if he remarries now."

"He's not interested in her," Louise said softly. "He's just being nice to an old friend."

"An old friend he's bringing up here." Anne shot a malevolent glance at Louise. "I expect one of us will have to move."

"No, no." Bremmer nodded toward the table next to them. "Look, he's sitting her next to his aunt. I must say, she's even more beautiful now than she was eight years ago."

"She's widowed, too." Camilla Houghton-Jones and her fiancé, Montague Pettigrew, had quietly joined them. "We use the same dressmaker. She's been back in London for several weeks now and she's no longer a penniless artist. Apparently, she married when she left here. Her late husband left her very rich." Camilla was a broad-faced, thin-lipped woman in her late twenties and wore her dull brown hair pulled into a bun at the nape of her neck. Montague Pettigrew, a good five years older than his intended, had thinning black hair, a widow's peak, and pale white skin.

James returned and took his seat. "Sorry." He smiled apologetically at the others. "I wanted to make certain Elise was seated comfortably. Now we can get the festivities started. Thank you all for being here on time."

"Of course." Louise nodded at the maître d', who was standing in the aisle leading to the kitchen. He stepped out and banged a gong, the signal for all to be quiet.

James stood up and waited a few moments for everyone's attention. "First of all, I want to thank all of you for coming tonight. My father would have been so pleased as he loved this annual event more than anything. I know it is usually a much smaller affair and I know some of you are missing the Morningtide Arms in Barking, where we had it for so many years, but this year I wanted it to be a genuine celebration of my father's legacy."

He paused as the crowd cheered. "As most of you know, my father started out as an apprentice lighterman and by hard work and a lot of luck he ended up owning the company. But Michael William Pierce never forgot where he came from and he never forgot that it was the hard work and honest labor of his employees which helped make us a success."

"Your father was a good man, treated his people decent," someone shouted.

James grinned. "He was indeed. Most of you know what's coming next, but as we've more guests tonight than we ever had at the

Morningtide Arms, I'll explain our custom. In the past, we toasted with beer or ale, but companies grow and change so this year we're toasting with champagne. The waiters will fill your glasses and then we'll all stand. The lights will go dark for two minutes; one in honor of my father and one to honor all brave men who lost their lives this year on the sea, the river, or the canals. When the lights come back on, we'll raise a glass in their memory."

Again, Louise nodded at the maître d' and a long line of waiters and bellmen carrying champagne bottles trooped out. They fanned out to the tables and began pouring.

Louise smiled at James as they sat down. "You've done your father proud. It was nice of you to be so gracious to Elise Newcomb. I'd not heard she was back in London."

"She's only been back a few weeks." James glanced at the dark-haired woman sitting between two elderly women. "She ran into my aunt Mary yesterday, and you know my aunt—she insisted Elise come tonight."

"Mary's such a thoughtful woman." Louise hated his aunt. The feeling was mutual.

The waiters finished, and as the last one retreated to the kitchen, James got to his feet and motioned for everyone to stand. The electric lights went out, and for thirty seconds there was coughing, chairs scraping, and the muted noise from the kitchen. Then the room fell silent, and as the seconds ticked by, the clip-clop of horses and the jangle from their harnesses could clearly be heard. All of a sudden, one of the light sconces sputtered and sparks flew off in every direction. Someone yelped in surprise, gasps were heard around the room, and people shifted in their seats. The lights came back on.

James was the first to react. "That was unexpected," he exclaimed. "And I'm not sure it was a whole two minutes, but nonetheless, we honored our people. Ladies and gentlemen, raise your glasses and toast to Michael William Pierce, the founder of Pierce and Son and the Lighterman's Ball, and to all those who are no longer here with us. May they rest in peace." James hoisted his champagne flute high and then drank. Everyone else did as well.

Louise motioned to the musicians and they struck up a lively tune. The waiters returned bearing covered silver serving trays and platters of food. They put them on the buffet table and took their serving stations as the maître d's staff began herding the guests to the food, table by table.

Montague started to rise. "Sit down," Camilla ordered. "We don't eat until everyone else is served."

"But that's ridiculous." He pointed to the crowd. "We're far more important than them . . ." He broke off as James fixed him with a hard stare.

"If you're equating human worth with social class," James said, "you're not going to be very useful to me as a director."

"He didn't mean it like that, James," Camilla interjected. "Monty's hungry and he says things he doesn't mean when he hasn't eaten. We're delighted you invited both of us to be on the board."

"And I'm pleased to have you both, I just need to ensure that Montague understands that at Pierce and Son, we value character and hard work, not social class or lineage—" James broke off as Bremmer began to cough and wheeze. "Are you alright?"

Stephen didn't reply. He sucked in huge gulps of air and shoved back hard in his chair. His eyes rolled up in his head and his feet kicked against the floor. Foam poured out of his mouth and his body jerked, his arms flailing up and down against the tabletop with enough force to make the centerpiece sway.

"Dear God, he's having a fit," Anne cried as she leapt up and grabbed his shoulders, trying to hold him down. "Someone do something."

James stood up. "Is there a doctor in the house?" he bellowed. "A doctor, is there a doctor here?" He shoved back his chair, intending to go to the lobby and have them send for a physician, when he saw an auburn-haired man leap up from one of the tables by the front window and race in his direction. Running flat out, the man shoved a young lad and a waiter out of his path.

"I'm a doctor," he shouted. "Help me get him on the ground," he ordered as he shoved Anne Bremmer out of his way. "Put him on his side."

The others at the table had scrambled to their feet, Montague stumbling backward while simultaneously trying to help Camilla out of her chair.

James and the doctor eased a now retching Stephen Bremmer onto the floor. The physician pried open the man's mouth, shoved his fingers inside and checked for obstructions, then loosened his tie and shirt collar and checked his pulse rate. By now, Bremmer's twitching had subsided, his skin had gone a deathly white, and his mouth was agape.

"What's wrong with him?" Louise cried. "Is he having a stroke or a fit?"

The doctor flopped him onto his back, balled his hand into a fist, and banged it hard against Bremmer's chest, once, twice, and three times.

Anne Bremmer screamed. "What's he doing?"

"He's trying to start his heart," James soothed. "I've seen it work on seamen who'd gone in the water."

But it didn't work on Stephen Bremmer. After a fourth unsuccessful try, the doctor shook his head. He bent close and ran his finger around Bremmer's mouth. He examined the matter for a moment before rubbing it gently between his fingers and then looking at it again. Finally, he stood up. "I'm so sorry, but this gentleman is dead."

"Oh my God." Anne Bremmer shook her head, her expression stunned. "This can't be happening. I told him he ought to exercise more. The doctor warned him to be careful of what he ate and drank because of his gout, but he didn't listen. He'd been warned his heart wasn't good as well." She looked at the doctor. "It was his heart, wasn't it?"

"Looked like a stroke to me." Camilla stared at the dead man. "He was twitching like a rabbit in a snare."

"It wasn't a stroke or a heart attack." The doctor looked at James. "Mr. Pierce, as the person in charge of this event, you'd better summon the police. What's more, I'd like everyone at this table to step away. Nothing here should be touched. It's now evidence."

"Of what?" Louise demanded. "This is outrageous. The poor man simply died. It's unfortunate, but hardly a crime."

"Who are you?" James demanded. "Why do we need to call the police?"

"I'm Dr. Bosworth. I'm on the staff of St. Thomas' Hospital, but more important, I'm also a police surgeon for the Metropolitan Police. And the reason you need to call the police is because this man has been poisoned."

* * *

Phyllis, the housemaid for Inspector Gerald Witherspoon, glanced at the window above the sink. "It's getting late, Mrs. Jeffries. Where's the inspector? Shouldn't he be home by now?"

"He said he might be delayed tonight," Mrs. Jeffries, the housekeeper, replied. "He had a court appearance at the Old Bailey today and then there was a meeting at Scotland Yard. But you're right, even with all that, he should have been here by now. It's almost nine o'clock."

Phyllis hung up the dishcloth and dried her hands on a clean tea towel. She was a slender young woman in her early twenties with dark blonde hair, porcelain skin that was the envy of most of her friends, and a sweet-natured disposition that had more than one young man hoping for a bit of her attention. But tonight her sapphire blue eyes were worried. "It's not like him to stay out so late without sending us a message. He's always so considerate. His supper will be ruined."

Mrs. Jeffries shook her head. She was a woman of late middle age with dark brown eyes and once-dark auburn hair that was now more gray than red. There was a sprinkling of freckles over her nose and a ready smile upon her lips. "Don't fret, Phyllis. Mrs. Goodge's stew can stand up to a warming oven and she's made fresh bread and his favorite pudding."

She understood the girl's concern. Gerald Witherspoon had solved more murders than anyone in the history of the Metropolitan Police Force and, of course, one didn't solve so many crimes without making enemies—and not all those enemies were in prison or had faced the hangman's noose. Many of them were walking the streets of London.

The fact that the inspector had substantial help with his cases wasn't common knowledge, even among the criminal classes. It was his name in the newspaper when a killer was brought to justice and his name bandied about on the lips of thieves, felons, and fences. It would be him who would face the consequences of his own success. Not her, not any of the household, even though they, along with some of their friends, were instrumental in bringing murderers to justice.

"But he always sends a message when he's going to be really late," Phyllis persisted. "I know I'm being a nervous Nelly, but I couldn't stand it if something were to happen to him. I've never worked for someone like him before. He's been so good to me."

"He'll be fine, Phyllis." Mrs. Goodge, the cook, came into the kitchen. A fat orange tabby cat followed at her heels. She pushed her wire-rimmed spectacles up her nose as she lowered her stout body onto a chair, moved it out from the table, and patted her lap. "Come on, Samson lovey, you come have a nice cuddle." The cat jumped up and gave the other two women a good glare before making himself comfortable.

"Then why haven't we heard from him?" Phyllis exclaimed. "And Wiggins isn't here tonight so we can't send anyone to the station to see what's what."

"Wiggins will be late tonight as well." Mrs. Jeffries glanced at the carriage clock on the pine sideboard. "But if the inspector isn't home or we haven't received a message by ten o'clock . . ." She broke off as they heard the back door open and footsteps pounding up the corridor.

Breathing heavily, Wiggins, the footman, raced into the room. Fred, the household's black and brown dog, got up from his spot on the rug by the cooker and trotted over to him. "Hey, old boy, we'll have to do walkies later." He petted the dog as he caught his breath.

"What are you doing home so early?" Mrs. Jeffries got up.

"There was a murder." Wiggins gasped. "At the hotel, the Wrexley. A bloke at the top table was poisoned."

"How do they know it was poison?" Mrs. Jeffries asked.

"Dr. Bosworth was there. He tried to save the fellow but he died. He made 'em send for the police. We'd just 'ad the toast when the man started gaspin' and twitchin' and makin' a right spectacle of himself. I slipped up to the front when the doctor went up, and when it was over, I heard him tell them the man 'ad been poisoned and to send for the police."

"Maybe that's where our inspector went," Phyllis said hopefully.

"The Wrexley," Mrs. Goodge muttered. "Wasn't that the same hotel where Thomas Mundy was murdered?"

"That's right," Mrs. Jeffries said.

"Goodness, that's a strange coincidence." The cook stroked Samson's back.

"Yes," Mrs. Jeffries agreed. "Apparently, that's not the only one. Wiggins and Dr. Bosworth were both on the scene, so to speak."

"Funny thing, coincidences, I'da not been there if Tommy hadn't sprained his ankle and he needed someone to escort his sister. She's a typist at the company that was 'aving tonight's do."

"You took Tommy's sister?" Phyllis stared at him in surprise. "You kept that a secret."

Wiggins grinned as he got up. "Well, I was a bit embarrassed to say much. Ellen, that's Tommy's sister, hadn't even made up her mind she was goin' until early this afternoon. She didn't have anyone else to escort 'er and she didn't want to show up on her own since the firm allowed single people to bring a guest. So she asked me. But I've got to get back. I've got to get 'er safe 'ome."

"But what if our inspector sees you?" Phyllis protested.

"That won't matter. Wiggins has a good reason to be there." Mrs. Jeffries turned to the footman. "It'll be faster if you take a hansom and use one to escort the young lady home as well."

She didn't need to tell him what else he should do; that was understood. As well as seeing the young lady safely home, he was also to find out everything he could about the murder. The Wrexley Hotel was in Witherspoon's district, and she was certain the inspector was now on the case.

As Inspector Gerald Witherspoon and Constable Barnes entered the front door of the hotel, William Stargill, the night manager, came out from behind the reception counter and rushed toward them. "This will not do, Inspector. The Wrexleys are going to be furious." Stargill's round, fleshy face was red and perspiration beaded along the top of his dark handlebar mustache.

Witherspoon was a slender man of medium height with a pale, bony face, thinning brown hair, and a mustache. Behind his spectacles, his deep-set blue gray eyes were sympathetic. "I understand, Mr. Stargill. It's a dreadful coincidence that your establishment has had another violent death."

"He's saying it's a murder, Inspector." Stargill's bluster disappeared and he looked like he was going to cry. "There's a police surgeon in there telling all and sundry that we've poisoned one of the party guests. Oh, goodness, this will be our ruin. We'll never recover from a second one."

"Mr. Stargill, please, I know this is upsetting, but if you'll give me some time, I'll speak to you when we've concluded the preliminaries."

His shoulders slumped and he nodded. "I'll be in my office."

Constable Barnes, a tall man with a ruddy complexion and a headful of wavy iron gray hair under his policeman's helmet, said, "Let's see what's what, sir." He led the way across the lobby and into the dining room.

Witherspoon had expected a scene of chaos, but the constables had the room in very good order. The ball guests were sitting at the tables, most of them talking quietly as they ate their meal. The musicians' platform was empty save for their instruments and music stands. Three constables were standing guard near a makeshift barrier composed of tablecloths draped between chairs, which the inspector assumed had been hastily arranged in order to conceal the body.

"Who is in charge?" Witherspoon asked as he and Barnes made their way forward. Constable Griffiths, holding a wooden box, stepped into view. "I took charge, sir," he explained. "The police surgeon for our district is on his way. I've segregated the guests away from those that were sitting at the head table with the victim." He nodded at the box he was holding. "Constable Reid and I have collected all the glassware and such from the table so it can be tested." He handed off the box to one of the constables standing guard. "The deceased is Stephen Bremmer, sir. He's one of the guests."

"Good job, Constable." He knew the young officer was familiar with his methods. "Let's see what we've got here." He and Barnes went around the barrier. The table still had the name cards, the tablecloth, and the floral centerpiece—everything else had been taken into evidence. He noticed the name cards were all on one side, facing out toward the room.

The body of the man was on the floor. Dr. Bosworth was kneeling beside it, his attention fixed on the florid face of the deceased.

"Dr. Bosworth. So you're the one who reckons this poor soul has been murdered." Witherspoon kept his voice low.

Bosworth stood up. "Unfortunately, yes. I did my best to save him, but it was impossible. At first I thought he might have had an epileptic seizure or possibly a heart attack. But when I had a close look at the mucus and the foodstuffs he had disgorged, I noticed white granules were present."

"And that led you to conclude he'd been poisoned?" Witherspoon clarified.

"Yes, Inspector, I'm certain those granules are arsenic."

"We'll soon know. I'd better have a look at the deceased." Witherspoon steeled himself; despite his many homicide investigations, he was very squeamish about corpses. But he knew his duty, so he knelt down beside the dead man.

Barnes spared his inspector a sympathetic glance before moving around to the spot Bosworth had just vacated and gingerly lowering himself onto his knees. "Have the constables searched his pockets?"

"No, sir," Constable Griffiths said. "Not yet."

Barnes nodded and opened the gaping dinner jacket so he could put his fingers into the inside breast pocket. "Nothing here, sir." He checked the trouser pockets and pulled out a silver cigar case, a gentleman's purse, and two half-crowns. He stood up and gave them to Griffiths.

Witherspoon looked at Bosworth. "How do you think the poison might have been administered?"

"Tests will need to be done before we can say for certain, but it was probably in the champagne flute. Arsenic won't dissolve in a cold liquid and the champagne was the only thing that had been served."

"What specifically happened here?" Witherspoon rose to his feet.

"James Pierce—he's the host for tonight—rose to give the toast. The lights went out, and then when they came back on, everyone drank their champagne and the poor fellow went into spasms. Mr. Pierce yelled for a doctor and I rushed up." Bosworth shook his head. "But it was already too late and there was nothing I could do."

"The lights went out?"

"It's our custom, Inspector." James Pierce stepped around the barrier. He winced as his gaze flicked to the body and then back to Witherspoon. "We do it every year at our annual party. We go into darkness to honor the lightermen and dockworkers who have lost their lives this past year. My father started the custom, and not only have I kept it up, but I've included additional time in order to honor my late father."

"May I have your name, sir?" Witherspoon asked.

"James Pierce. I'm the owner of Pierce and Son and the host for tonight. Inspector, I'll be happy to cooperate in any way I can, but can my guests be allowed to leave?"

"We've a few questions we must ask." Witherspoon could easily see over the makeshift barrier. There was a huge number of people out there and it would require dozens of constables to take each and every statement. "This could well be a murder investigation."

"I understand that, Inspector, but most of these people didn't even know Mr. Bremmer," Pierce argued. "And most of them have to work tomorrow."

The inspector considered his request. "I suppose we could take down their names and addresses as long as either you or someone from your company can verify no one is giving us false information."

"Offhand, there are very few here tonight I don't know." Pierce surveyed the room and then pointed to a table. "Wait, I tell a lie. There's a fellow with our typist that I've never met but I expect he's her guest."

Witherspoon looked at the sea of faces and blinked in surprise. "Goodness gracious, that's Wiggins."

The footman had by now realized he'd been spotted so he stood up, waved, and hurried toward the inspector.

"You know the young man?" Pierce stared at him curiously.

"Indeed I do. He works in my household." The inspector smiled as Wiggins approached. "Goodness, Wiggins, what are you doing here?"

Wiggins stayed on his side of the tablecloth. "My friend Tommy sprained his ankle so he sent me a message askin' me to escort his sister to this 'ere party tonight."

"So you saw what happened?" Barnes interjected quickly. The constable knew that the footman could and would be a valuable asset in the investigation. He was one of the few people who understood how much help Gerald Witherspoon received when he was investigating a murder.

"I did and it were right sad," Wiggins said. "Do you want me to make a statement now?"

"No, we'll do that later," Witherspoon replied. "Right now, we just need to get everyone's name and address so these people can go home." He turned to Pierce. "Can you have your office staff assist the constable in verifying names and addresses?"

"Of course, I'll see to it immediately," he said as he headed for the guest tables.

"I'll get the constables onto the task." Barnes circled around the table. "Wiggins, walk with me. I'd like to hear what you've seen tonight." In truth, he wanted a quick word out of earshot of the inspector. As soon as they were a few feet away, he whispered, "Have you found out anything?"

"Picked up some gossip, but the main thing I want to tell you is that no one here could have killed the bloke. The lights weren't out long enough for anyone to have gotten out of their seats, made it up to where he was, and then put some poison in the fellow's glass. What's more, when it went dark, it was like we were all blinded."

They dodged around an elderly woman who was on her way to the buffet table for seconds.

"So what are you sayin'?"

"I'm sayin' unless someone could fly, the only ones you should be lookin' at are the people at the 'ead table," Wiggins replied. "The only other ones that coulda got there might be from the table next to where the victim was sittin', but even that woulda been 'ard."

"But not impossible?"

"Not impossible." Wiggins shrugged. "But he or she would 'ave to be ruddy fast on their feet."

* * *

Behind the barrier, Constable Griffiths put the contents from Bremmer's pockets into another evidence box and glanced up. "Inspector, Dr. Beacham, the police surgeon, is here, sir."

"Good, I'll get out of his way. Where are the guests that were sitting at the table with Mr. Bremmer?"

"I sent them into the lobby, sir. I hope that's alright, sir."

"It's fine, Constable. As soon as Constable Barnes and Mr. Pierce return, send them into the lobby as well." He looked at Bosworth. "Is there anything else you can tell me? Anything untoward you noticed?"

Bosworth shook his head. "Not really. I was too far away. My table is right at the back. I didn't even notice that the man was in distress until Mr. Pierce called for a doctor. I'm sorry not to be more helpful."

"Are you acquainted with the host?" Witherspoon asked.

Bosworth grinned. "You mean what am I doing here? I'm here as a favor to my aunt Nellie. She's a widow and she needed an escort. She and her late husband own a chandlery shop and they've supplied Pierce and Son for years."

"So you'd never met the victim?"

"Never seen him before tonight," he said.

Witherspoon nodded and said a quick hello to Dr. Beacham before going to the lobby. There was a clerk on duty at reception and the door to the manager's office was wide open. Hotel guests had politely but firmly been asked to go to their rooms.

The lobby had been spruced up a bit since Witherspoon's last visit. The settees and armchairs were now upholstered in blue and pale green stripes, the old, worn carpet had been replaced by bright red and green patterned rugs, and the huge potted ferns were now in shiny brass urns.

Five people stared at him as he approached.

"Where's Mr. Pierce?" A lovely blonde woman stood up. "Why isn't he here? Are we expected to sit here all night? What's happening? Why did that doctor fellow say that Stephen had been poisoned?"

"I'm sorry to keep you, but there is evidence that a murder has been committed," Witherspoon said. "I'm Inspector Gerald Witherspoon and I'll be conducting the investigation."

"Good, you've an excellent reputation, Inspector," James Pierce said as he joined them. "I'm sure you've many questions for us, but that lady there"—he pointed to the woman crying softly into her handkerchief—"is Mr. Bremmer's widow. This must be very distressful for her."

Witherspoon hesitated. He'd have liked to interview everyone who was at the table, but they'd already had plenty of time to share information with one another so trying to separate them would be pointless. Perhaps it would be better to take statements from them tomorrow, when they were alone in their homes. Tonight he might gain more information from the hotel staff and James Pierce. "I'm sure it is difficult for the lady and she has our condolences. I'll have my constable take down everyone's address and we'll take formal statements from everyone tomorrow."

"Thank you, Inspector," Pierce said.

"If you wouldn't mind staying, I do have a number of questions for you." Witherspoon nodded to Barnes, who'd been standing behind Pierce and had heard everything.

The constable whipped out his little brown notebook and moved toward the weeping widow.

"I can stay as long as you need, Inspector." He sat down in an armchair.

It took less than ten minutes before the lobby was clear. Witherspoon and Barnes took a seat across from James Pierce. "Mr. Pierce, what relationship did you have with Mr. Bremmer?"

"Stephen Bremmer is, or was, to be on our board of directors. I've known him for a number of years."

Witherspoon noticed that Pierce hadn't called him a "friend." "In what capacity?"

"I own Pierce and Son. I inherited it from my father. He was a lighterman and worked his way up from being an apprentice on a barge to owning half a dozen of them. One of the reasons we've been successful is because years ago, my father got the contract to ferry cargoes from the Bremmer family's ships to the wharves. I felt somewhat obligated to offer Mr. Bremmer a seat on my board."

"Mr. Bremmer's family owns ships?" Barnes asked.

"Not anymore. The family had a series of misfortunes and lost their vessels, but by that time my father had expanded and we didn't just ferry cargoes off the big ships onto the wharves. We haul coal, oil, wool, anything that can be loaded onto a barge. We've recently raised additional capital to expand further."

"So except for his being on your board, you didn't have a business relationship with him?" Witherspoon wanted to be sure he understood.

Pierce smiled slightly. "I'd like to say it was more of a social relationship, but that's not quite true, either. Stephen was a dreadful snob, and though we have a number of friends and acquaintances in common, I'm a working-class lad who he'd never consider his equal. Mind you, I never considered him my equal, either."

"You thought him better than yourself?"

Pierce laughed. "No, sir, I thought him far less than me."

"You didn't like him, sir?" Barnes looked up from his notebook.

"Of course not. Stephen wasn't a likeable man. I only invited him tonight because he's on my board. Despite his upper-class roots and Oxford education, Stephen was practically illiterate. He could barely read a newspaper, married his wife because he needed her money, and generally took no interest in anything other than himself."

"Then why did you want him to be on your board of directors?" Witherspoon asked.

"Simple, Inspector. I asked him because my father made me promise to help out the Bremmers should they ever need it. My father was a wonderful man and he believed in paying one's debts. He always felt that he'd never have been successful if Stephen's grandfather hadn't given him that first contract. It laid the groundwork for everything that came later."

"I noticed there were only place settings on one side of the head table," Barnes said. "Why was that?"

"I wanted to be with my employees. I wouldn't have even had a head table, but Louise Mannion—she helped me make all these arrangements—insisted it was the proper thing to do. But I was adamant that none of us should have our backs to our guests."

"Who was sitting next to Mr. Bremmer?" Witherspoon asked.

Pierce thought for a moment. "I was in the middle, Louise was to my right, and Stephen was next to her."

"Where were the others sitting?"

"Anne Bremmer was on his other side. Camilla and Montague were on the other side of Anne, and Nicholas Parr was on my side of the table at the very end."

Barnes said, "Why did you insist the lights go out?"

"As I said earlier, it's our custom. We have this function every year. Mind you, this is the first time we've included so many guests. But we do it to honor those who died the past year."

"How long were the lights to be out?"

"It was supposed to be dark for a full two minutes, but there was a problem with the electricity and they came back on within"—he frowned—"I'd say a minute, perhaps a minute and a half."

"I see," Witherspoon said. "Do you know of anyone who might have wanted Stephen Bremmer dead?"

Pierce stared at him for a long moment. "Quite a few, Inspector. Stephen Bremmer was only good at one thing: making enemies."

CHAPTER 2

Wiggins wished he could put Ellen into a hansom cab and be done with it, but he was too much of a gentleman for that. He struggled to keep a smile on his face as he ushered Ellen to the cloakroom for her wrap. It was downright aggravating that he couldn't stay here and start asking questions; he'd overheard snippets from at least two conversations that sounded as if they might know something about the guests at the head table. "I'm sorry the evenin' turned out like this. But now that they're lettin' us go, we'll find a hansom and I'll see ya 'ome."

"Don't be sorry, Wiggins. This is the most exciting evening I've ever had." She laughed and patted his arm as he held her mantle. Ellen Duncan was a tall woman with brown hair, a long, narrow face, deep-set gray green eyes, and slightly buck teeth. She had dressed for the evening in her best maroon skirt, a cream-colored blouse with puffy sleeves and lace around the square-necked bodice, and a matching hat and veil. Wiggins slipped the heavy garment over her shoulders, took her elbow, and led her out into the street.

Many of the guests from the ball still milled about in front of the entrance, women swathed in heavy coats and scarves against the cold and workingmen wearing awkward-fitting dark suits deemed suitable for the evening's festivities.

"We don't have to take a hansom." Ellen grabbed his arm as they weaved through the crowd. "Mr. Pierce has arranged for omnibuses to take us back to the East End. There are four of them and they're the big ones as well. There's one for Barking and two for the Commercial Road and another for Dagenham."

Wiggins considered her suggestion. He wanted to learn as much as possible. If they took the omnibus, he might overhear something useful, but on the other hand, Ellen worked in the office of Pierce and Son, so she might know a good deal about the guests sitting with the victim. "No, I've got plenty of coin. We'll take a hansom. Tommy would want me to make sure you got home quickly after something as wicked as this."

"That's fine, then." She broke off and waved at a couple. "That's Margaret Chastain. She thinks she's so special because she and Ned had a right posh wedding last month. Ned handles the accounts in the office. I don't know why he married her; she's not much to look at and she can't do anything except scrub floors and peel potatoes. Mind you, her parents own the bake shop on the Barking High Street."

"Not everyone can be as clever as you." Wiggins knew a bit of flattery went a long way. "Sorry, don't mean to act forward, but you can work a typewriter and you've got a proper job."

"Oh, I'm not all that clever." She giggled. "And you're not being forward. My brother wouldn't have let you escort me tonight unless he knew you were a gentleman. Tommy's nose is going to be out of joint when he finds out what he missed. I mean, how often do you see someone being murdered right before your eyes? Whoever heard of such a thing?"

Wiggins relaxed. He'd made the right choice. Ellen had been on her best behavior earlier, but the strange turn of events seemed to have loosened her tongue. He hoped she'd keep it loose until he walked her to her door. "Did you know the gentleman that was killed?"

"He's not a gentleman." She snorted as they turned the corner. "He might be an upper-class toff, but he's a nasty pig. Oh no, I shouldn't have said that—you're going to think I'm a terrible person for sayin' such things about the dead."

Blast, he didn't want her going quiet now, not when he had her talking. "Don't be silly. Just because someone died, it doesn't mean you can't tell the truth about what they were like when they was alive. And what you was sayin' was right interestin'."

"Alright, then, but I don't want you thinkin' ill of me."

"I'd not think that," he assured her.

"Mr. Bremmer used to come to the office sometimes to see Mr. Pierce—now there's a right gentleman if ever I saw one and he's ever so nice. He never yells at the staff and always remembers everyone's name."

"Yeah, he seems like a nice fellow. Go on, then, what about Bremmer?"

She snorted again. "He's one of them men that thinks he's got a right to do what he likes with us and we're to just put up with it. Genelda, she comes in once a month to help me get the invoices done, twice he's cornered her in the cloakroom and put his hands where they don't belong. First time it happened, poor Genelda just stood there. She was shocked but scared if she said anything, she'd get sacked. She told me what he'd done and I marched right in and told Mr. Pierce. The second time it happened, Genelda slapped him away and run into Mr. Pierce's office. Mr. Pierce told him in no uncertain terms he was to leave the office girls alone. Usually, there's only me and Mrs. Taft—she does the correspondence typing and she's fifty if she's a day—but we've a right to work in peace. 'Course in a big company, we'd be safer. The large firms don't allow the men and the women to work in the same work area, so then Mr. Bremmer wouldn't have had a chance to bother us. But Mr. Pierce is a modern man and says that if we can share the same streets we ought to be able to share the same workplace. Besides, his own mother ran the office for years when they was building up the business, and from what I've heard, she'd have boxed Mr. Bremmer's ears right and proper."

Wiggins didn't think Genelda had much of a motive for murder, but it didn't hurt to find out as much as he could. "Was she there tonight?"

"No, she couldn't come."

"What did Mr. Bremmer say when Mr. Pierce told 'im off? Did he lose 'is temper and cause a fuss?"

"Of course not, he might think he's better than the likes of us, but he'd not want to make Mr. Pierce angry. He tried to make light of it. He laughed and said women shouldn't be working in the first place, that they should stay home." She stepped off the pavement as they came to the hansoms lined up by the cab shelter. "Bremmer was a fool. Does he think we're spending all our time poundin' them keys because we like it? We do it for the same reason everyone works; we need our wages. Tommy brings in decent enough, but there's seven of us in the house and every penny counts."

Wiggins guided her to the first hansom in the line, gave the driver the address, and then helped her inside. He climbed in and closed the door. "Why was he hangin' about your office? Did he have some sort of position there?"

"No, but he's known Mr. Pierce for a long time. He didn't start comin' around all that much until he found out the company was takin' in a limited number of investors."

"He was going to invest."

She shrugged. "I don't know about that, but I know he wanted to be on the board of directors. I overheard him talkin' to Mrs. Mannion about it the day after Mr. Pierce had me type up them letters. I remember it because Mrs. Taft had been home with a bad cold for days and I'd been stuck doing all the correspondence as well as my own work. Mr. Bremmer and Mrs. Mannion came into the office but they had to wait because Mr. Pierce was meetin' with half a dozen people in the conference room. They wanted to wait in Mr. Pierce's office, but Phillip, he's Mr. Pierce's secretary, said they couldn't because there was confidential papers on the desk and he didn't want to interrupt Mr. Pierce's meetin' to see if it would be alright to let them into the office. Mr. Bremmer got angry and started to make a fuss, but Mrs. Mannion shushed him and pulled him over to the little waiting area the other side of the freight cashier." She paused and sucked in a deep breath. "But Mr. Bingham, he's the freight cashier, was in the meeting. Mrs. Taft's desk, where I was sitting, is right behind the counter and I overheard Mrs.

Mannion tell him that if he wanted to be on the board with her and the others, he'd better learn to watch his tongue with the staff. James, that's what she called him, wouldn't tolerate him bullying the office help." She snorted for a third time. "That's what she called us."

Wiggins braced his feet against the floor as the cab swung around a corner. "How long ago was this?"

She thought for a moment. "Mr. Pierce wanted the final list of the board of directors confirmed before January fifteenth, so I think it was the first week of the new year. That's right, that's when Mrs. Taft was out and I was doin' her work and mine. Believe me, typing confirmation letters is a lot harder than doin' the invoices."

"Confirmation letters?" Wiggins repeated.

"Of course, the letters confirmed they'd agreed to be on the board and that there was an allowance of fifty pounds a year for each of them for their time and trouble."

"Do you remember who was asked to be on the board?" Wiggins knew nothing about the upper management of the business world, but he did know that events and actions that happened within a few weeks of a murder often had a bearing on the crime.

She grabbed the handhold as the cab gathered speed and started to sway. "Let me see, there was Mr. Pettigrew and Miss Houghton-Jones, Mrs. Mannion, and oh yes, Mr. Parr. Then, two days later, Mr. Bremmer was added."

"There were women on the board?" Wiggins pretended to be shocked, but in truth, from what he'd seen of females the past few years, he was of the opinion that most companies would be better run with women.

"Like I told you"—she grabbed his arm as the cab lurched

forward—"Mr. Pierce is a modern man. He's well educated and he even studied in America. I once overheard him telling Mrs. Taft that in San Francisco, they had women working in banks and running all sorts of concerns. Can you imagine that? Female bank clerks? Whatever will they think of next?"

William Stargill slumped in his chair. He'd taken off his coat, loosened his tie, and had an open bottle of whiskey on his desk. He held a half-filled glass in his hand. "Please tell me that the gentleman's death was an accident."

"For both our sakes, I wish I could, Mr. Stargill, but I'm afraid that both of the doctors who examined Mr. Bremmer agree that it's most probably a murder."

An expression of hope flashed across his face. "Most probably?"

"We won't know for certain until the official postmortem is completed," the inspector said.

"Oh, Lord." Stargill took a quick, huge gulp. "The Wrexleys are going to have a fit. They've spent hundreds of pounds upgrading the hotel, adding better electrics, redoing all the carpets, new upholstery in the lobby, and they were going to put in a lift this summer. Now that it's happened again, I suppose we'll be lucky to keep the doors open." He drained his glass and then poured another one. "Oh, sorry, Inspector, would you or the constable care for a drink?"

"Thank you, no, we're on duty," Witherspoon replied. "Mr. Stargill, I understand this is difficult, but I've some questions." He hoped the fellow wasn't too drunk to answer properly.

"Of course." Stargill gave him a drunken grin. "Ask away."

Witherspoon decided to continue. If the fellow's answers were obviously ridiculous, they could come back tomorrow and go through it again. "Did anyone go in or out through the kitchen either prior to or right after the electric lighting went out?" He thought it prudent to make sure the killer wasn't someone from the outside.

"No, the electricity went off in the kitchen as well, but as we knew it was scheduled, several gas lamps had been lighted. Kitchens by their very nature can be dangerous and I didn't want one of the under chefs chopping off a finger in the dark."

"You've asked the staff?" Barnes clarified.

"I've been through this before, Constable." He smiled cynically. "As soon as I heard the police had been sent for, I went to the kitchen myself. Everyone agreed that no one, not even the staff, moved about during the darkening. What's more, once the ball started, the double doors to the dining room were closed and the desk clerk assured me that no one went inside the room."

"When was this event planned?" Witherspoon asked.

"Mr. Pierce got in touch with me last month." Stargill reached for a stack of letters, thumbed through them, and pulled one out. He handed it to the inspector. "As you can see, he wrote to us on January seventeenth. He said he'd seen our ad in the newspaper offering our premises to be let for private meetings, parties, and other festivities."

Witherspoon nodded as he scanned the neatly typed page. "It's odd, isn't it, to have an outside function here at a hotel?"

Stargill shook his head. "Business has been off since that dreadful Mundy incident, and frankly, with all the money the Wrexleys have spent, they wanted to see a bit of return on their investment. It was their idea to let the premises for private functions. Apparently they got the notion when they were in New York. I checked the advance reservations and saw that we weren't particularly full for the night he wanted to use the dining room and our catering service. I wrote back saying we'd be pleased to host him. Mr. Pierce came by the following day. Mr. Cutler, our day manager, gave him a tour of our facilities and he made the booking immediately. Which reminds me, Inspector, the items you took into evidence, we'll get them back I presume? The champagne flutes are quite expensive and the cutlery is of the finest commercial quality."

"We'll get them back to you as soon as we ascertain what object contained the poison. That specific piece will have to be kept in evidence until a trial is over."

"I doubt our flatware is at fault," Stargill muttered. "Seems to me it would be hard to put poison on a knife."

"You're probably correct, sir, nonetheless, everything will need to be tested," Witherspoon said. Dr. Bosworth had told the police surgeon he was of the opinion the poison was in the champagne flute. The police surgeon had agreed. "Can you tell me, sir, exactly how long were the lights out?"

"The room was supposed to be dark for a full two minutes, but there was some sort of problem and Mr. Tibbet from the electrical company hadn't shown up, so when the sparks started flying in the dining room, I flipped the switch back on."

Barnes interrupted. "You were handling the electricals?"

He nodded. "That's right, there's a switch box in the passageway between the kitchen and the dining room. When Mr. Tibbet didn't show up, I was afraid something might go wrong so I did it myself. We've had some problems ever since they supposedly improved the system. The room was probably dark for no more than a minute and twenty or perhaps thirty seconds. I knew that Mr. Pierce might be disappointed, but once I saw the sparks flying off the sconce, I couldn't risk anything happening to the property."

"How many people knew about this?" Barnes asked

Stargill looked confused by the question. "Knew what?"

"About the lights going out," Witherspoon interjected.

"Mr. Pierce explained that going dark was their company custom, Inspector, so I assume everyone in the room knew about it beforehand."

"Yes, of course." Witherspoon nodded. "But how many people here at the hotel would have known?"

Stargill's jaw dropped. "Are you suggesting that one of our staff members had something to do with that man's death? That's absurd. None of the waiters or kitchen staff even knew Mr. Bremmer. I believe that's the dead man's name."

"You can't know that, sir," Barnes chided. "Have you added any new staff since Mr. Pierce booked your premises?"

"No, the Wrexleys will spend their money to tart the place up but they're far too cheap to let me employ additional staff. Having enough people on hand to service tonight's function was difficult enough—I had to press three chambermaids into service in the kitchen and two more to handle the cloak room. I tell you, this whole business has been nothing but a dreadful nightmare. It's even worse than the other time. God knows what the Wrexleys will say once they find out it's happened again." He closed his eyes and drained his glass. "I've sent them a telegram, and I expect by tomorrow, the situation here will be hideous, to say the least."

* * *

The moment he walked through the front door, Mrs. Jeffries could see the inspector was exhausted. "Oh, sir, you do look tired. Are you hungry or do you want to go right up to bed?" She glanced at the hall clock and noted it was ten past eleven. Wiggins still wasn't home, and though she trusted in his ability to take care of himself, it was still a worry.

"I'm ravenous, Mrs. Jeffries, so I'll eat and then get right upstairs."

"Go into the dining room, sir, and I'll bring your dinner right up. Mrs. Goodge has made a lovely lamb stew as well as an apple crumble for pudding. Would you like me to bring you a sherry as well?"

He gave her a wan smile. "You just bring me my dinner. I'll get us both a sherry, I've much to tell you."

Mrs. Jeffries had his dinner on the dining room table in less than five minutes. "Now, sir, do have a bite to eat before you say anything."

He shoved a forkful of stew into his mouth while she sipped her sherry. She had one ear cocked toward the back door. If the lad wasn't home soon, Mrs. Goodge was going to have a fit.

After several huge bites, the inspector put his fork down, reached for his sherry, and took a drink. He sighed in pleasure as he put the glass down next to his plate. "I tell you, Mrs. Jeffries, this has been a very tiring day. I was tied up in a trial at the Old Bailey, and when I finally got back to the station, there had been a bit of fisticuffs and the duty officer, Inspector Halloway, had been knocked over and ended up with a broken foot."

"That's dreadful, sir. Will he be alright?"

"Oh yes, he'll be fine but the consequence was that I was there when the call came in that there'd been a murder, and you'll never guess where it was." He took another quick sip.

"Where, sir?"

"The Wrexley Hotel." He speared a piece of lamb and carrot then shoved it into his mouth.

"The Wrexley? Gracious, wasn't that where Thomas Mundy was murdered?"

He nodded. "That's right."

"Who was killed? One of the guests?"

He thought for a moment as he chewed. "Not precisely. Actually, the hotel has had a difficult time recovering from the Mundy murder so they've taken to letting their premises for outside functions. The victim was a guest at an event called the Lighterman's Ball. It's an annual party that a company called Pierce and Son gives to their employees and suppliers. A chap named Stephen Bremmer was poisoned with arsenic. At least that's what Dr. Bosworth and the police surgeon both think."

"Dr. Bosworth?" Mrs. Jeffries realized how annoying it was to pretend ignorance. "What was he doing there?"

"Apparently, he was escorting his widowed aunt to the festivities. She's one of the company's suppliers. What I found strange was young Wiggins being on the scene, so to speak. Is he upstairs?"

"He's not home as yet." She decided to stick to the truth as much as possible. "I believe he was escorting the sister of one of his friends to the event. You know Wiggins, sir, he's very much a gentleman and he's probably late because he's seeing the young lady to her front door."

"Yes, yes, of course. Though I do want to have a word with

him. He's a very intelligent young man and he might have seen or heard something useful. Have him pop into the dining room tomorrow at breakfast."

"Of course, sir. With so many people in attendance, how on earth will you narrow down your suspects?" She cocked her head toward the back of the house as she heard a faint thump and then the barest hint of footsteps. Relieved, she knew that Wiggins had made it safely home and had the good sense to come in quietly.

He took another quick sip of sherry. "We had a bit of luck there." He told her about the lights going out. "So you see, if the timeline for the darkness is correct—and we've no reason to think it isn't—then the killer, if indeed this is a murder, could only have been at the same table as the victim or possibly the table beside it."

"And both the police surgeon and Dr. Bosworth were sure he'd been poisoned with arsenic?" She wondered how Dr. Bosworth could be so certain.

"They can only confirm it once the tests are performed, but they're both experienced doctors, and so until we learn differently, I'm going on the assumption they're correct."

Mrs. Jeffries refilled their glasses as they continued chatting. As Witherspoon ate the remainder of his supper, he told her everything that had happened at the Wrexley. He put the last bite of apple crumble in his mouth, chewed, and then sat back with a happy sigh. "That was a delicious meal."

"Mrs. Goodge will be pleased to hear you enjoyed it, sir, but I expect it was especially good as you were very hungry. What will you do tomorrow, sir?"

"I'll take statements from everyone at the head table and see what we can find." He yawned and got to his feet. "I'll see you in the morning, Mrs. Jeffries."

Downstairs, Fred butted his head against Wiggins. "You need to go walkies, old fellow?"

"He just wants your attention," Phyllis said. "I took him out earlier. He's fine."

Wiggins grinned at her. "That was nice of ya. Truth is, I'm tired. Mind ya, I'm glad I was there tonight, give us a head start on the investigation. I found out some bits and pieces when I was takin' Ellen 'ome."

"Mrs. Jeffries said you're only to rest tonight. You can tell us what's what tomorrow morning," Phyllis instructed. "So you took the young lady home. That was very kind of you."

"I was right tempted to let her go on one of the omnibuses the company provided to get their staff back to the East End, but she works as a typist in the office and I thought she might know something useful. Turns out she did, but I'll wait and tell it tomorrow." He gave Fred one last pet, yawned, and headed for the staircase. "See ya in the mornin'."

"Good night," Phyllis murmured as the dog went back to his spot by the cooker and curled up on his thick rug to sleep.

She stood there for a long moment, wondering what on earth was wrong with her. She wasn't interested in Wiggins. He was just a friend, she'd been very clear about that to everyone in the household. But if that was true, why was she so bothered that he'd been with Tommy's sister tonight?

It didn't make sense, simply didn't make any sense at all.

* * *

As was his custom when they were investigating a homicide, Constable Barnes stopped by the inspector's home so they could plan their day as they walked to the Ladbroke Road station together. As was also his custom, Barnes stopped in the kitchen first to have a chat with Mrs. Jeffries and Mrs. Goodge.

When he'd begun working with the inspector, it had come as a surprise when he realized Witherspoon was getting information about their murder cases from sources other than witnesses, suspects, or even informants. But he was a wily old copper and it hadn't taken long to figure out exactly where all the useful bits and pieces had come from. At first, he'd been annoyed because no one in the Witherspoon household was a properly trained police officer. But he'd soon seen the advantage they had: They could get people who would spit on a policeman's shoe rather than help him to not only answer questions but answer them honestly.

Servants of their suspects, scared of losing their position and the roof over their heads, would often become deaf, dumb, and blind when questioned by a constable but would chat a mile a minute to one of their own. Street lads who spent most of their lives ducking the local coppers could easily be persuaded to tell Wiggins or Smythe what they'd seen or heard. Betsy and Phyllis picked up gossip about victims and suspects from the local high street shop clerks as easily as buying a pound of potatoes. Even Mrs. Goodge contributed and she did her share without leaving the kitchen. She had a vast network of delivery boys, repairmen, and old colleagues that she plied with tea and treats as she discreetly questioned them. Then, of course, there was Mrs. Jeffries. He hated to admit it, but it was God's own truth, when it came to solving murders, that woman had more talent in her little finger than any of the detectives at Scotland Yard. She was blessed with a mind that could take seemingly unrelated facts and put them together so the truth could be found.

On one of their early cases, he'd decided it was foolish not to take advantage of the situation and so he'd boldly gone into the kitchen, plopped himself down at the table, and told the two startled women that sharing might be a very good thing. They'd been wary at first, but had soon learned he could be trusted.

This morning it didn't take long for Barnes to add some additional details to what Mrs. Jeffries had learned from the inspector. "If what we were told last night is actually true, then either the victim committed suicide or the killer was sitting at one of the two tables by the musicians' platform," he stated.

"But Wiggins told you that the room was in darkness for so little time, he's doubtful that anyone from the table next to the victim could have done it?" Mrs. Goodge said. "Isn't that right?"

"That's what he said and he's a sharp one, so he knows what he's on about so he's probably right."

"And everyone was sure that the lights weren't out for the full two minutes?" Mrs. Jeffries clarified. "Time can seem distorted when it's dark."

"Mr. Stargill was sure of it as was James Pierce." The constable drained his cup and stood up. "I'd best get upstairs. We've got to get cracking on this one. I've a feeling there's going to be pressure coming down from on high. My wife told me that Stephen Bremmer is the godson of Sir Elliot White Ridley."

"The cabinet minister?" Mrs. Jeffries exclaimed.

"That's him." Barnes nodded and then disappeared up the stairs.

Five minutes later, they heard the front door close so the two women began setting up for their "morning meeting." Mrs. Jeffries, who hadn't been able to sleep, had gone out before dawn to Betsy and Smythe's flat. She'd slipped a note through their letterbox telling them to be here by nine. She'd sent Wiggins to Knightsbridge with a similar message for Luty Belle Crookshank and her butler, Hatchet.

The clock struck nine just as the back door opened. There was a flurry of footsteps and Betsy, a beautiful blonde matron in her mid-twenties, dashed into the kitchen. Her husband, Smythe, was right behind her. He was a heavily muscled, brown-haired man a good fifteen years older than his wife. Betsy had once been the housemaid but had given that up when she had their daughter, Amanda. Smythe was still supposedly the inspector's coachman, but as Witherspoon rarely used the carriage, he did a number of other tasks around the household.

"Where's my baby?" Mrs. Goodge put the big brown teapot on the table. "Why isn't she with you?" The cook shared godparent duties with Luty Belle Crookshank and the inspector.

"We were going to bring her, but she wanted to play with Maisie, the little girl from across the road." Betsy hated disappointing Mrs. Goodge and she knew that Luty Belle would be upset as well. But Amanda didn't get many opportunities to play with other toddlers and she wanted her daughter to learn how to get along with other children. "I'll bring her for our afternoon meeting."

"But that's when she naps."

"Not anymore," Smythe muttered. "The little one doesn't sleep as much as she used to."

Again, they heard the back door open, and within a few minutes, everyone was present. Lady Ruth Cannonberry, their neighbor from across the communal garden and the inspector's "special" friend, was the last to arrive. A woman of middle age with dark blonde hair interlaced with gray, she was the widow of a peer and the daughter of a country churchman. Ruth sincerely believed in Christ's admonition to love thy neighbor as thy self. She worked tirelessly for the rights of women, the oppressed, and those that couldn't fight for themselves.

Luty Belle Crookshank was an elderly, wealthy, white-haired American. She'd been a witness in Witherspoon's second case. But she was no fool and she'd noticed the inspector's household asking questions in her communal garden and around the neighborhood at large. Soon after that case was solved, she'd come to them with a problem of her own and ever since then had insisted on helping with their work. Luty believed in justice. So did the man sitting next to her, Hatchet, her butler. He was a tall, white-haired man with a past he rarely mentioned and a number of sources he could call upon for information when they were "on the hunt."

"We've much to tell you," Mrs. Jeffries announced as everyone settled down.

"Your note said there was a murder last night at the Wrexley Hotel," Hatchet said. "Isn't that where Thomas Mundy was killed?"

"It was and that's not the only coincidence." Mrs. Jeffries gave them a quick but thorough report on everything they'd learned from the inspector and Constable Barnes before motioning to Wiggins. "Tell us what you found out last night."

"I did what ya told me this morning and I stopped in and spoke to the inspector while he was 'avin' his breakfast." Wiggins put his tea mug down. "So he already knows what I'm goin' to tell ya. When I took Ellen 'ome last night, she gave me an earful." He gave them almost a word-for-word recount of his conversation with the young woman. When he was through, he said, "I think it's a good idea to meet her again after she's finished work today. She might know more."

"But what about the Wrexley Hotel?" Phyllis protested. "You have sources there as well. Remember, those two footmen from the Mundy murder think you're a reporter and they might have seen or heard something useful."

He shook his head. "Nah, Ellen's a better bet. There's been a murder and there'll be lots of tongues waggin' at the office today."

"I agree with Wiggins," Mrs. Jeffries interjected. "And I also think we've no time to waste. Constable Barnes seems to think there's going to be a lot of pressure from the Home Office to get this one solved quickly." She got to her feet and the others followed suit. She didn't need to give them instructions; each and every one of them knew what they needed to do.

The Mannion home was located in the middle of a row of town houses on Barlow Square in Holland Park.

Witherspoon sighed heavily as he waited for Barnes to pay the hansom driver and join him. The flawless white façade of the five-story house reeked of wealth, privilege, and probably arrogance as well. He wasn't a pauper himself, but he'd grown up in modest circumstances, and despite his current financial situation, he still considered himself a working member of the middle class. "Let's see what the lady has to say," he muttered.

"Right, sir." Barnes charged up the short walkway and banged the polished brass knocker. A black-clad butler opened the door. "Yes? What do you want?"

The constable decided to take immediate control of the situation.

"What do we want," he repeated. "We want to speak to your mistress. We're investigating a murder here, not smarming around banging on doors for the fun of it."

The butler's mouth dropped open in shock.

"Surely Mrs. Mannion is expecting us," Witherspoon said quickly. "We made it perfectly clear we'd be here this morning."

The butler clamped his mouth shut and opened the door wider. "Wait here," he snapped as they stepped inside. "I'll tell the mistress you're here."

"I'm glad you set the fellow straight," Witherspoon said as he gazed at his surroundings. "We've already wasted enough time in this investigation. I'm afraid that letting the people at the head table go home last night instead of taking their statements properly might have been a mistake. Goodness, this place is amazing."

The floor was white marble, a lush pale green and gray carpet climbed up the curved staircase, and on the first-floor landing, he could see a set of double French doors topped with a huge fanlight. Against the wall was a trio of green and white Chinese-style porcelain on a rosewood library drum table. Directly opposite was a huge mirror with a carved rosewood frame.

"She's not hurting for money," the constable muttered.

The butler returned. "The mistress will see you now. Follow me." He led them past the staircase and down a long hall, passing two reception rooms and a huge dining room.

"The police are here, ma'am," he announced as they stepped into the drawing room.

The same white, green, and gray colors were evident in the ornate French-empire style furniture. Louise Mannion, dressed from head to toe in black, was seated on a pale green and white striped sofa.

"Good day, Inspector, I hope this won't take too long." She waved them toward two uncomfortable-looking chairs. "Poor Anne is in a state and I'd like to stay with her until her sister arrives."

"We'll be as quick as possible." Witherspoon sat down but waited until Barnes had pulled out his notebook before he spoke.

"Well, get on with it, man," she snapped. "I've not got all day."

"Neither do we, ma'am," the inspector replied. "And as you'll be seeing Mrs. Bremmer today, you might do her a kindness and remind her that we'll be along later today to take her statement."

Louise drew back. "Surely you're not going to speak to her today? She's just lost her husband."

"And she was sitting right next to him when he was poisoned." Barnes looked up from his notebook and gave her a cool, polite smile. "As were you, Mrs. Mannion."

She drew back, her expression outraged. "What are you trying to imply?"

"The constable wasn't implying anything, Mrs. Mannion," Witherspoon said. "He was merely pointing out that both of you were in a position where you might have heard or seen something important."

"I don't think I can be of any help to you. It was dark so I couldn't see anything and the only thing I heard were people coughing and scraping their chairs."

Witherspoon nodded as if he understood, but she, like most witnesses, heard more and even saw more than they knew. "When the lights went out, was everyone still seated at the head table?"

"Yes, we all knew that when the lights came back on, James was going to do the toast."

"And was Mr. Bremmer sitting back in his chair or was he right up against the table edge?" Barnes asked.

Her perfect brows drew together in thought. "I think he'd moved his chair back a bit. He was not a slender man."

"Can you estimate how far back he'd moved?" Witherspoon tried to picture it in his mind. "Was there enough space between him and the table so that someone could have slipped close and tampered with his drink without you or Mrs. Bremmer being aware of their presence?"

"No, there wasn't enough room." She frowned. "But I could be mistaken. A few seconds before the lights came back on, he pushed his chair further back."

"Did you hear anything unusual when he did this?" Barnes asked.

"I don't think so," she replied. "But as I said, for the first few seconds, it was actually quite noisy. Everyone had taken his or her seat but not everyone had settled down. You could hear chairs scraping, glasses clinking together, and someone had dropped a knife or a fork onto the floor. When the room finally went quiet, one could hear the traffic noise from outside. The hotel is close to the train station so there are always carriages and hansoms."

"Do you know of anyone who might have wished to harm Mr. Bremmer?" Witherspoon asked.

"Harm him? Of course not. He was a gentleman, not some street ruffian."

"It's odd you should say that, Mrs. Mannion," the inspector said. "Mr. Pierce said that Mr. Bremmer was good at making enemies and that there were a number of people who disliked him."

Her eyes widened in surprise and she took a breath. "Oh dear,

I suppose that now that James has let the cat out of the bag, I don't need to worry about being disrespectful to the dead. It's true, Stephen wasn't well liked. He could be abrasive and rude. I know that Camilla and her fiancé weren't particularly fond of him."

"Why did Miss Jones dislike him?" Witherspoon pushed his spectacles up his nose.

Louise smiled. "I wouldn't say it was dislike, Inspector. She simply found him to be a boor and said she hoped she and Montague didn't get seated next to him. When I was doing the place cards, I deliberately put the two of them on the other side of Mrs. Bremmer."

"Were he and Mrs. Bremmer happily married?"

Louise said nothing for a moment. "I don't know how to answer that question, Inspector. How can one tell if a marriage is or isn't happy? But as far as I could tell, they seemed most suited for each other."

"Did you see Mr. Bremmer arrive at the hotel?" Barnes asked. "It's important we establish his movements."

"Not really. James, Mr. Pierce, asked me to help plan the ball. He's a widower, you know. So I was checking with the manager to make certain everything was as it should be when Stephen arrived. He was standing near the head table when I first saw him."

"You knew about the darkening of the lights and the proposed toast?"

"Of course, Inspector. This is an annual event for Pierce and Son. In all the previous years, the festivities have taken place at a very large pub in the East End, but because the company has changed and grown so much, James wanted it in a much larger facility."

"I see. How did Mr. Bremmer seem last night?"

"How did he seem?"

"Was he nervous or did he appear upset or frightened?"

"Not in the least. He was a bit annoyed because one of the hotel staff had mistaken him for the man from the electric company, but other than complaining for a few moments, he was perfectly fine. No, that's not quite true, either; I noticed he was limping as he came around to take his seat, so I think his gout must have been bothering him."

"Gout?" Witherspoon repeated. "That's quite painful. I wonder why he didn't stay home."

"I imagine he didn't want to disappoint Mr. Pierce. James was adamant that the members of his board be at the ball."

"What did Mr. Bremmer do for a living?"

"He was a gentleman, Inspector, he lived off his family income."

"How was that income generated?" Witherspoon stared at her quizzically. "Mr. Pierce told us that the Bremmer family once owned Bremmer Shipping, but that's been gone for years."

"The family did lose all their ships, Inspector, but there was some investment income left."

"Are you certain of that, Mrs. Mannion?" Barnes interjected.

She looked momentarily confused. "I can't say that Stephen ever discussed his income specifically, but he certainly implied he wasn't destitute."

"Mrs. Bremmer's family has money, don't they?" Witherspoon asked.

"As far as I know. Again, Inspector, we're not the kind of people that discuss personal finances."

"Pity," Barnes murmured. "This is murder, and money, or the lack thereof, is often at the heart of a motive."

"How long have you known Mr. Bremmer?" the inspector asked.

"All of my life. My family is in the shipping business as well. Perhaps you've heard of us. Lyndhurst Shipping."

"Indeed I have, ma'am." He tried to think of another question, but until they got the police surgeon's report and verified that the death was a deliberate poisoning as well as how the poison had been ingested, he was wary of saying too much. She was, after all, a suspect. He glanced at Barnes, who gave a small shake of his head. He stood up and Barnes slapped his notebook shut and got to his feet as well. "Thank you, Mrs. Mannion. I may have more questions for you at a later time."

"Of course I'll do anything I can to help." She smiled sadly. "Stephen could be rude and obnoxious, but he didn't deserve to die so horribly."

They waited till they were outside the house before either of them spoke. "What did you think of her, sir?" Barnes flicked a quick look up and down the road, hoping to spot a hansom. "I think we'd best head for the high street if we want a cab."

Witherspoon thought for a moment as they began walking. "I'm not sure, Constable. She's certainly a beautiful woman and I imagine she is still somewhat in a state of shock."

"You think so, sir?"

"I do. When we first arrived, she was almost uncooperative. That comment she made that she hoped we wouldn't take too long—it was almost as if she blamed us for her friend's death. I've seen that before in witnesses. The police intrude and all of a sudden the whole nightmare becomes real. But then she seemed to come to her senses. Perhaps she realized we're only doing our job. What was your impression?"

"She wanted to protect Bremmer's reputation. But that's understandable considering her class and the fact that she's known the man all her life," Barnes said. But he wasn't sure he was willing to give Louise Mannion or anyone else who was at that table the benefit of the doubt. In his experience people were often murdered by someone they thought was a friend. "Mind you, sir, according to what Wiggins heard from the young lady he escorted home last night, Stephen Bremmer was heartily disliked by the women at Pierce and Son. But I doubt any of them could have done it. The one he'd molested wasn't there and Ellen was sitting with Wiggins. Where to next, Inspector?"

"Let's go and have a word with Camille Houghton-Jones. She lives in Belgravia. We know that she didn't like the victim. Perhaps she'll have something interesting to tell us."

"Right, sir. When do you think we can get the surgeon's report?" Barnes saw a hansom coming down the road so he stepped to the curb. "It's difficult asking the really useful questions. We need to find out how that bloke was poisoned." He raised his arm and waved until the driver spotted him.

"If we're lucky, it might be at the station when we check back this afternoon. Who did you put in charge of questioning the hotel kitchen staff?"

"Constables Griffiths and Evans, but I don't hold out much hope it was one of them. Unless one of the hotel workers is a lunatic, I don't think any of them would have a reason to kill off one of the guests. It's bad for business."

CHAPTER 3

Phyllis held fast to her shopping basket as she rounded the corner and headed into a strong gust of wind. The cold blasted through her thin jacket and she gasped as she stepped into the entryway of a bank to catch her breath. Today wasn't going well. She'd made a fool of herself at the morning meeting and now she wasn't even sure she was in the right place. Was this the closest shopping street for the Bremmer household? Perhaps there was a smaller high street somewhere in the depths of Belgravia that only the locals used. Drat, she should have asked Wiggins when he walked her to the omnibus stop; he knew this area like the back of his hand. But after raising a fuss about him wanting to question Ellen again, she'd been too embarrassed to say much at all.

There was no point in worrying about it; she was here now and she'd either find out something useful or not. She stuck her head out far enough to survey the street. A greengrocer's, a chemist's, a baker's shop, and an ironmonger's were on one side of the street. A grocer's, a butcher shop, a fishmongery, and a haberdashery were on the opposite.

Stepping out from the shelter of the entryway, she headed for the greengrocer's. The wind had quieted, but it was still miserably cold. Tomorrow I'm wearing my heavy overcoat, she promised herself as she dodged to one side to avoid a trio of matrons walking abreast. Pausing by the entrance, she surveyed the small, open-air shop. Only one customer was inside, and more important, the clerk was a young man. Phyllis stepped inside and, keeping a smile on her lips, walked up to the counter.

"May I help you, miss?" The shop assistant handed change to an elderly gentleman, who counted it carefully and pulled a coin purse out of his pocket.

"Miss?" the clerk prompted.

The other customer put the purse in his pocket, tucked his paper-wrapped vegetables under his arm, and turned to leave.

"Yes, thank you, yes." She stalled for time as she pretended to examine the bins of vegetables. Past investigations had taught her that people talked more freely when it was just the two of them. As soon as they were alone, she turned her attention to the young man.

"I'd like a pound of carrots, please." She widened her smile and he gave her a shy nod as he grabbed a newspaper from the stack by the till and moved to one of the bins farther down the aisle. She waited patiently till he'd weighed the vegetables and wrapped them securely. "Will there be anything else, miss?"

"Actually, I'm hoping you can help me." She dug some coins out as he shoved her order across the counter.

"Of course, miss, if I can."

She handed him the money. "I'm afraid you'll think me a silly person, but my mistress read in the morning paper that one of her acquaintances had passed away. She gave me a condolence card for his household but I've lost the address. I'm sure he lives nearby. His name is Stephen Bremmer. Would you happen to know his address?"

"He's dead?" The clerk's face fell. "He owes us for last month's account. Oh no, this is bad news. It'll take ages to collect now."

"Oh dear, my inquiry seems to have distressed you." She gave him what she hoped was her most sympathetic smile. "Please forgive me. I'm so very sorry." She picked up the paper-wrapped bundle. "I'll ask someone else."

"Not your fault, miss," he said quickly. "I was just shocked, that's all. We've had trouble getting our money the past few months. My guv isn't goin' to like this news."

"But surely his wife will see to it that the household bills are honored," Phyllis said.

"She will, but it might take her a while, dependin' on how angry she was. Accordin' to my auntie Peg—she works there part-time when the old girl will pay for a bit of heavy cleanin'—the Bremmers aren't what you'd call a happy couple. She's the one with the money, and when she gets annoyed at him, she don't pay the household bills. Auntie Peg says she does it deliberately, that she likes embarrassin' him, that she does it every chance she gets."

It was important to keep him talking, so Phyllis leaned toward him in a manner she hoped would flatter him. "Gracious, really? She did that? But if Mrs. Bremmer won't pay the household bills, what do the shopkeepers do? I don't know about such things." She gave him a shy smile. "Most shops can't afford to give their goods to someone who won't pay."

"Don't worry, miss, we get our money," he boasted. "Mind you, sometimes it's not easy and the guv himself has to go 'round to the Bremmer house to have a word with the housekeeper. But we don't get cheated."

She contrived to look confused. "Then why were you so concerned when you found out he was dead?"

He blushed a bit. "The guv said I was to get a raise in me wages next month, but if he can't collect everything that's owed for this month, he might put it off."

"And you're afraid that Mrs. Bremmer will delay paying?"

"She's done that before." He looked glum. "And I was countin' on that increase. It's not much, but every little bit helps. But she'll do what she wants; the rich always does. Just ask Mr. Bruce at the tailor shop. Last week, Mrs. Bremmer refused to pay him and the tailor told Mr. Bremmer he couldn't have his fancy suit until the tailor got his money. Mr. Bremmer stormed off in a rage and my auntie Peg was there when he got home. She says they had a blazing row about it."

Camilla Houghton-Jones lived in a six-story Georgian town house in Mayfair. "The mistress is in here." The housekeeper, clad in a severe black dress that swished noisily, led them into the drawing room.

The two policemen stopped just inside the open double doors. Witherspoon surveyed his surroundings while Barnes pulled out his notebook.

The room was dark and dismal. Walls papered in a dark gold rose above wood paneling so old it looked black, and the scuffed oak floors were covered with a set of faded Oriental rugs, half of which were missing the fringe. Dozens of paintings cluttered the walls and two huge potted ferns in corroded brass stands stood sentry on either side of the mantelpiece, above which was a portrait of the Queen as a young woman. The windows were draped with heavy cream and brown striped curtains and the old-fashioned mahogany carved furniture was upholstered in a dull russet material patterned with some sort of gigantic flower.

A man wearing a navy blue suit and a woman dressed in a high-necked gray blouse and black skirt stared at them from the settee. "I'm Camilla Houghton-Jones, Inspector. I understand you've some questions for us."

"Indeed, I do, ma'am." He nodded toward Barnes. "This is my colleague, Constable Barnes."

Both of them ignored the constable and kept their attention on the inspector. "I'm Montague Pettigrew," the man said. "Miss Houghton-Jones is my fiancée. I knew you'd have questions for me so I thought I'd come along as well; kill two birds with one stone, so to speak."

Witherspoon acknowledged the introduction with a slight inclination of his head. He didn't approve of interviewing those who might be suspects together, but at this point in the investigation, he wasn't sure objecting would do any good. If he felt it necessary, he could always come back at another time. "We generally prefer to take witness statements separately, but as you're already here, for the sake of efficiency, we'll take both your statements."

She gestured to the two chairs on either side of the settee. "You may be seated."

They moved in separate directions. Barnes took the chair on the left and Witherspoon took the opposite one. The constable balanced his notebook on his knee, took out his pencil, and looked expectantly at the inspector.

"Miss Jones," he began.

"Houghton-Jones," she corrected. "My mother was one of the Sussex Houghtons."

"Sorry, Miss Houghton-Jones, you and Mr. Pettigrew were seated at the head table with the victim, Mr. Stephen Bremmer. What time did you arrive at the hotel?"

"We got there just before seven." She smirked. "Normally a ball would never start that early."

Her fiancé snickered. "I would hardly call it a ball. That's a rather silly affectation that James' father adopted years ago."

"Are you referring to your host, James Pierce?" Barnes asked. He knew who they were talking about, but he wanted to rile them a bit to see if he could loosen their tongues.

"Don't be rude, Montague," Camilla chided him. "And yes, he was talking about Mr. Pierce. I do hope that the comments made here will remain confidential. James is very sensitive to any implied criticism of either of his late parents, especially his father."

Barnes wanted to tell them if that was true, they should have kept their sneers a bit more private; instead, he just glanced at the inspector and said, "That's up to the inspector, Miss Houghton-Jones. He determines what information gets shared with the other witnesses."

"Now see here," Pettigrew snapped. "You've no right to speak to us like this. It's a simple enough request."

"Montague, please." Camilla frowned at him before turning to Witherspoon. "Inspector, my fiancé should have chosen his words more carefully. We've no wish to cause James any distress. We're both going to be on the Pierce and Son board of directors and sometimes people can misconstrue a silly remark and blow it completely out of proportion to what the speaker intended."

"I understand, Miss Houghton-Jones." Witherspoon knew exactly what his constable was doing. It was a good technique and it had shown him something very important. They both wanted to be on the board, but they certainly didn't consider James Pierce one of them. "I've no wish to repeat unkind comments unless there is a specific and necessary reason to do so."

"Thank you, Inspector."

"Both of you are going to be on the board?" Barnes queried. "Not just Mr. Pettigrew? Isn't that unusual?"

"It's unusual but not unheard of." She smiled slightly. "Mrs. Mannion is also going to be on the board, as is Anne Bremmer. James is a very modern man. You know, he allows the women typists to work in the same office as the male clerks. I'm not sure I'm all that modern, but I think being on the board of his company is appropriate. The world is changing."

"And sometimes not for the better." Pettigrew patted her hand. "But in this case, it's very much the right thing to do and I'm very grateful to James for including me."

Witherspoon nodded. "When you arrived at the hotel last night, did you see Mr. Bremmer?"

Montague answered. "Yes, he was standing across from the musicians' platform near the head table. He appeared to be speaking to one of the hotel staff."

"Then Mrs. Mannion went over to speak with him," Camilla added.

"Did Mr. Bremmer take his seat then?"

"No, he walked toward the front of the room, but I didn't pay any attention to where he went. We were a bit late, so we gave our coats to one of the hotel staff and took our places. James had been adamant that all the board members be there on time."

Barnes stopped writing and looked up. "Exactly when did Mr. Pierce tell his board he expected them to be there and on time?"

"At the board meeting earlier that afternoon," Camilla replied. "James made it clear that we had specific duties and obligations to the company. One of them was being at the ball and on time for the toast."

"What time did the board meeting end?" Witherspoon asked.

"About half past three." She looked at her fiancé. "That's right, isn't it?"

"It is, dearest. I remember checking my pocket watch as we left. I wanted to make certain I had time enough to pick up my new shirt from the tailor's on Bond Street."

"Were either of you aware that the lights were going to go out?" Witherspoon relaxed back against the chair and then shoved his foot onto the carpet to keep from sliding off the slippery seat.

Camilla nodded. "Everyone was aware of it, Inspector. Not only was it the custom at this affair but Mrs. Mannion had told us about it. She was helping James with the arrangements. He's a widower, you know."

"Had you been to the Lighterman's Ball previously?" Barnes asked.

Both of them gave a negative shake of their heads.

"Please understand, Montague and I lead very quiet lives. Despite the impression we may have given you, we liked and respected

James, but neither of us particularly like that sort of social occasion," Camilla explained. "We only went because James insisted. Previously, the event was a small affair held at some sort of pub in Barking and it was just for the employees. It's only been this year that James opened it up to their suppliers and allowed the employees to bring guests."

The constable nodded, as if he understood their point of view. "Is being on the board a paid position?"

Neither said anything. They just looked at each other with shocked, rather confused expressions.

"It seems a simple enough question." Barnes already knew the answer. "Is Mr. Pierce payin' you?"

"We're not getting paid." Montague sniffed. "But our time is very valuable and there is an honorarium of fifty pounds annually. James insisted on it."

"I understand you weren't overly fond of the deceased." Witherspoon directed the question at both of them. "Why was that?"

Again, both of them looked surprised. It was Camilla who recovered first. "I don't know who has told you such a thing. But it most certainly isn't true."

Montague interrupted her. "You know perfectly well it was Louise who told them. You shouldn't have asked her to seat us as far away from Stephen as possible." He looked at the inspector. "It's true. Neither of us cared for the man but it was worse for my dearest Camilla; she's actually related to that boor."

"Montague, please, do have some respect for the dead," Camilla pleaded.

"Just because he's managed to get himself poisoned is no reason for us to pretend we liked him," Montague shot back. "As for respecting him, on what grounds should he be respected? Can you name one virtue the fellow possessed? Was he kind, was he decent, was he charitable? No; he was none of those things. Just because he's gone I'm not going to pretend he was worthy of being mourned."

Witherspoon cleared his throat. "Could you explain why you disliked Mr. Bremmer?"

"It isn't just us, Inspector." Montague snorted in derision. "I can't think of one single person that actually liked the man, and that includes that poor woman that was married to him. He was rude, mean-spirited, cheap, obnoxious, and constantly lording his 'heritage' over the rest of us."

"The Bremmers came over with the Conqueror," Camilla added. "They were a very wealthy family for many, many generations."

"I thought they owned ships?" Barnes interjected.

"Yes, yes, they did," she hastened to explain. "But at one time they owned more than just a few ships. Over the years they lost most of their landholdings. Stephen's great-grandfather managed to buy a few vessels and he did quite well with them. They'd grown into a large fleet but then Stephen's father took over and, well, by the time Stephen was old enough to take over the firm, it had gone out of business."

"And you're related to the Bremmer family?" Witherspoon said.

"He's a distant cousin," she replied. "But I've known him all my life. We've all known one another for years."

"By 'all,' who do you mean?" the inspector asked.

"Everyone at the head table."

Barnes stopped writing again. "Does that include James Pierce? I got the distinct impression he's not, uh . . . how can I put this . . . one of you?"

"Admittedly, Mr. Pierce has working-class roots, but his family has done exceptionally well in business, which afforded James an excellent education. As I've already told you, we're not dreadful snobs. James is genuinely liked and respected."

"Oh, do tell the truth, Camilla, dearest. That's what you say now but I can recall that when Louise first began inviting the fellow to her dinner parties, you were appalled. The only reason you let James Pierce into our social circle is because Louise Mannion insisted he be included." He broke off with a snicker. "I don't think she'll be too happy this morning, though, not since Elise Newcomb showed up last night."

"Montague, really, watch your tongue," Camilla snapped. "Louise would be very upset if she knew you said such things. It's not decent; Osgood hasn't been dead a year."

"Osgood?" Witherspoon repeated. "Who is that?"

"Osgood Mannion," Camilla replied. "Louise's late husband. He drowned in a boating accident last March."

"And who is Elise Newcomb?" Barnes added.

"She's an artist, Constable, and she used to live next door to the Pierce family, but for the past eight or so years, she's lived in the United States. She and James were once very close."

"And now that she's back in England, it looked to me as if he was doing his best to bring her close again." Montague chuckled. "She might have been gone for years, but I happen to know that she loathed Stephen Bremmer."

"Could you repeat her name, please?" Barnes put down his pencil and stretched his right hand out flat, wiggling his fingers to relax the muscles.

"Elise Newcomb."

"Cory," Camilla corrected. "She's now Elise Cory. She married while she was away and apparently she's come back a rich widow."

Montague looked at her. "How did you find that out?"

"We share the same dressmaker and Madame Verlaine is a dreadful gossip." She smiled. "Of course, her chatter does relieve the tedium of getting one's dresses fitted."

"Do you know why Elise Cory loathed the deceased?" Witherspoon asked.

Montague gave a negative shake of his head. "Afraid not, Constable. You'll have to ask the lady yourself, but mark my words, it was common knowledge eight years ago that she hated him."

"That's one of the worst-lookin' boils I've ever seen." Luty Belle Crookshank clucked her tongue as she examined the ugly growth on Harry Meeker's right hand. She reached into her cloak pocket, yanked out a handful of coins, picked out a shilling, and handed it to the young man standing next to her. "Take this and run down to the butcher shop on the corner. Buy a couple of rashers of bacon and then get back here lickety-split."

Donald Callendar looked uncertainly at the money in her outstretched hand.

"Luty, what on earth are you doing to my clerks?" John Widdowes stood in the door of his office. He watched the group crowding around the elderly American with an amused expression on his broad face.

"I'm trying to help this young feller. So you tell this here one"—she pointed at Donald—"it's okay to go buy that bacon."

John stifled a laugh and then nodded at his clerk. "Go on, do as she says. She might know what she's talking about."

"Might know?" Luty winked at Harry as she moved toward her friend. "I know exactly what I'm doin'. Once I get finished doctorin' this one, he'll be as fit as a fiddle and happier than a hog in a corn patch."

"Bring us tea, Jeremy," John called to his private secretary. The dark-haired lad had been hovering outside John's office so he could see Luty. The staff at Widdowes and Walthrop, Merchant Bankers, loved it when the American came to visit. She livened the place up and the guv was always in a good mood after she'd gone. Luty patted Jeremy on his arm as she passed him and stepped into John's office.

John followed her inside and settled her into the chair across from his desk. "I'm so glad you've come by, Luty. I've some news."

"Good news, I hope." Luty grinned. She'd heard gossip and she hoped what she'd heard was true.

John actually blushed. He was a middle-aged man with a burly build that was muscle and not fat and a head full of honey-colored hair that made him the envy of his friends. Born in the Limehouse Workhouse, his intelligence and hard work had led to his being a founding partner of one of the premier merchant banks in London. Honest, ethical, and decent, he was one of the few bankers in London that Luty trusted wholeheartedly; he didn't let social class determine his opinion of people.

"Most definitely." His cheeks reddened even more. "Actually, I was going to send you a note, but as you're here, I'll tell you."

"Tell me what?" she demanded. "Come on, spill it. I'm an old woman and time's a'wastin'."

"We got married. Chloe and I, we got married in Paris. We've just come back."

Luty laughed in delight, jumped up, clapped her hands together, and then threw her arms around him in a big hug. "You can thank me now." She poked him in the ribs. "I had a hand in you two coming together. You'da not met her if it hadn't been for me cornering the two of you at the Pattisons' ball."

"Thank you, Luty." John laughed and gave her a good squeeze before letting her go. "Chloe is dying to see you so you must come to dinner soon. As a matter of fact, I think I know why you're here, so why don't you come tomorrow night? There might be a bit more news and some very pertinent gossip to be had."

"You're a clever one, aren't you." She gave him another poke in the ribs and then plopped down in her chair.

"I didn't need to be clever to figure out why you've come." He went around his massive desk and took his seat. "Stephen Bremmer's death is all over the newspapers. If you read between the lines, there's substantial speculation that he didn't die of natural causes. Some of the bolder papers hinted he'd been poisoned, but no one has confirmed it."

"And no one will until the police surgeon's report is finished," Luty said. "But we've got it on good authority that it was murder."

"How can you be so sure?"

"Because one of our friends, Dr. Bosworth—he's helped us on a few of the inspector's cases—happened to be there that night, and when Bremmer fell ill, he ran to help him. He saw something that made him insist on callin' in the police. Wiggins—he works for the inspector and does a bit more than that if you take my meanin'—he was there, too."

John's heavy eyebrows rose in surprise. "That's quite a coincidence."

"They do happen." Luty shrugged. "I've got a whole list of 'em rattlin' around somewhere in my head, but as I said, I'm an old lady and time's a'wastin'. Let me tell ya what we know. Bremmer was attendin' the Lighterman's Ball at the Wrexley Hotel and was sittin' at the head table." She told him what they knew thus far, taking care to mention every detail and hoping she'd not overlooked anything. "Accordin' to Wiggins, who is a sharp one, it was probably one of the guests sitting either at the top table or the one next to it that murdered the feller," she finished.

"But you just said James Pierce called for two minutes of darkness. Surely that means anyone could have crept close enough to do it," John said. "Or am I missing something?"

Luty cringed inwardly. Nell's bells, she was getting forgetful. "Sorry, my mistake. I shoulda told ya, it was dark but not for the whole two minutes. Sparks started flyin' off one of the electric lights and the manager turned everything back on. Wiggins is sure the lights weren't out long enough for anyone from the other tables to have snuck up, tampered with the victim's drink, and then made it back to their seat."

"That makes sense," John murmured.

"I've not read the morning papers so I don't know if any of 'em listed the names of the ones sittin' close enough to Bremmer to kill him," she began.

But he held up his hand. "I know who was there. Chloe, who is an early riser, had already read all the papers by the time I joined her for breakfast. And when I say all the newspapers, I mean it literally. She has a real fondness for what some people call the 'gutter' press, and they published the names. She knew one or two of them, so do come to supper tomorrow evening."

"What time?" Luty asked.

"Come at six and we'll eat at seven. Chloe and I don't hold to the ridiculous custom of eating a full meal at half past eight."

"Good, I don't like eatin' late, either. Now, what can you tell me about Stephen Bremmer?"

John had provided important information on several of their past cases. He was discreet and dedicated to the notion that only guilty people should be punished. Growing up poor and friendless, he'd seen firsthand how the rich, the powerful, and the connected got away with the most heinous of crimes.

"Not much, I'm afraid. His family used to be one of the largest landowners in England, but that was generations ago. They ended up owning a shipping company but Reginald Bremmer, Stephen's father, drove that into bankruptcy. I've heard rumors that he's completely broke."

"So what's he livin' on?" Luty asked.

"His wife's money," John replied. "Chloe told me this morning that he only married Anne Bremmer, who is a good ten years his senior, because she was rich."

"How about James Pierce? Know anything about him?"

"Yes, but I can't say a word as he's one of my clients and I won't discuss them . . . No, that's not right; I will tell you that he's honest, decent, and incredibly talented in business."

"Well, hell's bells, John." Luty crossed her arms over her chest and gave him a frown. "That's not tellin' me much."

"I'm telling you all I can about him." He grinned. "You know my rules, Luty, I'll not discuss my clients. That's why I want you to come to dinner tomorrow night. Believe me, by then Chloe will have found out every morsel of gossip there is to be had about the people at Bremmer's table. But I can tell you this much: Chloe dropped a few tidbits about Montague Pettigrew this morning at breakfast."

"What did she say?" Luty demanded.

"Enough to make his ears burn." He broke off as Jeremy entered. The secretary crossed the room and put a loaded tea tray on the side of the desk. "Thank you, Jeremy." He poured their tea and held up a dainty blue and white china cup. "Sugar?"

"Two lumps, please."

He put the sugar in and stirred the tea with a delicate silver spoon. "According to my lovely wife"—he handed Luty her tea—"Montague Pettigrew is the heir to a rather large fortune, a fortune which now belongs to his uncle, Frederick Montague Pettigrew. The gentleman currently provides his nephew a very generous quarterly allowance and that is what he lives on." John picked up his cup and took a sip. "Pettigrew is engaged. He's to be married later this spring. I can't recall his fiancée's name."

"Camilla Houghton-Jones," Luty said quickly, delighted that she'd remembered.

He nodded. "I hope this won't shock you, Luty, but there were rumors that Pettigrew was in love with an actor."

"I notice you didn't say actress," Luty replied. "And I'm not shocked. Live and let live, that's my motto. But even if Pettigrew was in love with someone other than his intended, what of it? It's not like he could marry this actor, and the class he comes from marry for property, not love."

"True, but Pettigrew is desperate for his uncle to remain in the dark about his, er . . . predilections. Old Mr. Pettigrew is very religious and doesn't even approve of drinking. If he found out his nephew and heir was involved with another man, he'd cut him off without a penny."

"Hence, the engagement." Luty shook her head. "That makes sense. But if Chloe has heard the gossip, surely his fiancée has heard it as well, so why'd she say yes?"

John shrugged. "It's possible she doesn't know. Many young women are very sheltered from the true nature of the world."

"And even if she is aware of it," Luty muttered, "a nice fat fortune goes a long way to easing whatever qualms she might have."

John laughed. "Goodness, Luty, you are cynical. Perhaps the young lady is actually in love with Pettigrew."

"If she is and he's in love with someone else, then she's in for a world of hurt," Luty said.

Jeremy stuck his head back into the office. "Excuse me, sir, but Mr. Connolly is here for your meeting."

"I'll be right there," John said.

Luty stood up and put her cup on the tray. "Thanks for takin' time to see me, and you tell that wife of yours I'll be there tomorrow with bells on!"

He walked her to the outer office. "Six o'clock, then."

Jeremy was standing with an elderly white-haired man wearing an old-fashioned black frock coat and holding a top hat. He bowed politely to Luty and then followed the secretary into the office.

"You don't need to see me to the street. You're busy and I've got business with this young feller here." She pointed at Harry. The lad was gaping at an open sheet of brown paper, on top of which were two rashers of raw bacon.

John laughed. "I wish I could stay and watch, but I don't want to keep Mr. Connolly."

Luty waited till John's office door closed behind him and then she marched to Harry's desk. "Hold out that hand," she ordered. She shoved her fingers into her cloak again and yanked out a huge, pristine white handkerchief.

"Is it goin' to hurt?" Harry asked as he extended his arm toward her.

"Nah, you'll feel it a bit later today, but it ain't goin' to hurt ya none." She picked up a slice of bacon, folded it in half, and plopped it directly on top of the boil. Then she grabbed her handkerchief and wound it around his hand, pulling it tight before topping the material into a knot. She wrapped the paper around the unused rasher. "Hang on to this one, and tonight before you go to bed, pull the other one off and put this one on. Now, you leave the bacon on until lunch tomorrow, and when you take it off, the boil will have squirted its pus and you'll be fit as a fiddle. But just in case this don't work, if you ain't better, go to St. Thomas' Hospital tomorrow and see a feller named Dr. Bosworth. He knows what he's about and he'll take good care of that hand."

"But I can't take your handkerchief, ma'am." Despite the lack of lace or embroidery, Harry could see it was an expensive item.

"Don't be silly. It's only a handkerchief, and what's more, it don't even belong to me. Belongs to Hatchet, my butler. I hate them dainty little female hankies. One good blow and they're as useless as tits on a bull."

The moment she entered the Hanover Gallery, Ruth spotted Octavia Wells. The tall red-haired woman was on the far side of the room, standing between two elegantly dressed women and chatting. She was smartly dressed in a gray suit with a matching gray felt hat trimmed with emerald green feathers.

As the treasurer of their women's suffrage society, Octavia knew almost to the penny how much a man or woman in London's high society was worth. She made it her business to know such things. She worked hard to convey the impression she was simply a society matron, obsessed with gossip, clothes, and parties. In reality, she kept her eyes and ears open and her opinions to herself when she was gathering information about which women might or might not be sympathetic to their cause or angry enough at an errant husband to hand over a nice-sized donation.

At the meeting this morning, Luty had volunteered to find out about the financial situations of those sitting at the head table with the victim, but Ruth knew that Octavia could help with that as well. She'd mentioned it to Luty as they'd crossed the communal garden to Luty's carriage, and the elderly American had given her blessing.

Ruth watched her friend for a moment and then opened her catalogue. She didn't want to interrupt so she'd wait till Octavia was free. Besides, it had cost a shilling to get inside so she might as well look at the paintings.

Moving to her left, she stopped in front of the first picture and angled her body so she could keep an eye on Octavia while simultaneously looking at the painting. It was a still life of a vase of wildflowers sitting in a window. She neither liked nor disliked it very much. She moved on to the next one and then the next until she'd seen every single one on this side of the gallery. Finally, the two women moved away from her friend. Ruth waited till they'd gone through the door before she spoke. "I hope you don't mind that I've tracked you down? Please say you've a few moments to spare for me."

Octavia laughed. "Of course I do. How on earth did you know I'd be here?"

"Your housekeeper told me."

She motioned to a bench halfway down the long gallery. "Let's sit, my feet are killing me." She took Ruth by the arm and marched her toward the seat. "I think we're going to get a sizeable donation from one of those ladies." She nodded toward the exit door. "The mother won't give us so much as a ha'penny because she's got ridiculous views about what women should and should not do. But the daughter has money of her own and she is quite sympathetic to our cause. I imagine she'll be very generous. She wants to be an artist. But as you'd expect, Mama won't hear of it. But you didn't track me down for a report on our finances."

"No, I didn't, though I hope they're in excellent shape."

"They are, but we can always use more money. Unfortunately, most of the wealth in this country is controlled by a bunch of reactionary old men who seem to think giving women the right to vote will cause the ruination of the British Empire. Now, what can I do for you?"

"I was hoping you might know something about a man named Stephen Bremmer. He died last night at the Wrexley Hotel and it appears his death might be murder."

"I take it your inspector got the case?"

"He did." Ruth trusted her implicitly. Octavia had provided information about suspects in a number of their other cases. Her knowledge about the finances and the habits of London's monied classes had proved invaluable. Additionally, she was committed to both the rights of women and the rights of the poor. More important, she knew how to be discreet. "We're trying to find out as much as we can about both the victim and the others who were seated at his table."

"It was the Lighterman's Ball, wasn't it?" Octavia asked.

"You've heard of it?"

"Oh yes, it's a ball put on every year by Pierce and Son. Mrs. William Pierce was one of our biggest supporters. She was a busy woman so she rarely came to a meeting, but she sent us a generous donation every quarter. After she and her husband died, the son, James, continued doing so. I do hope he isn't the murderer; I should hate for us to lose that money each quarter. It's a hefty amount."

Ruth tried not to laugh, but couldn't help herself. "Well, then, I hope it's not him as well. He was sitting at the same table as Bremmer, but not right next to him. His wife, Anne Bremmer, was at the table as well." She rattled off the names of the others.

"Let's start with Anne Bremmer," Octavia said. "She's the one with the money and it is completely in her control, not her husband's."

"Really." Ruth's eyes widened. "How on earth did she manage that? Even with the Married Women's Property Act, it is still difficult for females to manage their own financial affairs."

"She didn't, her father did. I don't know all the details, but before he let her marry, he supposedly took all the family money and set up a series of trusts that she controls and that specifically exclude her husband."

"That must mean he didn't want Stephen Bremmer to get his

hands on it," Ruth murmured. "That's strange; Bremmer is from one of the oldest and most distinguished families in England."

"Yes, but sometimes that isn't enough; apparently it wasn't for Anne's father. She was older than he was and was well on her way to being a rich spinster when he suddenly appeared in her life. I know this because I had my eye on her before she married. I thought she might be a good candidate for our group, or if she didn't want to join us, she might help financially." She broke off and grinned. "But I was way off the mark there. She has no interest in women's rights."

"That's a pity," Ruth muttered. "But she's luckier than most married women; she controls her own money."

"From what I've heard, she might have been happier if she'd stayed a spinster," Octavia said. "Supposedly, her marriage has made her miserable. She controls the purse strings while he constantly taunts her."

"How so?"

"Apparently, Bremmer is one of those pathetic creatures who waste their lives boasting about their ancestors instead of doing anything useful themselves. According to him, she's simply a rich man's daughter while he's from one of England's oldest and most distinguished families. He torments her by telling her she'll never get her life's wish."

"Which is?"

"You're not going to believe this." Octavia snickered. "That silly woman wants to be presented at court."

Witherspoon got out of the hansom and stared at the redbrick building that housed James Pierce's offices. The place was a stone's throw from Liverpool Street Station and one of many warehouses in the area. Two flatbed wagons were pulled up and unloading in the bay doors.

Barnes paid the hansom driver and then joined Witherspoon. They walked between the two wagons and into the warehouse proper. On the wall of the left side of the cavernous space the word INBOUND was written in huge letters and on the opposite one the word OUTBOUND was in even bigger script.

A ten-foot-wide aisle separated the two sides. Barrels, tea chests, covered furniture, roped bundles, bales of wire, wooden crates, trunks, and all manner of goods covered the floor down the length of the room on both sides. Men in flat caps and open shirts hauled wheelbarrows, pallets, and handcarts from the wagons to the outbound side of the room. Tally clerks, both male and female, moved among the cargo, shouting at young lads to move various boxes and crates from one spot to the next. On the outbound side, a rope had been strung halfway up the wall and hung with signs of exotic place names like Singapore, Hong Kong, and Jakarta.

The worker closest to them stopped and leaned on his handcart, his gaze moving from Witherspoon to the constable's uniform. "You lookin' for the guv?"

"Yes, is he here?" Barnes asked.

"Offices are upstairs." He nodded toward a staircase on the other side of the open bay door. "He's there. Mr. Pierce is the first door on the left. He's expectin' you lot."

"Thank you." Witherspoon nodded politely.

Upstairs, they reached a corridor with offices on both sides. They could hear the clatter of typewriter keys as they approached Pierce's office. Witherspoon glanced in the open door. A middle-aged man sat behind a high counter above which hung a sign saying FREIGHT CASHIER. Behind him were three desks running down the center of the room, two of them occupied by women typing while the last one sat empty. Next to them was a row of male clerks, all with open ledgers on their desks.

James Pierce's office door was open. He sat behind an enormous desk with an open file in front of him. Glancing up, he spotted his visitors and rose from his seat. "Come in, Inspector, Constable, I'm all ready for you. Would you like tea?"

"That's kind of you, sir, but no," Witherspoon said as he and Barnes stepped inside. Bookcases filled with books, ledgers, and box files lined the walls. Light filtered in from the huge window and a bright Oriental rug covered the floor in front of the desk.

"In that case, have a seat and we'll get started." Pierce motioned to the two straight-backed chairs in front of his desk.

"Thank you, Mr. Pierce." Witherspoon sat down and winced as his bony backside flattened what little stuffing was left in the thin maroon cushion. He glanced at Barnes and saw that he had pulled out his brown notebook and was at the ready. "Mr. Pierce, you told us last night that Stephen Bremmer had a number of enemies."

"I did. It was truly the only talent the man had."

"Were any of his enemies sitting at the table with him last night?"

Pierce sat back in his chair. "I don't wish to cast aspersions on any one particular person, but I know that most of us at the table didn't like him. I've already told you my reasons for putting him on the board."

"You did, sir, but once he was on your board, how could you be sure he wouldn't try to influence your management of the business?" Witherspoon asked. He didn't think wanting to rid oneself of an interfering board member was much of a motive for murder, but he wanted to lay it to rest if possible.

Pierce laughed. "Because he's a lazy sod. I've known him for years, Inspector, and he'll show up for the quarterly board meetings, but he'll not take any interest in business. His father was the same way. He's the only one on the board who hasn't invested in the business."

"The other board members are also investors?" Barnes asked.

"Correct. We've raised a substantial amount of capital so that we can expand the business. Admittedly, some of the new board members didn't invest very much, but they invested enough to have a genuine interest in the business continuing to grow."

"But you retained a controlling interest, is that right?" Witherspoon wished he knew more about the business world.

"Of course. But I don't think my business affairs are why Stephen was killed," Pierce said. "As I said, he wasn't interested in the business."

"When the lights went out, did you hear anyone at your table moving about? Did anyone get up?" the constable asked.

Pierce thought for a moment. "No, I don't think so."

"Is it possible someone from the next table could have quietly slipped past you to get to Mr. Bremmer?" Witherspoon asked.

Pierce's expression changed. He now looked wary. "I doubt it."

"Who was sitting there?" Witherspoon shifted again, trying to get comfortable.

"Phillip, my secretary; Mr. Bates, the operations manager, and his wife; Mrs. Taft, she types the correspondence; my aunt Mary and her son, Paul. Mr. and Mrs. Bingham, he's our freight cashier; and Mrs. Cory. None of them would want to harm Stephen."

"Not even Mrs. Cory?" Barnes asked softly. "We understand that she loathed the man."

"Whoever said such a thing is lying," he snapped. "Mrs. Cory has only recently returned to England. She's lived in America for years. What reason could she possibly have to murder Stephen Bremmer?"

"That, sir, is precisely what we need to find out."

CHAPTER 4

Wiggins watched the back door of the Wrexley Hotel from across the street. He was cold and confused and wondering why he'd decided to come here instead of going to Ellen's office. He'd planned on having a quick word with her when she came out for lunch. But when he'd arrived at the Shepherd's Bush, instead of taking the train to Liverpool Street Station, he'd sent Davey Marsh, a street lad, to the inspector's home with a message saying he'd be late tonight. Then he'd hopped on an omnibus and come here.

He cupped his gloved hands under his chin and around his nose, breathing hard to generate a bit of warmth. He'd not changed his mind because of what Phyllis had said, no, absolutely not. He'd come here because he could learn more from a chambermaid or one of the kitchen workers than he could from Ellen. Besides, he didn't even know if Ellen left the office for lunch. She might have brought food from home—lots of people did—and what's more, he told himself, if he showed up when she got off work, he'd find out everything that Ellen had seen or heard the entire day. Yeah, that's why he'd come here, he assured himself. Just because Phyllis stared at him like a wounded puppy this morning didn't mean she had any influence on what he did or didn't do.

Across the busy road, the back door of the Wrexley flew open and a woman wearing a gold and gray striped wool hat and an oversized gray coat charged out and raced down the stairs. He stepped onto the pavement to get a better look and then took off at a dead run across the road. He caught up with her just as she reached the end of the mews. "Hello, miss, remember me?"

She stopped for a moment and stared at him. Her eyes were blue, her jaw square, and beneath her hat, he could see tendrils of brown hair sticking to her forehead.

"You're that reporter, aren't you? The one who was here when the other bloke got murdered?"

"I am," he admitted. He tried to remember her name, but it wouldn't come. "I'm Albert Jones. Do you mind if I walk with you?"

She shrugged nonchalantly. "If ya like. But I know the only reason you've turned up is because of that man droppin' dead. Mr. Cutler, he's the day manager, said we're not to say the fella was murdered even though we had the police there half the night."

"So you weren't there when it happened?"

"Nah, only Mr. Cutler's special favorites got asked to work extra last night."

Wiggins wasn't sure what to say, so he took her elbow and started toward the front of the hotel.

But she jerked to a stop. "Not that way. I don't want anyone seein' me with a reporter, and that nasty Bendal is right there at reception."

"Right, that's fine. We'll go whichever way you like. I'm grateful you're willin' to talk to me. My guv will 'ave my guts for garters if I don't show up with something for 'im to write about today. Who is Bendal?"

"He's that smarmy little desk clerk at reception. I used to think he was nice but he's a right old tattletale, always running to Mr. Cutler or Mr. Stargill, the night manager, tattlin' on someone about some silly thing."

"He sounds a right nasty sort." Wiggins walked slowly, his hand politely but firmly on her arm. There was a lot of time to kill before he needed to get across town and meet Ellen. He might as well use it to find out what he could. Pity this one hadn't been there last night, he thought, but he knew that people liked to talk. Hopefully, this young lady had listened closely.

"He is and he's worse now that we've had another"—she broke off and sneered—"*incident* at the hotel. Everyone is as nervous as a cat in a room full of hungry hounds. Honestly, it was bad before, you know, since Mundy was murdered. Business has been so awful they've cut everyone's work hours. Look at me, I got less than half me shift today, only two hours! Who can live on that? But do they care that I need my full wages to help keep a roof over our heads and food on the table? No, they bloody well don't."

Wiggins glanced at her as they rounded the corner onto a residential street filled with prosperous town houses. Her lips trembled and her expression was pure misery. He looked away. Like everyone in the inspector's household, he was grateful he'd ended up working for a man who was not only decent, but would take the food out of his own mouth to make sure the people who depended on him could eat. He heard her sniffle and he peeked at her again. Cor blimey, the poor girl was crying. "I'm sorry, that sounds like it's a terrible place to work."

"It is." She swiped at her face. "It's awful but we all need our jobs so there's naught we can do about it. But no matter what we do, no matter how hard we work, it is never enough for that lot. They didn't use to treat us like this, but this past year, ever since Mundy was murdered, they've become horrid and cheap. They're always watchin' us, waiting for us to make a mistake or say the wrong thing to a guest. But you know what's worse? If one of them, one of the customers, steals a towel or a bar of soap, they take it out of our wages. Can you believe it? It's just goin' to get worse now that we've had another death. It's already started."

"How do ya mean?"

"The Wrexleys are havin' a fit because of the stuff the police took away."

"What stuff?" Wiggins thought he knew, but he wanted to be sure.

"The china and cutlery and the champagne flutes from the head table. God, from the way Mr. Cutler was carryin' on this morning, you'd think we're waiting to get the bloomin' crown jewels returned."

"Maybe that's just because everyone was still upset because of last night," Wiggins suggested, hoping to comfort her.

She shook her head. "No, like I said, it's goin' to get worse. The Wrexleys spent a fortune tartin' the place up and hiring Mr. Sherwood to bring in a bit of outside business, but they've taken the cost out on those of us who work there. Poor Joey Finnigan is scared that he's going to get the sack because there's some missing glassware, and Boris—he's the maître d'—is terrified the police will tarnish the silverware or break one of them expensive champagne flutes that they took away." She sniffed and wiped her cheeks again. "I don't know what I'm goin' to say to my gran when I get home. We live in her house and this is the second time in a week they've sent me home early so I'll not get all my wages."

Wiggins stopped and pulled her around to face him. It was time to be a decent person, not a pretend reporter. "I'm so sorry you and the other people who work there are goin' through such misery. It's not right and it's not fair. But I can tell you something that I know for certain, because I've been through misery as well."

"And what's that?" She stared at him, her expression skeptical.

"It'll get better, miss, it really will. Because nothin' lasts forever, not even bad things."

"That is a ridiculous assertion," Pierce argued. "Mrs. Cory has been out of the country for the last eight years!"

"Hatred can last longer than that, sir," the constable replied calmly. "Do you have Mrs. Cory's address?"

Pierce got up. "Why do you need her address? I've just told you, she's nothing to do with Stephen Bremmer."

"We heard what you said, sir." The constable stared at him expectantly. "And if you refuse to tell us, we can easily find out where she lives. Our constables wrote down the addresses of everyone who was at the ball. I thought it might be faster to get it from you."

Just then there was a sharp knock and the door opened. A young man stuck his head inside. "Sorry for interrupting, Mr. Pierce, but you've a visitor."

"Not now, Phillip," he ordered.

"But it's Mrs. Cory. She says it is urgent, sir."

"That's a coincidence," the constable muttered.

For a few seconds, Pierce said nothing but then he nodded. "Send her in, Phillip."

He looked at the two policemen. "We might as well get this over with. You can speak to Mrs. Cory now."

"Coincidence or not, we'd prefer to interview her alone," Barnes said.

"That is our general policy," Witherspoon added, "but as she's here, I see no reason not to take her statement."

"Mrs. Cory, sir." Phillip ushered a dark-haired young woman into the room and stepped back.

She stopped and stared at the two policemen for a moment before turning her attention to Pierce. "Oh dear, James, I've interrupted you. I'm so sorry."

"Don't be, it's actually good that you've come." James' face softened as he smiled at her.

Witherspoon found himself gawking. She was lovely. Her hair was a deep, rich brown and her eyes the same shade. High cheekbones, a perfectly proportioned nose, and a mouth that was full enough to save her face from being too perfect. Slender and petite, she wore a hunter's green fitted jacket with matching skirt and hat. He shifted in the uncomfortable seat as an image of Ruth Cannonberry popped into his head.

"The police are here about Stephen Bremmer's death. They'd like to speak with you as well," James explained. He glanced at his secretary. "Bring in another chair, Phillip."

A few moments later, the introductions had been made and

Elise Cory was seated next to Witherspoon. "I don't see how I'll be very helpful, but I'll do my best to answer your questions. Please go ahead," she said.

The inspector nodded; he was a tad distracted by the faint scent of her perfume. He got himself under control. This would never do. This young woman was very beautiful, but there was no one in the world like his dear Ruth. "Ah, er . . . I understand you were once acquainted with Stephen Bremmer?"

"I was, but that was many years ago," she replied. "I've only recently returned to England from the United States."

"Have you had any contact with Mr. Bremmer since you've returned?" the inspector asked.

She shook her head. "No, the Lighterman's Ball was the first time I've seen him since I've been back."

"Did you speak to him when you saw him?" Witherspoon shifted again, still trying in vain to get comfortable.

"No, I was preoccupied. There were so many of my old friends and acquaintances there that I was rather busy greeting everyone," she answered. "I didn't even realize he was in the room until Mrs. Pierce, James' aunt, mentioned him."

"What did Aunt Mary have to say about him?" James demanded.

"Nothing, James. Mrs. Bingham asked who he was and your aunt Mary answered her," she clarified. "It was perfectly innocent."

"Mrs. Bingham is the wife of our freight cashier," he explained.

"Mrs. Cory"—Barnes looked up from his notebook—"can you tell us why you came back to England?"

"That's a personal question, Constable, and I don't see what it has to do with Stephen Bremmer's death," Pierce protested.

"It's alright, James. I don't mind answering. The constable isn't the first person to wonder why I came home now."

"But you shouldn't be subjected to answering questions about what are essentially private matters." He shot the constable a glare. "It's no business of the Metropolitan Police why you came back to England."

"It's our business if her coming home has anything to do with Stephen Bremmer's death," Barnes argued. "I'm not saying Mrs. Cory has anything directly to do with it. What I am saying is her showing up in London at this time might have been the spark that set the fire. All the rest of the guests at the top two tables have been in London all along; Mrs. Cory is the only new element in the mix."

Witherspoon nodded. He knew exactly what the constable was saying but wasn't sure if James Pierce or Elise Cory understood. "Er, what the constable means—"

"I know what he means," she interrupted. "And he's right, perhaps my coming back to London did act as a precursor to Stephen Bremmer's death. I would hate to think so, but it is possible."

"That's nonsense," Pierce muttered. "You've had nothing to do with him for eight years."

"Thank you for understanding, Mrs. Cory," the constable said.

"To answer your question, Constable, my husband passed away January a year ago. He had a number of business interests in both California and Nevada so it took me some time to take care of everything. When everything was finally sold, my mother-in-law and I returned to England. Without Bartholomew, Nevada was just too lonely for both of us."

"Your mother-in-law is English?" Witherspoon asked.

"She's originally from Stepney." Elise smiled broadly. "And she has two sisters still living in her old neighborhood, so she's very happy to be home and close to family."

"Are you happy to have come back?" The constable pretended to look down at his notebook, but he kept his gaze on Pierce's face. He wanted to watch the man's expression as he listened to Mrs. Cory answer his question.

"I am," she declared. "I loved my time in America, but I'm glad to be home."

Pierce smiled slightly and looked relieved.

"When did you first become acquainted with Mr. Bremmer?" Witherspoon thought it wise to learn as much background information as possible. It often came in very handy.

"Years ago, Inspector. My father was hired to do a series of murals for Lyndhurst Shipping. I don't recall the exact time or place, but think it was about then that I met Mr. Bremmer."

"Elise's father was the artist Dounton Newcomb," James interjected. "He did excellent seascapes. His work was commissioned by a number of shipping lines."

"Were you and Mr. Bremmer friends?" Barnes looked up from his notebook. He wanted to see her face as she answered.

"Not at all." She grinned. "My father was simply the hired help, Constable. Stephen Bremmer barely spoke to us if we happened to be in the same place at the same time."

Barnes tried not to smile, but he couldn't help himself.

"When the lights went out," Witherspoon continued, "did you hear anyone leave your table?"

"No, but there was a lot of noise and I wasn't really paying all that much attention."

"Did you leave your seat?" the constable pressed.

"See here, Constable." Pierce leapt up again. "This is getting absurd. You can't possibly think that Elise had anything to do with Bremmer's death. That's ridiculous."

"It's a standard inquiry in cases like this," he replied.

"Why would it be a standard inquiry?" Pierce sat back down, his expression hard. "She's got nothing to do with him."

Both policemen ignored him. "Ma'am, we've been told that you disliked Mr. Bremmer," Witherspoon said. "As a matter of fact, the exact words our witness used to describe how you felt about Stephen Bremmer eight years ago was that you loathed him. Is that true?"

"Don't answer that, Elise," Pierce commanded. "I'm going to send for my solicitor immediately. They've no right—"

She interrupted him. "There's no need for that, James. I had nothing to do with Bremmer's death so I'll answer whatever they ask." She looked at the inspector. "It is true, at one point in my life, I loathed Stephen Bremmer."

"Can you tell us why?"

"A number of reasons, but mainly, I objected to how he treated my father. He was disrespectful and rude. My father was a brilliant artist and often obtained commissions such as the one for Lyndhurst Shipping. But he always wanted a show at the Bryson Gallery in the West End. He did a series of seascapes and Bryson's was going to show them when all of a sudden, they rescinded the offer. I'm an artist as well, Inspector, but my specialty is portraits. I found out from one of my clients that it was Stephen Bremmer who had pressured Bryson's to withdraw the offer."

"Why did Bremmer do it?"

"Because he liked to strut around pretending that he was refined and cultured. At some stupid tea, Bremmer made some comments about art and my father exposed his ignorance. He couldn't have the 'hired help' making him look like a fool so he took his revenge by making certain the show was canceled."

"No wonder you hated him," Pierce murmured. "Why didn't you come to me, Elise? I might have been able to help."

"You were busy building the business with your father."

"Did you confront Bremmer?" Barnes asked.

"Yes. He laughed at me and said that there was nothing I could do about it."

"Except hate him," the constable said.

"I did. I was young and idealistic and I took things very much to heart. Bremmer was a boor and a bully who enjoyed hurting others. But over the years, I find that those particular characteristics manifest themselves in a large number of people."

"So you didn't hate him when you came back to England?" Witherspoon pressed.

"I haven't given him a thought, Inspector. Why should I? Life, as they say, teaches us that the passions of youth often become the embarrassments of the present."

"I'm not sure I understand," Witherspoon admitted.

She laughed. "My father was very philosophical about it. He told me I was a fool if I let the actions of a man like Bremmer control my emotions. As he put it, a show at the Bryson would have helped his career, but not having one certainly didn't hurt him."

"So you no longer had a grudge against Mr. Bremmer?" Barnes clarified.

"Not anymore, Constable. He simply wasn't important to me."

* * *

Ida Leacock picked up her fork and eagerly attacked the apple tart. "Mrs. Goodge, you've still got the touch. Your tarts were always miles ahead of anyone else's."

"Why, thank you, Ida. I'm pleased you still like them. How have you been?" Mrs. Goodge poured them both a cup of hot, strong tea.

"Excellent." Ida grinned. "Business is doing well, the family is good, and frankly, I'm enjoyin' life."

Though close to each other in age, she and the cook couldn't be further apart in appearance. Her curly hair still had enough brown in it to be called salt and pepper, she was as thin as Mrs. Goodge was portly, and instead of wearing spectacles, her deep-set hazel eyes saw everything going on around her.

Ida Leacock and Mrs. Goodge had worked together years earlier. Ida had left service and managed to save enough money to open a tobacconist shop that had proved successful. She now owned three tobacconist shops, but the reason Mrs. Goodge wanted to see her was simple: Ida loved to gossip. She'd talk the paint off a fence post if she couldn't find a person to chat with. She had the ability to get complete strangers to tell her the most intimate stories about their family, friends, lovers, and employers. She also kept up a steady correspondence with her former colleagues who lived far away and made sure to take tea or have a pint with those who lived close.

"So am I, which brings me to the reason I wanted to see you." Mrs. Goodge helped herself to a slice of tart. "You've heard about the man that was poisoned last night."

"The one at the Wrexley Hotel." Ida clucked her tongue. "Two murders in as many years; Lord, that must be killing their business.

But yes, I have heard about it. I dropped by my shop in Deptford this morning and got an earful. What do you want to know?"

"Anything you know," Mrs. Goodge replied. Ida, though a talker, was discreet about the information she passed along about the inspector's cases. The woman believed in justice and, like the Witherspoon household, was sick and tired of the rich and powerful getting away with murder. "Sorry, I should say I'd like to know anything you've heard about the people sitting at the dead man's table." She took a breath and then rattled off their names.

Her guest listened carefully. "Some of those names sound very familiar, but not all of them. I've never heard of Nicholas Parr. But everyone in Deptford knew the Bremmer family. At the shop this morning everyone was sayin' that Stephen Bremmer had so many enemies it'll be hard for the police to sort it out. The Bremmer family had a big house out toward Greenwich, and when old man Bremmer passed away, he left a string of debts that never got paid." Ida frowned thoughtfully. "Let me think for a minute, I know I've heard of some of those people . . . yes, that's right." She nodded to herself. "Louise Mannion, she's one of the Lyndhursts—you know, the shipping people."

"Rich, then?"

"Very," Ida replied. "Oh yes, now I recollect. She had a brother named Leonard and he almost drowned. Yes, yes, that's right. The Pierce boy, James—his family owned a barge business—he pulled him out of the estuary. Old Mr. Lyndhurst was so grateful to the Pierce boy for saving his son that he gave them a lot of business after that."

"He'd not been doing business with Pierce and Son before?" Mrs. Goodge asked.

"I don't know," Ida admitted. "But I do know that the accident caused a lot of talk. Leonard Lyndhurst claimed he'd been pushed into the water."

"Couldn't he swim?"

"I don't think so." Ida shook her head. "Otherwise, he'd have just swum to the edge and pulled himself out. But he didn't, and if young James Pierce hadn't been there, the boy would have drowned."

"Wouldn't he have seen who shoved him in?" Mrs. Goodge demanded.

"I think it happened at night." Ida frowned again. "It's an old story, Mrs. Goodge, and I could easily have the details wrong. But I do know that afterward, Leo and James became fast friends. What's more, Lyndhurst claimed he'd been shoved into the water till the day he died."

"He's dead?"

Ida nodded. "He died about eight or nine years ago. I think it was from one of those tropical diseases; he'd just come back from the Far East. His passing just about killed old man Lyndhurst. Leonard was the heir to the company as well as being the favorite."

"Men often favor the brother over the sister," Mrs. Goodge commented.

"True, and Louise Lyndhurst was rumored to be a bit of a wild one. Mind you, the young man's death kept all the tongues from wagging about the other scandal."

"What scandal?"

"Supposedly Louise had fallen in love with someone most unsuitable. Someone who she insisted she was going to marry whether the family liked it or not."

"Do you know who it was?"

"I wish I did." Ida forked another bite of tart. "Maybe when her brother died, she came to her senses and broke it off. She must have; she ended up marrying Osgood Mannion and he was a prime catch. He had more money than the Bank of England. But wanting someone unacceptable happens a lot these days. Just look at Camilla Houghton-Jones. Everyone thought she'd be a spinster till her dying day—God knows the woman doesn't have much going for her except a good lineage and that big house. Yet she's now engaged to Montague Pettigrew and he's going to inherit a ruddy fortune."

"Why would Montague Pettigrew be unacceptable?" Mrs. Goodge asked. "They're both from the same social class."

"It has nothing to do with his class." Ida cackled. "Remember that footman that worked at the Deeney house? The lad that was so handsome that every lady in the household would stop and stare when he came out the Deeneys' front door?"

"Oh, goodness, he was a handsome one." Mrs. Goodge smiled as she recalled the man's perfect face.

"And remember how he never even noticed the ladies taking note of him?" Ida continued.

"Gracious me, yes, now I remember. He ran off with that Italian count."

"He did quite well for himself." Ida shrugged. "The count left him a lot of money."

It took a moment for Mrs. Goodge to understand. "So you're saying that Pettigrew is unsuitable . . ."

"Because he's like the Deeney footman and the Italian count."

"That's right, but apparently he's rich enough that Miss Houghton-Jones either doesn't know, or if she does know, she doesn't care."

* * *

"We'll have better luck getting a hansom at the station." Barnes frowned at the steady stream of loaded and empty wagons moving up and down the road in front of the warehouse.

Witherspoon pulled on his gloves. "Right, then, let's go. I'd like to interview Mrs. Bremmer before it gets too late today."

"We'd better get crackin', sir." Barnes started across the road. "She lives on the other side of town and the traffic this time of day is fierce."

"Constable Barnes, Inspector Witherspoon."

The two policemen stopped as Constable Griffiths, who'd just come around the corner, hurried toward them.

"Looks like the police surgeon's report came in, sir," Barnes said.

The inspector had left instructions at the station that if the autopsy report arrived, Constable Griffiths was to read it and then track them down. He'd left a list of the witnesses, their addresses, and the order in which the witnesses were going to be interviewed so that Griffiths needn't run all over London trying to find them. Both Witherspoon and Barnes knew it was important to find out if Bremmer had indeed been poisoned.

"Sorry to shout, sir," Griffiths said breathlessly. "But I was afraid you were heading to the station. I'd never find you there."

"Take a moment to catch your breath," the inspector said.

"I'm fine, sir," he replied. "The report arrived, and as instructed, I read it. Dr. Bosworth and the police surgeon were both right, sir. The victim was poisoned with arsenic. There were traces in his stomach, his mouth, and his champagne flute."

"Thank you, Constable," Witherspoon said. "I hope you didn't have too difficult a time finding us."

"Not at all, sir. If it's all the same to you, sir, I'll head back to the Wrexley Hotel. We've not finished interviewing the staff."

Witherspoon nodded and the three men went to Liverpool Street Station. Griffiths went inside to catch a local while the inspector and Barnes found a hansom.

"What did you think of Mr. Pierce and Mrs. Cory?" Barnes braced himself as the hansom took the corner too fast. They were on their way to Belgravia to interview the widow.

"I'm not certain what to think. James Pierce made it quite clear he had no liking for the victim, but perhaps he's only being honest because he knows we'd find out anyway."

"You could say the same about Mrs. Cory, sir. She gave the appearance of being forthright about her previous feelings toward Bremmer while at the same time dismissing his importance to her current circumstances. Seems to me both of them were workin' a bit too hard to convince us they considered the victim nothing more than a borin' nuisance. What's more, it's as plain as the nose on your face that James Pierce was doin' everything he could to protect Mrs. Cory."

"Agreed. I think the man is in love with her. Camilla Houghton-Jones and Montague Pettigrew gave us the same impression." Witherspoon tapped his chin with a gloved finger. "But it could well be that any or all of them are lying. Constable Griffiths just confirmed that the arsenic was in Bremmer's champagne glass, and from what we've learned of the man's character, he didn't do it himself."

"Maybe the widow will be able to shed some light on the situation." Barnes grabbed the handhold as the hansom lurched to a hard stop.

"Let's hope so." Witherspoon dug both his heels into the floor to keep from tumbling forward. "It's odd, isn't it?"

"What is, sir?"

"The number of coincidences there are in this case. The Wrexley Hotel, Dr. Bosworth and Wiggins being on the scene so to speak."

"Mrs. Cory showing up here unexpectedly," the constable added.

"And all the widows and widowers there were at that table." He stared out the window, his expression thoughtful. "Mrs. Mannion is a widow, Mrs. Cory is widowed, and Mr. Pierce is a widower. What's strange about it is they're all relatively young."

"Mrs. Cory was at the next table," Barnes corrected. "But I see what you mean, three of 'em, all without a husband or wife and all of them with a bit of history between them."

"Do we know how their respective spouses died?"

The hansom jerked forward again. "No sir, we don't, but I'll make it a point to find out."

They discussed the case as the cab drove through the crowded afternoon traffic. By the time the rig pulled up in front of the Bremmer home, the sky had gone dark and mean. "Looks like a storm is coming," the inspector said.

The widow Bremmer lived on a small street off Eaton Square. The house was a six-story white town house at the end of the row on Rotwell Place. A black wrought-iron fence enclosed the staircase leading to the lower ground floor, the front door was painted a shiny black, and the brass door knocker was so highly polished, Barnes could see his reflection. He lifted the knocker and released it.

When the door opened, a butler stared at them. "Yes, what do you want? This house is in mourning and the mistress isn't receiving visitors."

"We are well aware that there's been a death in the family," Barnes said. "That's the reason we've come."

"Please tell Mrs. Bremmer it's imperative we speak with her," Witherspoon added quickly.

"Wait here." He slammed the door.

Neither of them spoke as they stood on the stoop. Witherspoon looked up as he felt a drop of rain splat against his spectacles. It began to rain in earnest just as the door reopened and the butler waved them inside. "She'll see you."

The foyer was impressive. The walls were a bright white, the floor an intricate hex pattern of black, white, and brown diamond-shaped tiles, and the staircase was a polished dark wood that climbed to a first-floor landing before gracefully curving upward. A red ceramic umbrella stand decorated with gold Celtic knots stood by the door, and next to it was a huge hall stand complete with mirror and a bench seat upholstered in crimson velvet.

The butler led them down the long hallway to a set of open double doors. "The police are here, madam," he announced.

They stepped inside and the inspector took a quick moment to survey his surroundings. The walls were pale green and liberally covered with portraits and paintings. Black runners were draped over the fireplace and mantel as well as on all the many tabletops and cabinets. The heavy velvet curtains were closed and the only spot of real color was the emerald green and cream striped upholstery on the empire style furniture.

Anne Bremmer, wearing high-necked widow's weeds, sat in the center of the sofa and stared at them. "Don't just stand there, come in and get about your business."

Witherspoon moved toward her. "I'm Inspector Witherspoon and this is Constable Barnes. You're Mrs. Stephen Bremmer."

"I am. Was Stephen murdered?" She didn't ask them to sit down.

"Yes, ma'am, he was," the inspector replied. He saw Barnes take out his notebook and pencil. "Unfortunately, that means we must ask you a number of questions."

"Get on with it, then. I've a lot to do now."

"First of all, please accept our condolences for your loss," the inspector began, but she interrupted.

"I said to get on with it."

"Do you know of anyone who wanted your husband dead?" Barnes asked.

"Many people probably wanted him dead," she retorted. "He was not a nice person. What exactly killed him?"

"Arsenic, ma'am, there was arsenic in the champagne flute." Witherspoon saw no reason not to tell her. Despite their best efforts, most details of a murder ended up in the newspapers. "Were you sitting next to your husband the entire time the lights were out?"

"Of course. It was dark."

"Did you hear anyone moving about in the darkness?" Barnes asked. "Anyone coming close to your table?"

She cocked her head to one side. "There might have been someone walking behind us, but I can't be sure. It wasn't noisy per se, but it wasn't quiet, either. I could hear the kitchen noises and there were people scraping chairs and coughing; that sort of thing."

"Do you think it possible that if indeed there was someone moving about behind you, that person could have successfully put arsenic in Mr. Bremmer's glass?" Witherspoon didn't think such a scenario likely, but it had to be addressed.

"Only if they could see in the dark, Inspector." She gave him a slight smile. "We were all blinded when the electricity was turned off. It took a few seconds for my eyes to adjust to what little light came in through the lobby and the street."

"What time did you and your husband arrive at the ball?" Barnes wished he could sit down.

"I arrived a few minutes before it was due to commence," she replied. "I've no idea what time Stephen arrived."

"You came separately?" Witherspoon couldn't keep a note of surprise out of his voice.

"We did. Stephen had things to do that afternoon and I presume he came by hansom cab. I took the carriage."

"What exactly was your husband doing before he came to the ball?" Barnes asked.

"I don't know. He wasn't in the habit of explaining his comings and goings to me." She shrugged as if it didn't matter.

"Wouldn't he have had to come home to change into his evening clothes?" Witherspoon knew the corpse hadn't been wearing daytime attire.

"I suppose, but if he did, we didn't see each other. I was busy getting ready myself."

"So you've no idea what he was doing in the hours before he was murdered?" Barnes was incredulous. He knew many marriages weren't happy, especially upper-class ones where the principals were more interested in property than passion, but she was the coldest woman he'd ever seen.

"I believe he muttered something about going to his tailor," she shrugged. "You can ask Rankin if he knows."

"Who is Rankin?" Witherspoon asked.

"He's a footman. Sometimes Stephen tells him where he'll be. I don't know why, but I've heard him do it a time or two."

"Do you keep arsenic in the house?" Barnes fixed her with a hard stare.

"Of course. We use it to kill vermin."

"Where do you store it?"

Again, she shrugged. "I've no idea. That would be something you'd need to ask Mrs. Martin. The housekeeper takes care of that sort of thing. Shall I ring for her?"

"No, ma'am, we'll speak to her and the footman after we've finished here. I presume we can talk with them downstairs?" Witherspoon wasn't going to question a servant in front of their employer.

"If you must." She sighed and glanced at the clock on the side table. "How much longer will you be? I've got to speak to the vicar and send a number of telegrams telling the family what's happened."

"Not much longer, ma'am," Witherspoon assured her. "Was your husband at the head table when you arrived?"

Considering how everyone they'd interviewed had described the events leading up to Bremmer's death, Witherspoon didn't think it likely that the killer could have put arsenic in the victim's champagne glass when the lights went out so quietly and stealthily that he or she was neither seen nor heard.

"No, when I arrived, he was standing near the table but he'd not sat down."

"Was anyone sitting at the head table?" Barnes had realized the same thing as the inspector, that the glass might not have been poisoned when the lights went out.

She thought for a moment and then shook her head. "I don't remember."

"Did you see anyone in the vicinity?" Witherspoon pressed. The arsenic hadn't leapt into Bremmer's flute on its own. Someone had to have put it there. "Please, Mrs. Bremmer, I understand this is dreadful for you, but please, think hard. It's very important."

She looked confused. "But there were so many people there that night, I don't know . . . Oh, let me think, give me a moment."

"Take as much time as you need, ma'am."

She closed her eyes. "I'm trying to remember. I'm trying to think back to mentally retrace my steps. Yes, now that you've brought it up, there was someone there, someone hovering near the tables. Oh my Lord, she wasn't just hovering, she was right there. How could I have forgotten? Of course, I knew the moment I saw her that it was going to raise eyebrows."

"Who did you see, Mrs. Bremmer? Who was it?" Witherspoon asked.

"I remember now." She shook her head incredulously. "I can't believe I forgot because just a few minutes later after we'd all sat down, James made a spectacle of himself and then Stephen taunted Louise and even Camilla was talking about her."

By this time, both policemen could guess the identity of the woman Anne Bremmer claimed to have seen.

But the inspector wanted to be sure. “Please tell us the name of the person you saw.”

“It was Elise Cory.”

“You’re certain?” Barnes wasn’t sure he believed her. “A few moments ago you couldn’t remember.”

“Thinking about it brought it all back,” she replied. “And it was definitely her. She was standing right in front of the table reading the place cards. I saw her pick one up and then put it down.”

“Could you tell which card it was she picked up?” Witherspoon asked.

“From where she was standing, it could have been anyone who was sitting near the center. Mine or Stephen’s or even Louise’s card.”

CHAPTER 5

Smythe stepped into the Dirty Duck Pub and stopped for a moment so his eyes could adjust to the dim lighting. He'd spent most of the day at pubs and hansom cab shelters near the Bremmer house and the only thing he'd found out was what they already knew: No one liked the man. He didn't want to show up with nothing to say at this afternoon's meeting, so he decided to get help from his old friend Blimpey Groggins.

Blimpey, a portly, ginger-haired man with a ruddy complexion and a face as round as a pie plate, was sitting at his usual table reading a newspaper. He owned the Dirty Duck along with a number of other properties in London but he made his living buying and selling information. He had people working for him at the newspapers, the shipping lines, the courts, the customs houses, all the pawnshops used by fences, insurance companies, estate agents, Parliament, Whitehall, and—rumor had it—he even had a source or two planted at Buckingham Palace. His enemies claimed he'd sell to anyone, but that wasn't true; he had a hard-and-fast rule that he'd never sell information that he knew would harm a woman or a child.

He knew what was going on in London's upper echelon of society as well as who was doing what to whom in both the criminal underworld and the business community. Blimpey charged his clients a pretty penny but Smythe never haggled over the expense. He had plenty of money. Years earlier, he'd returned from Australia a rich man and he'd invested wisely, so his wealth had continued to grow. Blimpey, Betsy, Mrs. Jeffries, and his bankers were the only people in London who knew the truth about his finances.

Blimpey looked up from his paper as Smythe approached. "I wondered if you'd be along." He put the paper to the side. "Your guv must've caught that Bremmer case."

"How do you know there's a case?" Smythe slid onto the stool. "They only think it's a murder. They'll not know for certain until the postmortem is finished."

"The postmortem is finished and the report is already at the Ladbroke Road Police Station." Blimpey laughed. "Bremmer was poisoned. There was enough arsenic in his gut to kill a ruddy elephant."

Smythe wasn't surprised that Blimpey already knew the contents of the report. Considering how he made his living, that was only to be expected. "You find out how it got into said gut?"

"The champagne flute," Blimpey replied. "But your guv will give those details to Mrs. Jeffries and she'll pass them along to you lot. You're here because you're wantin' to find out about who might have wanted to put the arsenic inside Stephen Bremmer."

"True. What can you tell me?"

"A lot of people hated him."

"That's what I 'eard today." Smythe stared at him curiously. "You're good, but how did you find out so fast?"

"It pains me to admit that it's a coincidence rather than brilliance on my part, but Bremmer's name has come up before in my inquiries. Generally, I keep my customers' inquiries confidential, but in this case, it'll be alright to tell ya." He broke off as Eldon, his man-of-all-work, came out from the storage room carrying a keg.

"You want somethin'?" Eldon called to Smythe. He went behind the bar and eased the small barrel onto the counter.

"Nothin', thanks," Smythe said quickly. He was good at holding his liquor but he'd already had to down several pints today and another glass would be sure to muddle his mind.

"Like I was sayin', I generally keep my clients' business private, but the client in this case is long dead."

"And who would that be?"

"Vincent Lester. He's the father of Anne Bremmer, Stephen Bremmer's wife. He hired me to get the goods on Stephen as he didn't want his daughter marryin' the fellow. The Lesters are rich and he was sure Stephen was marryin' her for her money. He was dead right about that."

"But she ended up marryin' 'im anyway?"

"That's right. They say love is blind but in her case it must have been deaf and dumb as well."

"What 'ad he done?"

"It wasn't what he'd done—though that was bad enough—it was what he was: mean-spirited, foulmouthed, arrogant, and worst of all, poor. Vincent Lester did everything he could to keep him away from his daughter, but Bremmer latched on to her like a ruddy leach and wouldn't let go."

"Why didn't the old man threaten to cut her off if she married him?" Smythe asked. "Isn't that what rich fathers usually do to make their daughters see sense?"

"He threatened her, but she called his bluff and as she was of age she married Bremmer. But Vincent Lester had the last laugh. He made sure everything she inherited was hers and hers alone. She has complete control of her money. Supposedly, when Bremmer found out he had a right fit. He threatened to take the estate to court, but as he had such a bad reputation for not payin' his bills, there wasn't a competent solicitor in London who'd take his case, nor a decent barrister to argue it in court."

"What a miserable way to live your life." Smythe shook his head, thinking of the happiness he'd found with Betsy and their child. Luck had been with him when he'd come back from Australia and on the spur of the moment decided to go to Upper Edmonton Gardens. He'd wanted to pay his respects to his previous employer, Euphemia Witherspoon, Inspector Witherspoon's aunt.

That decision had changed his life.

He'd found the poor woman deathly ill and being cared for by a very young footman, Wiggins. The other servants were robbing her blind so he'd sacked them all, sent Wiggins to find a doctor, and set about taking care of his old friend.

But medical help came too late, and despite the doctor's best efforts, Euphemia Witherspoon couldn't be saved. Before she died, she made Smythe promise that despite his not needing employment, he'd stay on at Upper Edmonton Gardens and see that her nephew, Gerald Witherspoon, was properly looked after. Smythe agreed to remain long enough to make certain he had a household that wouldn't take advantage of him. He'd stayed on as Witherspoon's coachman, and before long, Mrs. Jeffries, Mrs. Goodge, and then his beloved Betsy had been added to the household. Then they'd started investigating murders and they'd become a family. The only fly in his ointment now was the worry that Wiggins and Mrs. Goodge would find out he'd not told them the truth about his circumstances and had continued to keep it secret for such a long time.

"It was and, believe it or not, it gets worse," Blimpey said. "Anne Bremmer is a good ten years older than Stephen, and as she's aged, she's gotten as mean and nasty as he is. My sources told me she torments him by keeping him on a short leash financially, and when she really wants to embarrass the fellow, she'll deliberately not pay his bills. Despite his ancient lineage, he's been tossed out of several men's establishments for not paying the subscriptions. But—and this is the important bit—it turns out Stephen Bremmer has a source of income that's apart from her. He's actually managed to pay his way back into one of the best clubs in London."

"What do ya mean? Is there some family money that's come to 'im?"

Blimpey looked doubtful. "I don't think so, but I suppose it's possible. The Bremmers were once one of the wealthiest families in England, but that's long gone and I've not heard of any other rich relations poppin' out of the woodwork."

"Do ya know how long Bremmer's had this second source of income?" Smythe had an idea of what it might be, but he'd keep his opinion to himself until he had some facts.

"Not yet, but I've got my people workin' on findin' out, and I should be able to give ya more details in a day or so."

He nodded. "Right, if you could find out about the other people who were sitting at the table when he was poisoned, that'd be good, too." He started to rattle off the names of the suspects, but Blimpey stopped him.

"I know who was sitting with him and I know who was sittin' at the next table. I've already got my people workin' on 'em. I also know exactly what happened at the Wrexley Hotel. One of my sources works there and she told me about the lights goin' out but the room not stayin' dark as long as they'd planned. So you don't need to waste your breath goin' over old news."

"You found out more than just a few bits and pieces, Blimpey." Smythe eyed him skeptically. "As soon as you 'eard about the murder, you knew I'd be coming here."

Blimpey laughed. "'Course I did. You're not one to waste time larkin' about."

"You know I can find out a few facts on me own," Smythe said defensively.

"'Course ya can, but let's be honest 'ere. You're not as good at gettin' people to chat as your lady is. She's just like my Nell; they can both sweet-talk the devil into tellin' his secrets."

Smythe laughed. "And how is your good wife and your little one?"

"They're both right as rain and I couldn't be happier. I look forward to goin' 'ome each night to be with 'em. I can't imagine my life without the two of 'em. Look at Stephen Bremmer; he spent his life chasin' nothin' but money and he ended up livin' in misery before bein' murdered by someone who hated him. My money is on his wife. She was sittin' right next to him."

"Why didn't Bremmer just walk out? With his family connections, he could 'ave gotten a divorce, and with a rich wife, she'd probably have given him a settlement to avoid a scandal."

"Maybe, maybe not. People are strange, Smythe." Blimpey gazed off into the distance. "Sometimes the most important thing in their life is hangin' on to their hatred, and supposedly she told him the only way he'd get anything out of her was over her dead body."

Wiggins pushed away from the lamppost as he spotted Ellen coming out of the double doors of the warehouse. He ran around an empty wagon and across the road. He was less than twenty feet away from Ellen when she caught sight of him. She gave him a huge, delighted smile, and in the flash of a second, he realized he might have made a mistake. Cor blimey, he wasn't conceited about his looks, but he knew he wasn't ugly. From the expression on Ellen's face, it seemed she might be getting the wrong idea. He liked her well enough but only as a friend. Blast a Spaniard, this could be a problem. Toying with a lady's emotions wasn't right, not even in the cause of justice. But he was here and he wanted information.

"Did you come to see me home?" Ellen called loudly enough so that the two girls walking ahead of her would take notice.

"In a way. I was seein' a friend off at Liverpool Street Station and I need to speak to Tommy," he lied. "So I thought I'd walk 'ome with you, if you don't mind."

Her face fell. "Oh, it's him you're wantin' to see, then. Right, he should be home by the time we get there."

"And I wanted to see if you was alright." Wiggins couldn't stop himself; if she had the wrong idea about his intentions, he'd deal with it later. But right now she looked so miserable he felt like he'd kicked a kitten into the Thames. "Seein' someone die like that isn't very nice."

She brightened and took his arm. "I'm fine, but it's nice that you were concerned."

Wiggins hoped she wouldn't mention anything untoward to Tommy. That would be even harder to handle than her thinking he was sweet on her. Tommy would expect him to do right by her and Wiggins was no more interested in her than he was in one of them statues at the British Museum. "How was everyone else today at your office? Were people upset?"

"It was all anyone could talk about," she replied. "Mind you, we've so much work to do there weren't much time to chat, but no one was all that bothered it was that awful Mr. Bremmer that got killed."

"Guess he weren't well liked, huh." He stopped as they reached the corner and waited for a break in the traffic.

"Not really. None of us could understand why he kept comin' about the place but he was here all the time. Every time Mrs. Mannion came, he was like her lapdog and trotted in behind her. Malcolm, he's the lead inbound clerk, says it was because he needed to suck up to Mr. Pierce, 'cause he really wanted the honorarium that comes with bein' on the board and Mr. Bremmer knew that Mr. Pierce didn't like him very much."

"Mrs. Mannion was there a lot?" Wiggins tugged her away from the curb as a four-wheeler took the corner fast.

"Yes, she was always comin' by to try and take him to lunch or to make certain the plans for the ball were goin' along properly." She giggled. "Poor Mr. Pierce didn't stand a chance against her.

She was always at him to let her take over. I know because I overheard her telling him she'd be pleased to see to the details, that he was so busy and she had plenty of free time. She about had a fit when she found out he'd gone to the Wrexley on his own and booked their premises for the Lighterman's Ball."

"So did he let her do it?" Wiggins looked both ways and then tugged her across the busy street.

"She finally wore him down. I think she's sweet on him." She looked at him out of the corner of her eye. "A woman can always tell when someone is sweet on someone, don't you think?"

"What else happened today?" he asked quickly, hoping to distract her.

"Truth to tell, it was a bit of a miserable day."

"What 'appened?"

"To begin with, Phillip—he's Mr. Pierce's secretary—he was in a bad mood." She grimaced. "He's generally so good natured, but he was right put out this morning when he saw that the tea things were still dirty. I overheard him telling Malcolm that yesterday afternoon right after the board meeting here, Mr. Pierce told Phillip he and the rest of us could leave as soon as the tea things were tidied up, you know, so we could get ready for the ball. Mrs. Mannion insisted she'd take care of it and Mr. Pierce let everyone leave right then. But the only things she washed were the cups and mugs. She'd not touched the pot, and when Phillip grabbed it off the sink, he thought it was empty and he wasn't careful and he ended up spilling cold tea all over his best shirt."

"That's not nice," Wiggins replied. They rounded the corner onto a residential street lined with a row of small two-story brown brick houses. This road wasn't as bad as some in this part of

London; the pavements were cracked, but for the most part, it was in decent repair. The houses were covered with old soot from the local factories and none of them had gardens, but there wasn't any laundry strung across the road and most of the doors were painted and the stoops in good nick. Tommy and Ellen's family was one of the lucky ones; their father had a decent job on the railway and their mother didn't need to take in washing.

"The day only got worse when the police showed up," she continued. "And that set Mr. Pierce off something fierce."

"Your guv didn't want to speak to the police?"

" 'Course he did. He's got nothin' to hide," she retorted. "He was all ready for them and had even told Phillip to bring them right in when they arrived. No, it was Mrs. Cory comin' in that set him off."

Wiggins had to be careful here. He couldn't let on that he knew who she was. "Who's she?"

Ellen wrinkled her nose in thought. "I'm not sure. I heard Mrs. Taft telling Malcolm that Mrs. Cory and Mr. Pierce used to know each other. Mrs. Taft has been with the company for ages. I think Mrs. Cory was Mr. Pierce's late wife's cousin or somethin' like that."

"So she's a relation of Mr. Pierce's?" He wanted to make certain he understood who was who.

Ellen shook her head. "Not really. I think Mr. Pierce was sweet on her before he married his wife, at least that's what Mrs. Taft was sort of sayin' to Malcolm."

"Sort of saying?" he repeated. They were almost at the end of the block, close to Ellen's home and he realized she had slowed down and was now walking at a snail's pace.

"Oh, you know what I mean. Sometimes people won't come right out and say what they mean, they just hint around. That's what Mrs. Taft was doin' today. She wouldn't come out and say it properly because she didn't want to be accused of gossipin' in the office, but Malcolm told me that she said everyone was surprised when Mrs. Cory up and left for America because everyone thought she and Mr. Pierce were more than friends. Anyway, what I do know is all the men were staring at her like they'd never seen a woman before when she showed up and asked to speak to Mr. Pierce."

"How come? Is she funny looking?"

"Just the opposite. She's very pretty and Mr. Pierce told Phillip to bring her right in the minute he announced she was waitin' to see him. The police were there but Mr. Pierce still acted like he was afraid she'd disappear."

"What happened then?" He pulled her to one side as they came to a huge hole in the pavement.

"She went inside, and a few minutes later Mr. Pierce started talking so loud you could hear it all the way to the cashier's counter."

"He was shoutin'?"

"I wouldn't call it that, but we could hear him, and Mr. Pierce never raises his voice. He was het up about something. As soon as the police were gone, he slammed his door shut. Then he and Mrs. Cory were inside the office for over an hour."

"Was he still talking loud enough for you to 'ear him?" Wiggins asked.

"No, it went real quiet."

"I wonder what they were chattin' about?" They'd reached her house and Wiggins saw Tommy waving at him through the small front parlor window.

"I don't know, but it must have been important. He didn't even open the door when Phillip went to tell him the Tadish shipment had come in. Mr. Pierce always checks that shipment himself but this time he yelled for Phillip to take care of it."

"Wiggins sent word that he'll be late and for us to have the meeting without him," Mrs. Jeffries announced as she took her seat. "I'll bring him up to date before our morning meeting. Now, who would like to go first?"

"My report won't take long," Hatchet said. "Despite my best efforts, I found out very little and I'm not even certain that it has anything to do with this case."

"What did you learn?" Mrs. Jeffries helped herself to a piece of brown bread and slathered it with butter.

"Only that Bremmer had made inquiries at his club about finding a solicitor, but that could mean anything. The other tidbit I learned was that Bremmer was frequently threatened with being sued. Tomorrow one of my best sources will be back in town so I'm hoping to find out more."

"Don't take it to heart, Hatchet." Luty poked him in the ribs. "We all have bad days. I didn't find out much, either, and I had to doctor a boil."

"Doctor a boil?" Mrs. Goodge exclaimed. Amanda, who was sitting on her lap, giggled. "What does that mean?"

"When I was at my source's office, I fixed this young feller's boil. It was on his hand and just about the biggest one I've ever seen. But the boil ain't that important; like I said, he was a young one so he'll be just fine. What I did find out is that James Pierce is considered a decent, honest businessman who treats his employees well. But that's the only thing I heard about him. I did find out a few things about Stephen Bremmer's family and none of it was good." She repeated what she'd heard from John Widdowes. She was sure her recitation was correct because as soon as she'd climbed into her carriage, she'd made notes. Luty knew her memory wasn't as good as it used to be and she didn't want any of them making a mistake on this case because she'd forgotten something that ended up being important.

"So Stephen Bremmer lived on his wife's money and had no fortune of his own," Hatchet murmured. "Yet he's from one of the oldest families in England."

"And he lets everyone who'll stand still for ten seconds know it," Luty said. "But that's not all. I got a nice juicy tidbit about Montague Pettigrew." She cast an anxious glance at her goddaughter. "How much does our baby take in? What I'm about to tell ya ain't meant for little ears. Oh, Nell's bells, what am I thinkin'? She's too little to understand." She took a deep breath and then plunged ahead, telling them about Pettigrew's supposed love for an actor and the consequences to his inheritance prospects if his rich uncle caught wind of it.

"I heard that, too," Mrs. Goodge said. "Not about the rich uncle, but about his er . . . uh . . . leanings, shall we say."

"We found this out right quick," Smythe said, "so it's a good bet that Bremmer knew it as well. Could be that Bremmer held it over Pettigrew's head and Pettigrew got tired of it. He was sittin' at the same table as Bremmer; he was close enough to poison him."

"Isn't poison usually a woman's weapon?" Ruth asked.

"Not necessarily," Mrs. Jeffries said quickly. "But really, we must not speculate. We all know how that turns out. Once we get an idea fixed in our heads, we sometimes end up not seeing or understanding additional evidence that's right in front of us."

"I'd think that Camilla Houghton-Jones had a better reason for killing Bremmer," Phyllis said. "She'd not want the world knowing that she and her fiancé only married so he could inherit a fortune."

"That may be true, but really, conjecture about who may or may not have poisoned Bremmer will do more harm than good," Mrs. Jeffries insisted. "Besides, we don't know for certain that the man was deliberately poisoned."

"We do, Mrs. Jeffries." Smythe shifted uneasily. "My source found out the contents of the police surgeon's report. He was murdered."

"You must have a really good source," Phyllis said.

"Luty, were you finished?" Mrs. Jeffries asked quickly. She knew exactly who Smythe's source was.

"More or less, but tomorrow night I'm going to have dinner with someone who knows a thing or two about what goes on in this town and I plan on gettin' an earful then."

"You've found out a lot." Betsy grinned. "I spent half the day pushing Amanda's pram up and down the streets by the Bremmer house and not so much as a housemaid or footman stuck their noses out."

"But I'll bet Amanda loved it." Luty laughed. "And she's got such pretty rosy cheeks to show for it."

"So you heard nothing?" Phyllis said.

"The only person I spoke to was an elderly matron who stopped because the little one"—she jerked her chin toward her daughter—"kept waving at her."

"I take it the elderly matron didn't know anything about the Bremmers?" Mrs. Jeffries commented.

"She didn't even know who they were," Betsy replied. "But Amanda and I will be back at it tomorrow and perhaps we'll have better luck then."

"I'm sure you will." Mrs. Jeffries glanced around the table. "Who'd like to go next?"

"I'll have my turn now." Mrs. Goodge cuddled her goddaughter closer. She told them everything she'd learned from Ida Leacock.

"So Bremmer's father died with a string of debts," Smythe muttered. "That sounds a lot like what I 'eard."

"Well, at least that solves one puzzle," Mrs. Jeffries said. "Now we know why James Pierce was so readily accepted into his circle. He'd saved Louise Lyndhurst Mannion's brother."

"Do you think it was James Pierce that was the unsuitable attachment the Lyndhurst family feared?" Betsy asked.

Mrs. Goodge shrugged. "My source didn't know and I doubt that an old attachment from years ago has anything to do with Bremmer's death. At that time, she was only eighteen or nineteen years old. That's it for me."

"I'll go next, it won't take long," Phyllis offered. She told them about her encounter with the greengrocer's clerk. When she'd finished speaking, she helped herself to another cup of tea.

"I heard that as well," Ruth added. "My source said the same, that Anne Bremmer deliberately torments her husband by not paying his bills. Apparently, it's a miserable marriage." Without mentioning Octavia Wells by name, she repeated their conversation. "But she was bound and determined to marry him, even though she was a good ten years older than him. I also found out that it was Anne Bremmer's father that set up her inheritance as a series of trusts so that Stephen Bremmer couldn't touch it. Everything, even the house they live in, belongs to her and she doesn't let him forget it."

"Bremmer was so angry when he found out about not bein' able to touch his wife's money, he tried to take old man Lester's estate to court," Smythe added. "Oh, sorry, Ruth, I didn't mean to jump in front of you."

"I was finished. You go on and tell them what you found out."

He told them the rest that he'd learned from Blimpey.

"You mean he's got such a miserable reputation he couldn't even get a danged lawyer?" Luty cackled. "Nell's bells, that's about as low as a person can go."

"True." Smythe leaned forward aggressively. "But as the father of a daughter, I know why her father did it the way he did. Let's be honest here: There's some men that'll 'unt down a woman with a fortune and won't care about her feelin's at all. All he'll want is her money."

"Yes, but most women aren't mindless children," Ruth protested. "And from what my source told me, Anne Bremmer was no innocent girl. Her father made it perfectly clear that Bremmer was a fortune hunter but she wanted to marry him anyway."

"That's my point. If the woman is desperate enough and hasn't had a chance to marry, she'll be an easy mark," he argued. "But it's man's duty to do what he can to protect the ones he loves. I'd die before I'd let some rotter like him marry my little . . ." He broke off as his wife gave him a sharp kick under the table. The others were staring at him and he realized he'd raised his voice and been a tad too intense for someone just reporting what they'd heard. Most of those here at the table had no idea he was rich, and right now, he wanted to keep it that way. "Sorry, didn't mean to get carried away, it's just that men like Bremmer give the rest of us a bad name." He gave a nonchalant shrug. "Accordin' to my source, he's been a foul-mouthed, mean-spirited fellow for years. What's more, he gets his own back on his wife by lordin' it over her that she only comes from money and he comes from landed gentry. He's been trying to get a divorce or a settlement out of her for years. But she made it clear he'd only get one over her dead body."

"But he's the one who was probably poisoned," Hatchet pointed out.

" 'E was definitely poisoned." Smythe leaned forward. "Bremmer had enough arsenic in him to kill a ruddy 'orse."

"Arsenic?" Mrs. Jeffries said. "Was your source sure?" Something tugged at the back of her mind, some fact or idea, but she couldn't recall exactly what it might be. Smythe nodded. "He was."

Amanda suddenly heaved a cranky cry as her good mood vanished. "Now, now, pet, don't get upset." Mrs. Goodge tried to soothe her. "It's alright, whatever's wrong with our baby, we'll fix you right up."

"That's not going to work, Mrs. Goodge. She's wanting her supper." Betsy got up. "We'd best get home. Tomorrow I'll have another go at finding someone from the Bremmer household, and if I can't find anyone, I'll have a go at one of the others who were at the table when he was killed."

"I'll go 'round the pubs near the Pierce and Son offices." Smythe got up. "And I've a few other ideas as well."

Phyllis rose. "I'll do the Mannion neighborhood, which I think is also close to Camilla Houghton-Jones' home."

"And I'm goin' to see a bunch of stuffy old bankers." Luty grinned and chucked Amanda under the chin. "But then I'm goin' to dinner, and like I said, I'm goin' to git me an earful."

"As I reported earlier"—Hatchet made his way to the coat tree to get Luty's peacock blue cloak—"I'm seeing several sources, and hopefully, one of them will know something useful."

"I've people coming tomorrow." Mrs. Goodge reluctantly handed a now frowning Amanda over to her father. "And we'll see if a bit of madeira cake and plenty of tea will loosen a few tongues."

Inspector Witherspoon came in the front door only moments before Wiggins came in the back.

"Inspector, you must be exhausted." Mrs. Jeffries reached for his bowler and his heavy black overcoat. "It's already past eight."

"It's been a very full day, Mrs. Jeffries, and though I'm tired and hungry, I'm more in need of a glass of sherry and a chat before I have my dinner."

"Of course, sir." She led the way to his study. "Mrs. Goodge has a pot roast in the warming oven and it will keep until you're ready and there's a lovely rice pudding as well."

Witherspoon headed for his chair while Mrs. Jeffries went to the cabinet and pulled out a bottle of Harveys Bristol Cream sherry and two glasses. She poured their drinks, crossed the small space between them, and handed him his glass. "Here you are, sir. Now, you must tell me all about your day. You know how I love hearing about your cases."

He took a sip. "To begin with, I want to tell you that the postmortem report revealed that Dr. Bosworth was correct. Stephen

Bremmer was poisoned with arsenic. The grains were still visible in the poor fellow's stomach."

"How was the poison administered, sir?"

"The champagne flute tested positive. They found five grains in the bottom of his glass," he replied.

"And they knew for certain it was the glass that Mr. Bremmer had been drinking out of?" She had no idea why that question had popped into her head and out of her mouth, but she'd learned to trust her instincts.

"Absolutely." Witherspoon took another drink. "Luckily for us, Dr. Bosworth is a police surgeon. He supervised the collection of the evidence and the items taken from each place setting were clearly marked. It was most definitely the victim's glass that contained the arsenic and it was a massive dose." Witherspoon frowned slightly. "Though the report did mention that it was odd the victim didn't disgorge what was in his stomach rather than going into spasms. Still, the report also mentioned that could have been caused by any number of other factors including Mr. Bremmer's general health. Apparently, he was in the habit of taking a number of medicines for gout and arthritis."

Mrs. Jeffries sipped her sherry. Again, there was a tug at the back of her mind, and once again, the thought escaped before she could grab it.

"We interviewed Louise Mannion. I thought it wise to see her first as she was sitting beside the victim," Witherspoon continued. "At first she was rather uncooperative but then she seemed to realize that this was a murder inquiry." He told her what they'd learned at the Mannion home. "She helped James Pierce arrange the ball and had been to the Wrexley earlier that day to make certain things were going to run smoothly."

"Who decided upon the seating at the head table?" Mrs. Jeffries took another sip of her sherry.

"She did, but she made it clear she made the arrangement based on what the others who were going to be at the table requested. Apparently, Camilla Houghton-Jones and her fiancé didn't wish to be seated next to Stephen Bremmer."

"Did she say why?"

"They thought him a boor," he replied. "But the one question I was most interested in was how close to the table the victim was sitting."

"You mean you wanted to know if he was back far enough for someone to have slipped in and put the arsenic in his champagne?"

"Mrs. Mannion wasn't certain about it. When the lights went out there was a good bit of noise and, to some extent, confusion, so she simply couldn't say one way or another. After we saw her we took statements from Camilla Houghton-Jones and Montague Pettigrew. Unfortunately, though I usually don't approve of questioning witnesses together, Mr. Pettigrew was in Miss Houghton-Jones' drawing room when we arrived. Frankly, to my way of thinking, they'd already been together long enough to concoct any sort of story they wished, so insisting on taking their statements separately seemed rather like closing the barn door after the horses have bolted."

"I see your point, sir."

He took another drink. "In this case, it worked out quite well." He told her about his visit, taking care to repeat all the details. Repetition helped him keep things arranged properly in his own mind. Sometimes, when discussing the witness statements with his housekeeper, he'd found a completely different way to assess what people had told him.

"How so, sir?"

"Miss Houghton-Jones was defensive when I asked them about not liking Stephen Bremmer," he continued, "but Mr. Pettigrew stepped up and told what sounded like the truth. He verified Louise Mannion's comment. Neither of them liked the victim, but it sounded to me it was just a general dislike rather than a true hatred of the fellow. Actually"—he frowned and ran his finger along the rim of his sherry glass—"all of the witnesses we spoke with gave us that impression."

"I'm sorry, sir, I don't quite understand?"

"Well, everyone seemed to want us to think that though they didn't like Bremmer, they saw him more as a boor and a nuisance rather than an enemy."

"In which case, it means that none of them would bother to murder him; most people don't kill just because someone is a boor or a nuisance."

"Exactly my thoughts, Mrs. Jeffries. But despite what they all have told me, we'll keep digging. Someone hated him enough to kill him." Witherspoon sighed, took another drink, and drained his glass. "What's more, I'm not sure I believe any of them. Take for instance Elise Cory: She'd been in the United States for years and only recently came back to London. According to Montague Pettigrew, before she left England, she made it quite clear she hated Stephen Bremmer. Yet she also was careful to give us the impression that he no longer mattered to her in the least."

"Is she a suspect now?"

"I'm afraid so. When we spoke to Anne Bremmer, she stated

that when she arrived at the hotel, she saw Elise Cory hovering at the head table before everyone sat down."

"So you think she could have added the poison to Bremmer's glass?"

"It's possible," he replied. "As a matter of fact, both Constable Barnes and I are beginning to doubt that Bremmer's glass was poisoned while the lights were out."

"Why did you come to that conclusion?" she asked.

"For a number of reasons." He repeated what Anne Bremmer had told them. "She was very sure that no one could have slipped close enough to put anything in Bremmer's glass. When the lights went out, everyone was blinded. She wasn't the only one to make that assertion; I believe Wiggins told Constable Barnes the same." He glanced at his now empty glass. "I say, let's have another one, it's been a very trying day."

"Of course, sir." She refilled their glasses and returned to her seat.

"Thank you, Mrs. Jeffries." He took a long drink and sighed in pleasure.

"When did Mrs. Cory return to England?"

"A few weeks ago. She'd been living in Nevada, in a town called Carson City."

"Nevada; where's that, sir?"

"In the West, right next to California," he said. "She's widowed and when her husband died, she and her mother-in-law, who was originally from Stepney, decided to return to England. Apparently, her late husband left her quite well-off."

"Is there any evidence she's had any contact with the victim since she's been back in England?"

"Not so far, but it's early days yet. I must say, Mrs. Jeffries, she is a remarkably lovely woman." Witherspoon stared off into space with a dazed half smile on his face.

"You saw her?" Mrs. Jeffries suspected it was the two glasses of sherry on an empty stomach talking rather than the inspector.

He gave himself a small shake. "She came to James Pierce's office when we were interviewing him. I think he's got very strong feelings for the young woman."

"Why is that, sir?"

"Before she arrived, he was most cooperative and answered all our questions quite easily," Witherspoon replied. "But once she was there, when we asked her about her dislike of the victim, he got very aggressive and tried his utmost to shield her."

"How do you mean, sir?"

Witherspoon repeated as much of the interview as he could now recall. When he was finished, he put his glass on the table and stood up. "Gracious, Mrs. Jeffries, I'm quite light-headed."

"You've had a very busy day, sir." She got up. "Go on to the dining room. I'll bring your dinner right up."

Downstairs, Wiggins was tucking into his own meal. "Cor blimey, I'm hungry enough to eat a 'orse." Fred, who was sitting next to him, bumped his head against his knees. "I'll take you walkies as soon as I've finished, boy."

"I already took him out." Phyllis hung the dishcloth she'd been using on the bottom edge of the plate rack so it could dry.

"That was nice of you." Wiggins stuffed another bite of stew into his mouth.

"He gets lonely for you and I couldn't stand to see him pacing back and forth along the back hall." She sat down across from him. "You were very late tonight."

"I know and I didn't want to be. Cor blimey, I thought I'd never get out of there. I met up with Ellen after she got off work because I wanted to find out what was what."

"And did you?" Phyllis knew she had no right to question him but she couldn't help herself. Mrs. Jeffries had left strict instructions that no one was to pester the lad and that he was to have his supper and then go up to bed.

"'Course I did." He grinned. "You know the day after a murder they'd all be talkin' about it at her office and I was dead right." His smile disappeared. "But I think I might have made an awful mistake."

"What was that?" Phyllis struggled to keep her tone casual. In truth, she was dying to know more.

Wiggins tried to think of the best way to put it so he didn't sound like a conceited idiot. "It's hard to say it straight out."

"Just go ahead and tell me," she demanded.

"Alright, I will, but before I do, you've got to promise me you won't think I'm bigheaded or thinkin' too 'ighly of myself."

"I'd never think that, Wiggins," she promised. "Give me a little credit. I know what kind of person you are."

"Well, when I first got to the warehouse and she saw me walkin' toward her, she got this big, bright smile on her face and it weren't just a friendly, nice smile. It was the special sort that someone might give someone they were a bit sweet on. That's when I realized she might 'ave got the wrong impression. So as soon as I got up close, I told her that I was seein' one of me mates off at Liverpool Street Station and that I needed to speak to Tommy and could I walk home with her."

"You didn't want her thinking you were interested in her as a sweetheart or anything like that." Phyllis was incredibly relieved. "Is that it?"

"That's it exactly. Mind you, once I got to 'er 'ouse, Tommy was there and he bent me ear for over an 'our talkin' about football." He took another huge bite.

"That must have made things easier," she murmured.

He chewed and swallowed, all the while shaking his head. "Nah, it got right awkward after that. Ellen disappeared into the kitchen to help her mum with supper while Tommy and I was chattin' in the sittin' room. Then Tommy's dad come home and he went upstairs to change his clothes, then the minute he came back down, Tommy's mum came out and asked me if I wanted to stay for supper. I didn't know what to say, Phyllis. I know they've not much money, and truth to tell, even Tommy and his dad looked surprised by her invitin' me. Tommy's always complainin' that food is scarce at his house."

"So what did you do?"

"I told them the household here would be waiting dinner for me. That none of you would eat until I got home." He sighed. "I lied."

CHAPTER 6

Mrs. Jeffries sat up, tossed the covers to one side, and climbed out of her warm bed. She put on her house slippers and grabbed her thick wool dressing gown from the foot of the bed. Slipping it on, she moved to the window and stared at the gas lamp across the road. Sleep was impossible. She'd spent hours tossing and turning, trying to decipher and make sense of what little they knew about this case, and the only conclusion she'd reached was they had some facts but not as many as they needed.

Her eyes unfocused as she gazed at the pale light and thought about the meeting they'd had this afternoon. On the surface, it appeared they'd learned quite a bit, but had they? There had already been indications that Stephen Bremmer was heartily disliked by everyone from his spouse to the local shopkeepers, so getting confirmation of that fact didn't add to what they knew about the victim.

A town coach went by, momentarily blocking the lamplight, and she blinked. To begin with, what did they *really* know about the victim? He was rude, obnoxious, cheap, and arrogant. But half the aristocracy in London shared those same characteristics and they didn't end up poisoned. But Bremmer had, so he probably wasn't just murdered over a general dislike of his character. No, someone wanted him dead for a specific reason.

This afternoon, Smythe reported that Bremmer had a separate source of income from his wife. She let that idea play in her head for a moment and then shoved it aside. Until they knew exactly where the money came from, it was pointless to speculate. For all they knew, he might have been selling off trinkets he'd found in his wife's attic.

A wave of tiredness washed over her and she gave up thinking about the case. Instead, she let the bits and pieces she'd learned today come and go as they would. The inspector thought everyone was trying a bit too hard to pretend that the victim was nothing but a boor and a nuisance, but was that the truth? Bremmer was more than an obnoxious pest to someone. Perhaps one of them at that table hated him enough to want him dead. Perhaps someone did manage to put poison in his glass or perhaps they put it in their own glass and then made a quick switch when the lights went out.

Bremmer wanted to leave his wife but Anne Bremmer wouldn't give him a settlement, and until proven otherwise, he'd no money of his own. She was prepared to put up with a miserable marriage to get what she wanted, but if there was so much as a breath of a scandal attached about her, she'd never be presented at court. But now it seemed that Mrs. Bremmer's troubles were over. She was a respectable widow, and as long as she didn't remarry, she could have her moment at Buckingham Palace. Thus far, she was the only one who actually benefitted from Bremmer's death.

Of course, they'd also found out that both Camilla Houghton-Jones and her fiancé, Montague Pettigrew, might have reasons to be glad that Bremmer no longer walked among the living. Especially if he knew about Pettigrew's past indiscretions. From what they had learned about the victim, he had the sort of character that delighted in the misery of others. But they had no evidence Bremmer was aware of the situation.

She smiled as she remembered the inspector's expression when he spoke about Elise Cory. For a moment, he'd looked like a lovestruck lad. But it was Mrs. Cory who was the unknown quantity in the mix. As the inspector had said when she'd brought up his dinner tonight, all the others at the top two tables had been here all along, but she'd just come back from America. Perhaps she was the ingredient that finished the recipe, perhaps her appearance had either caused someone else to commit murder, or perhaps she still hated Stephen Bremmer enough to kill him.

Mrs. Jeffries realized she was jumping to conclusions. Don't be a fool, she told herself, Elise Cory coming to London might just be another coincidence. God knows this case was simply full of them. Yawning, she got back into bed and pulled up the covers. But just as she was falling asleep she realized what that nagging feeling in the back of her mind was trying to tell her.

"That's all I've got this morning, Mrs. Jeffries, and you've probably already heard most of it from the inspector." Constable Barnes picked up his tea.

"You've added a bit more detail," Mrs. Jeffries assured him. "That's always helpful."

"We've heard a few bits that might be useful to you and the inspector," Mrs. Goodge added. "I had a word with my friend Ida Leacock yesterday and found out a few things." She told him everything she'd learned and then glanced at Mrs. Jeffries. "Your turn."

"Let me start with what Wiggins told me this morning," she said. "He wasn't here for our meeting yesterday afternoon, but he did find out a few things." She told him what the footman had reported and then added to the narrative by repeating what the others had found out. "The last thing I'd like to mention, Constable, is the number of widows and widowers who seem to be suspects."

"I know; the inspector and I were talking about that yesterday," Barnes replied. "Three people under the age of thirty and they are all widowed. It's odd to say the least."

"It might just be coincidence," the cook suggested. "We've had a bushel full of them in this case."

"True." Barnes put his cup down. "But I'm still going to look into the circumstances of how they died."

"Even Mrs. Cory? From what I understand, her husband died in Nevada."

"Are you going to send a telegram to the local sheriff?" Mrs. Goodge asked eagerly.

"I don't think I'll need to go that far." The constable chuckled. "Her mother-in-law came back to England with Mrs. Cory. I'm going to ask her how her son passed away."

"That sounds like an excellent idea," Mrs. Jeffries murmured. "I imagine if there was any foul play suspected in her son's death, she'll tell you about it." In truth, she had completely forgotten that the widow Cory's mother-in-law had come back with her.

Barnes got up. "I'll leave you to it, ladies. See you tomorrow morning."

He disappeared up the stairs. The two women tidied up the kitchen and readied it for the morning meeting.

Everyone was at the table only a few moments after the inspector and Barnes had left by the front door.

"You go first, Wiggins," Mrs. Jeffries instructed, "and when you've finished, I'll report what the inspector told me last night as well as what the constable told Mrs. Goodge and I this morning."

Wiggins told them about his encounter with the maid from the Wrexley Hotel. "At first I was disappointed when she told me she'd not even been at the hotel when Bremmer was murdered, but after Mrs. Jeffries told me everything you've all found out, I'm thinkin' I ought to go back again," he concluded.

Mrs. Goodge put her elbow on the table and rested her chin on her fist. "Sorry, I'm not following. Why would you go back to the hotel?"

"It's 'ard to explain, but when Mrs. Jeffries was tellin' me all the other bits and pieces we've learned so far and then she said that it was even possible that Bremmer wasn't poisoned when the lights went out, it made me think that maybe someone played about with the flute before the party even started . . ." His voice trailed off as he saw the skeptical expressions on their faces. "I didn't say it made sense, but seems to me it makes more sense than someone droppin' the poison into his flute in full view of the musicians and everyone else in the room."

"But it wouldn't have been possible for anyone to know which glass Bremmer was going to have," Mrs. Jeffries pointed out. "What's more, the only two people who were even at the Wrexley prior to Bremmer's murder were James Pierce, who was there several weeks earlier, and Louise Mannion. She was there that day, but thus far, she's the only person who doesn't seem to have a motive for the murder. What's more, I doubt she was given leave to roam the hotel's pantry or storage rooms at will."

"I know that," he protested. He couldn't put his finger on it, but he was certain there was something they weren't seeing, something right under their noses, and he was determined to find it. "But look, it'll not take long to go back and do a bit of snoopin'. Who knows, I might find out somethin' useful."

"I suppose it couldn't hurt." Mrs. Jeffries looked doubtful. "But there is a lot more territory to cover on his case. It's important that someone makes contact with the households of the others that were at Bremmer's table."

"I can try the Mannion household and perhaps I'll even have time to do Camilla Houghton-Jones today," Phyllis offered.

"Nicholas Parr lives off the Marylebone High Street"—Betsy shot the footman a quick smile—"and I've been wanting to do a bit of shopping."

"You're not takin' our baby, are ya?" Luty hugged the child so close she giggled. "It's too cold out there today."

"The girl from upstairs is going to watch her," Betsy lied. In truth, she'd hired Mrs. Packard, who was from upstairs but was hardly a girl, to help out now that they had a case. But as her new employee wasn't just a nanny, but a proper housekeeper as well, Betsy didn't want anyone around this table wondering how she and Smythe could afford it.

"I might have a go at James Pierce's neighborhood," Smythe offered. "I've got to meet another source today, but I should have time to do both."

"The only one left is Elise Cory," Mrs. Jeffries murmured.

"She's only been in London a few weeks," Mrs. Goodge said. "Maybe her servants won't know anything."

"Why don't you let me try to find out about Mrs. Cory?" Hatchet proposed. "She's an artist, so my source might know something about her."

"So I'll go to the Wrexley this mornin'." Wiggins grinned and started to get up.

Phyllis grabbed his arm and he flopped back into his chair. "Aren't you forgetting something? You've still got to tell us what you found out from Ellen."

"Cor blimey, I almost forgot." It didn't take long for him to relate what he considered the pertinent details of his meeting. The only thing he left out was his feeling that Ellen had gone a bit sweet on him. They didn't need to know that. There were simply some things a fellow could only share with a sympathetic soul like Phyllis.

Nicholas Parr lived in the top flat of a four-story redbrick town house in Marylebone. Barnes reached for the shiny brass door knocker just as the door flew open and a middle-aged woman wielding a shopping basket and wearing a checked cloak stepped out.

Surprised, she gaped at them. "Oh dear, you're the police. You're here bright and early today."

"Yes, ma'am, and we're here to speak to—"

"You're here to see Mr. Parr," she interrupted. "Mr. Parr told me to send you up. He's right at the top. Go on, then, he's been expecting you."

They entered the foyer and started up the carpeted staircase. By the time they reached the final landing, both men were out of breath. Barnes waited till they'd stopped panting before he knocked. A dark-haired man who appeared to be in his early thirties wearing navy blue trousers and a white shirt opened the door. "Excellent, you're here at last. Did Mrs. Guthrie let you in?" He waved them inside.

"Yes, she was just going out to do her shopping," Barnes explained as he and the inspector stepped across the threshold. The sitting room was furnished with an overstuffed green and gold chesterfield sofa, a matching chair, two end tables, and three bookcases filled with books.

"I'm Nicholas Parr." He motioned them toward the sofa. "Please, make yourself comfortable."

Witherspoon made the introductions as they sat down. "Mr. Parr, you obviously know why we're here."

"Of course. It was a dreadful business, Inspector." Parr sat down across from them. "I've seen death before, but that was my first time witnessing a murder."

"It's never an easy thing to see, sir," Witherspoon said. "Mr. Parr, I understand you are on the board of Pierce and Son?"

"That's correct, that's why I was at the Lighterman's Ball."

"How long have you known Mr. Pierce?"

"Several years," Parr replied. "We've been in partnership with Pierce and Son since James took over after his father died. My family's company, Parr Customs Brokers and Freight Forwarders, is in

New York; we're agents for Pierce and Son. I met James when he came to New York to find a firm to handle his business interests."

"And that's your company?" Barnes said.

"Correct. When James found out I was moving to London, he invited me to be on his board. My company is hoping to expand into Europe, and England is a very good place to start."

"Thank you, sir," Witherspoon said. "Background information is always helpful to us. Was this your first time at the Lighterman's Ball?"

"Yes. I've been to London several times, but this was the first time I'd been invited to the ball."

"Did you see or hear anything unusual when the lights went out that night?"

"Nothing, Inspector. I was blinded when the room went dark."

"What about hearing something?" Barnes added.

"I heard plenty, but there was nothing that sounded unusual or out of place. It was what one would expect to hear; chairs scraping, people coughing, someone dropped some silverware, that sort of thing."

"Can you recall if you saw anyone hovering around the head table prior to everyone sitting down?"

Parr's eyebrows drew together. "That's a difficult question to answer. I saw a number of people around the table, including the victim. But I don't remember seeing any one person specifically."

"What time did you arrive at the ball?" Witherspoon asked.

"It was just past six forty-five. I wanted to get there early to have a word with James Pierce."

"Was Stephen Bremmer there when you arrived?" Barnes asked.

"I don't recall seeing him, but I wasn't paying all that much attention. I wasn't looking for him. I needed to see James. I wanted to let him know that the letter of credit from New York had arrived."

"I see." Witherspoon nodded. "How long have you known Stephen Bremmer?"

"I met him on January eighteenth of this year," Parr replied.

"You recall the exact date?" Barnes looked up from his notebook.

"Of course. It was the first meeting of the proposed board for Pierce and Son. We didn't do any official company business; it was organized simply to introduce me to the rest of the board."

"That was your first encounter with Mr. Bremmer?" Witherspoon asked.

"No, but that was the first time I met the man." Parr smiled slightly. "I had 'encountered' his reputation previously. Would you care for some tea?"

The inspector shook his head. "No, thank you. What do you mean, you'd encountered his reputation?"

Parr looked down at the floor and then took a deep breath before raising his chin. "I don't like to speak ill of the dead, but in this case, I'll make an exception. When I walked into that first meeting and was introduced to Bremmer, I was quite shocked. Unfortunately, I'd heard some very unsavory things about the fellow and I'd heard them from a source that I trusted implicitly. Naturally, I couldn't raise any objections to the man coming onto the board publicly, because what I'd heard was just gossip, but it was the sort of gossip that I felt James needed to hear."

"What did you do, sir?" Barnes pressed.

"I waited till everyone had left the meeting and then I told James what I'd heard about Stephen Bremmer."

"And what was that specifically?" the constable urged.

"That Stephen Bremmer was a blackmailer and that his victims were members of his own social circle." Parr's lip curled in disgust. "That's right, he preyed on his friends, people who trusted him."

Witherspoon leaned forward. "What did Mr. Pierce say when you passed along this information?"

"At first he just stared at me, then he sighed and said, 'I know.' "

Phyllis walked as slowly as she dared around Barlow Square. It was cold and miserable but she was determined to do her best to find someone from the Mannion household. But so far, no one had come out the lower ground-floor servants' door of number fourteen. She wasn't sure how much longer she could last. Not only was the weather not cooperating, but she'd already had to duck behind an oak tree when she'd seen Jenny Marshall striding toward her swinging a shopping basket. This neighborhood was too close to Upper Edmonton Gardens for her liking. There were too many like Jenny who knew her and could get in her way if someone happened to come up those servants' stairs.

She rounded the square, her gaze on number fourteen, when she heard a door slam and, a second later, footsteps pounding up the heavy metal steps. She stopped and looked at the pavement, pretending she'd dropped something. A blonde-haired young woman wearing a maid's cap and a short red jacket stepped onto the pavement. She carried a wicker basket on her arm.

Phyllis dawdled for a few seconds before she dashed across the empty road after the girl. She followed her, waiting until they'd both turned the corner and were out of sight of the house before she made her move. Servants were more likely to speak freely if there were no prying eyes watching from their employer's windows. "Excuse me, miss," she called.

The girl stopped and looked over her shoulder, her expression wary. "Were you speaking to me?"

Now that she was closer, she could see the girl had brilliant blue eyes and even, pretty features.

"I was." Phyllis smiled. "I'm so hoping you can help me. You see, I'm lost and my mistress will be ever so cross with me if I'm late getting back. But I don't know this part of London. I told her that before she sent me here but she insisted I come anyway."

The girl's expression grew a bit less wary. "Where are you lookin' to go?"

Phyllis was ready for this question. She reached into her pocket and pulled out a slip of paper. "Patton's, it's her dressmaker's. My mistress wants me to pick up her new gloves."

"I know the place. You're not far from there. Come along, you can walk with me. I'm going that way as well."

"Thanks ever so much." She fell into step next to the young woman. "My name is Phyllis Jones."

"I'm Marie Parker." The girl gave her a shy smile. "It's nice to meet you, Phyllis. You don't work around here?"

Phyllis hesitated before she answered. There was a good chance that if she lied, she might run into Marie at some time in the future and that wouldn't do at all. "Actually, I do work nearby, I just didn't want to sound like a country bumpkin so I fibbed a bit. I'm so sorry, but I've not been here long and I didn't want you thinking I was stupid. I get enough of that where I work. I'm a housemaid."

"Your mistress a harsh one, then?" Her steps slowed.

Phyllis adjusted her pace. Perhaps Marie wasn't in a hurry to get back to work. "Not as harsh as some, but she gets angry easily."

"She'll be angry if you're late?" They'd come to the corner and stopped, waiting for a break in the heavy traffic.

"I exaggerated a bit, well, because I needed your help. I really was lost, and if I can be honest, I wanted someone to talk to. Do you ever get like that? I mean, there's another housemaid, and of course, there's a scullery girl who helps the cook, but they've both been there for a long time and I just got hired a few weeks ago. They're not real friendly." She was making it up as they walked, hoping that her pathetic tale would loosen Marie's tongue. "What's it like where you work?"

"The girls are friendly enough," Marie replied. "But the mistress can be hard. She's a sharp tongue and likes to find fault."

"Oh dear, it sounds like your mistress might be worse than mine," Phyllis exclaimed.

"I'm thinking of looking for another position." Marie shifted her shopping basket to her other arm. "But finding work isn't easy and I'm not sure I can get a reference."

"Without a reference, finding another place is almost impossible." Phyllis yanked her handkerchief out of her pocket and swiped at her nose.

"Impossible or not, I'm going to try," Marie vowed. "I'm fed up. She's gone too far this time and now she's having a fit over a stupid serviette, can you believe it? Ever since the master died, she's gotten meaner and meaner with money. Right after his funeral she started takin' the cost of our tea and sugar from our wages, but this is too much." She came to a halt and turned to Phyllis. "I've looked all over the ruddy house for her stupid serviette, but it isn't anywhere to be found, but she keeps on at me about it, telling me over and over that I've got to find it, that it was handmade in France 'specially for her." She snorted. "That's a bloomin' lie. It's just a plain white serviette like every other one in the house. I can't afford to keep workin' for her. Last quarter I had to pay for a plate I dropped and a cracked cream pitcher that I swear was already damaged before I touched it."

"Oh dear, that sounds dreadful. How awful for you. When did this serviette go missing?" Phyllis felt bad for the girl. "Sometimes when I lose something, I retrace my steps. Perhaps that will help."

"Not this time. The stupid serviette disappeared three days ago when she had that awful man who just got murdered to tea. I was tidying up like I always do and I'm real careful these days, but before I could finish clearing up properly, Mr. Pierce came to the house unexpectedly and she shoved me and the serving cart out of the drawing room so she could entertain him. By the time I got back in the room, the serviette was nowhere to be found."

"Someone was murdered?"

"Mr. Bremmer was killed the next day. He was poisoned." She shot Phyllis a curious glance. "Don't they get newspapers where you work?"

Phyllis lowered her eyes, hoping she looked embarrassed. "They do, but I don't read very well."

"I'm sorry, that was mean of me." Marie touched her arm. "It's just the last few days have been a misery."

"It's okay." Phyllis kept her head lowered as she swiped at her dry eyes and then gave Marie a shy smile. "I'm fine. At least my mistress hasn't had one of her friends murdered."

"Mrs. Mannion was actin' peculiar well before Mr. Bremmer was killed." Marie started walking again. "The day he was comin' to tea she had me running up and down the back stairs like she was expecting the Queen and not an old friend she's known most of her life. First the silver jam pot wasn't good enough so I had to go down and fetch the old china one, then she wanted the matching ceramic spoons that haven't been used in donkey's years so I had to spend half an hour in the butler's pantry findin' the ruddy things, and then, mark me, if she didn't split the scones and slather them with cream. She was probably afraid Mr. Bremmer would use too much." She heaved a sigh.

"You poor thing." Phyllis nodded sympathetically. "I tell you what, if you've time, there's a café on the high street; I'll treat you to a cup of tea and you can tell me all about it. Believe me, I know what it's like to work for someone bad-tempered, unpredictable, and miserly."

It was early in the day, not yet half ten, and Wiggins knew he was taking a risk by coming to the Wrexley. Mid-morning wasn't a normal time for changing shifts, but he knew that the hotel was cutting their employees' working hours so there was a chance someone might come out.

A cold, damp wind slammed into him and he wished he were back in the warm kitchen of Upper Edmonton Gardens. If they didn't have a murder, he'd be sitting down to morning tea next to Phyllis. The others would be there, too, but it was only the housemaid he wanted to think about now. He couldn't understand the lass—one moment she was treating him like her brother but then the next she was getting her nose out of joint because he was hanging around Ellen. She'd tried to hide it yesterday but he could tell she'd been really irritated when he announced he was going to Pierce and Son. Last night, he'd made it clear that he wasn't interested in Tommy's sister but now he wasn't so sure it had been a good idea for him to be so honest with Phyllis. Maybe she'd like him more if she thought he liked someone else? He caught himself as the idea raced through his mind. Nah, that was stupid, and he was headed for a fall if he read too much into Phyllis's attitude. Across the road, the back door opened and a young man wearing a black coat and flat cap stepped out and hurried down the stairs.

Wiggins caught up with him as he was turning out of the mews. "Can I 'ave a quick word?" he asked.

"If it's about that ruddy murder—" The fellow looked over his shoulder toward the hotel. His face was narrow, his skin pale, and his hair brown. "We're not to talk about it."

"I'll make it worth your while." Wiggins gave him a confident smile. "I'm a reporter and if I don't show up with somethin' my guv's goin' to be right annoyed. Come on, there's a pub just up the road. You look old enough, I'll buy ya a pint."

He hesitated. "Alright, but not that pub. I don't want anyone seein' me talkin' to a stranger. There's a crowded one by the station, let's go there."

They didn't talk as they made their way to the pub. The place was full but Wiggins saw two men at a table at the end of the bar get up. "Grab that spot and I'll get us a couple of pints."

A few minutes later, Wiggins put their beer on the table and sat down on the stool. "My name is Albert Jones."

"I'm Joey Finnigan." He took a sip of his beer and closed his eyes in pleasure. "This 'ere is just what I needed. Thanks."

The name sounded familiar to Wiggins. "What do ya do at the hotel?" He took a quick sip as well.

"I'm supposed to be a waiter, but these days they 'ave us doin' all sorts of things. I spent half me time this mornin' workin' in the storage room." He took another drink. "What's more, this bloomin' murder is makin' what was already a bad situation even worse. We've had two big cancellations since that bloke was poisoned and Mr. Sherwood—he's the new catering manager—is having a right old fit about it. It's not fair, I tell ya, just not fair."

"So the staff is havin' a tough time," Wiggins suggested.

"That's puttin' it mildly. I was supposed to work till noon today but they sent me off at half ten. They're on the warpath about every little thing, cuttin' back people's work time, countin' every bit of glass or plate that we need to use. We've got to serve people. Honestly, a ruddy glass or two disappears and Mr. Sherwood and Mr. Cutler both think we've a thief in the kitchen. But we don't. The police took away all the stuff that was on the table where Mr. Bremmer was murdered, that's what happened to the missing glasses. I know, I was there and I saw them take 'em away."

Wiggins was beginning to think he'd made a mistake. Joey was telling him the same bits and pieces he'd heard yesterday. "Speakin' of the murder—" he began only to be interrupted.

"We weren't talkin' about that, there's naught left to say on the subject," Joey declared. "Poor bloke got himself killed and it's all of us workers at the Wrexley who are payin' the price. Mr. Cutler and Mr. Scargill have both hinted that if business doesn't pick up soon, some of us will be let go and I know it'll be me. Tableware is expensive, and when the police send the items back, it 'ad all better be there. Especially them damned champagne flutes, they cost the earth. Mind you, Hilda Jackson—she helps Mr. Sherwood—she claims one of the flutes went missing before the ball that night, but Hilda likes to talk and make herself sound important, you know, like she knows more than the rest of us, so I don't know if I believe her."

"I do hope that Mr. Pierce will still be in his office when we finally get there." Witherspoon grabbed the handhold as the hansom swung hard around the corner and into the heavy traffic of Oxford Street. "I know it makes sense to interview Mrs. Cory first. Her home is in Kensington and much closer than Pierce's office, but I'm very anxious to speak to him."

Barnes braced himself with his feet. "I don't think it'll take that long to interview Mrs. Cory. Look, sir, I know you want to ask Pierce about Mr. Parr's claim that Bremmer is a blackmailer, but I think it's important we have a word with Mrs. Cory as well. You were right, sir, there is and was something strong between Pierce and Mrs. Cory and it could have some bearing on this case. As we discussed before, sir, she's the only new factor that was introduced into this mix of suspects. All the rest of them have been part of the same social set for years."

"That's true."

"The gossip I heard was that James Pierce was fixing to marry Mrs. Cory and then she up and left the country. Could be her leaving had something to do with our victim."

"You were told specifically that the two of them were going to get married?" Witherspoon pushed his spectacles up his nose. "Who told you this?"

Barnes cringed inwardly. He was exaggerating a bit as no one had really confirmed the two of them were going to marry, but considering the information he'd learned from the household, he knew he was on the right track. The worst that could happen was that Elise Cory would deny the rumor. "My wife's cousin. She visited last night and she couldn't wait to tell me. She's a real talker, sir, and she's got the best memory I've ever seen. Truth to tell, Mary only came to see us because she lives in Dagenham and wanted to tell me what she knew."

"Do you think her information is reliable?" Witherspoon jammed his heel into the floor as the cab hit a pothole.

"Absolutely. She and her late husband used to run a pub on Crown Street and as I said, sir, she loves to chat."

"And your wife's cousin claimed that the previous relationship between Pierce and Mrs. Cory was far more serious than either of them have admitted."

"That's what she said."

"Do you think Mrs. Cory returned to England because she knew Pierce was now a widower?"

"Well, there's something strong between them. As you pointed out, sir, Pierce did his best to protect her when we started askin' questions," Barnes said. "And I got the feelin' she answered us so quickly to make sure we didn't poke him too hard, if you get my meaning. I've just got a feelin' about it, sir, a feelin' that we need to take a closer look at how everyone who was there that night might be connected. You know, sir, it's like that 'inner voice' of yours."

The inspector nodded. "I understand exactly what you mean. I think all policemen have a sort of instinct, or as you and Mrs. Jeffries put it, our 'inner voice.' So, let's hope that Mrs. Cory isn't out shopping or visiting."

Elise Cory lived on Rutherford Way, a quiet street off the Kensington High Street. They stepped out of the hansom and Witherspoon studied the house while waiting for Barnes to pay the driver. It was a two-story brown brick house with a cream-colored ground-floor façade and a lower ground floor surrounded by a black wrought-iron fence.

Barnes led the way up the short walkway and banged the knocker. A moment later, a young housemaid opened the door. "You're the police. Mrs. Cory said you might be coming." She opened the door wide and ushered them inside.

The foyer was narrow with white walls, a mirror in an intricately carved wooden frame, a coat tree, and a polished oak parquet floor that stopped at the carpeted staircase.

Witherspoon swept off his bowler. "Mrs. Cory was expecting us?"

"Not particularly, sir, but she said you might be coming to ask her more questions and if she was home, I was to show you in. I'll take your hat, sir." She hung it up and led them past the staircase and into the drawing room.

Elise Cory rose to her feet. "Hello, Inspector, Constable, please come in and have a seat."

Witherspoon nodded politely. It was difficult not to stare at her. She was as lovely as he remembered, and to avoid looking like a fool, he focused his attention on the room.

The walls were painted a pale yellow, the carpet a muted shade of patterned gold, and the furniture a mix of armchairs upholstered in bright flowered prints, side tables stacked with books and magazines, and a hunter's green settee. The furnishings were neatly arranged around a white-painted stone hearth. A beautiful seascape held pride of place over the mantelpiece and on the opposite wall was a portrait of a man. A painter's easel and worktable were next to the window. Despite the gloomy overcast day, the room was cheerful and inviting. "Thank you, ma'am." He sat down on one of the overstuffed chairs. "I hope we're not keeping you from anything, but we do have a few more questions for you."

"I expected you would." She sank down on the settee. "You're not keeping me from anything, Inspector. I've got a luncheon engagement later today but that's not until one o'clock. Would you care for tea or perhaps coffee? I have both."

"Nothing, thank you," Witherspoon assured her. "Mrs. Cory, exactly how long have you been back in England?"

"I arrived here on January fifteenth. My mother-in-law and I came on the *Lucania.* We landed in Liverpool, spent the night there in a hotel, and then came to London. I'd already rented the house and arranged for a small staff, so after a stop at the estate agent, we came straight here."

"Your mother-in-law lives here as well?" Barnes balanced his notebook on his knee.

"That's right. She's in Stepney at the moment, visiting."

Barnes made a mental note to come back and have a word with the other Mrs. Cory. "Was the Lighterman's Ball the first time you'd seen Stephen Bremmer since you've been back?"

"My answer is the same as when the inspector asked me that question when we were in James' office. That night was the first time I'd seen him since I returned home. The truth is, I've tried to avoid running into some of my old acquaintances. But in his case, it couldn't be helped."

"What do you mean?" Witherspoon asked.

"I couldn't avoid going even though I suspected Bremmer might be there. When I accompanied my mother-in-law back to her old neighborhood in Stepney, I ran into James' aunt and she insisted I go to the ball. Unfortunately, my mother-in-law joined in, and before I knew it, I'd agreed to go."

"Was there any particular reason you wanted to avoid your previous friends and acquaintances?" The inspector deliberately added the word "friends" to see how she'd react.

"Of course, Inspector." She laughed. "I was very angry and upset when I left England. My father had died and circumstances had forced me to move in with my cousin. Nora treated me as well as can be expected, but one doesn't like living as a poor relation. When I was given an opportunity to leave, I took it."

"You were offered a position?" Barnes asked.

She nodded. "As a governess. I'd been giving drawing lessons to Abigail Franklin, and when her parents decided to go to San Francisco, they offered me a position. I worked for them for a year."

"You told us before you were an artist," Barnes reminded her. "You do portraits."

"Before my father died, I'd done two portraits, but neither of them paid very well. Frankly, once he was gone, I didn't have the heart to go on painting. It took me several years before I picked up a brush again. So when I moved in with Nora, I started giving drawing lessons."

"What did you do after leaving the Franklins?"

She looked amused. "I got married and moved with my husband first to Sacramento and then to Carson City."

"Mrs. Cory, you previously told us your dislike of Stephen Bremmer was because you blamed him for your father losing the chance to show his work at a gallery," Witherspoon said.

"He was also a boor, a brute, and a bully," she added.

"But according to your previous statement, you weren't in the same social circle," Barnes pointed out. "So how often were you even around him?"

Her expression hardened. "Too often for my liking. I know it sounds ludicrous, but due to some very odd circumstances, we often found ourselves at the same events. My father's work was constantly in demand by the shipping companies for their ships and their offices. When a painting was being displayed for the first time, there was usually a small celebration and, as my mother passed away years ago, I often accompanied my father. Stephen was almost always a guest at these events, probably because of his family's previous involvement in the industry. Add to that, I lived next door to the Pierce family and they were socially acquainted with the Lyndhursts. So we'd find ourselves at the same village fetes, teas, that sort of thing."

"I see," Witherspoon muttered. "When you arrived at the Lighterman's Ball, did you go to the head table before the festivities started?"

"That's an odd question." She cocked her head to one side. "Why do you ask?"

"Because we have a witness who says they saw you looking at the place cards ten minutes before the ball started."

"They were mistaken. It wasn't me," she insisted.

Barnes looked up from his notebook. "Forgive me, ma'am, but

I think that someone mistaking another woman for you is unlikely. You've a most memorable and lovely face."

She stared at him for a moment and then burst out laughing. "There isn't a woman alive who wouldn't like to hear a compliment like that, Constable. You're right, of course, I did go to the table and I did it to look at the place cards. I was hoping against hope that Bremmer wouldn't be there that night. I didn't want to see him. His very presence brought back old and uncomfortable memories."

"If you were *that* afraid of seeing Bremmer, why did you give in and agree to attend?" Barnes persisted. "Was it because you wanted to see James Pierce?"

"Leave James out of this."

"Mrs. Cory, we know you and Mr. Pierce were very, very close before you left the country," Witherspoon began.

"That is in the past and irrelevant to anything. I'll admit that I loathed Stephen Bremmer and didn't wish to see him. I should never have let Mary Pierce talk me into attending that night. But I didn't realize that James had put him on the board so I wasn't absolutely sure that Stephen was actually going to be there."

"Why didn't you tell us this before?" Witherspoon watched her carefully.

"Why?" She stared at him in disbelief. "I loathed the man and he was murdered the very first time I was near him. I didn't wish to become a suspect and I knew that once you found out the history between the two of us, you'd cast your eyes upon me. But I had nothing to do with his death."

"But you hated him, didn't you," the constable charged, "and not just because of what he'd done to your father. Tell us the truth, Mrs. Cory. We're going to find out eventually."

She took a deep breath and looked toward the window. The curtains were tied back and the bare winter garden was visible. "He tried to make me his mistress. That's the reason I actually left. When my father was alive, Bremmer didn't have the nerve to accost me. But once he was dead and I had to sell our home and move in with Nora, he changed and became very aggressive—" She broke off and swallowed. "He told me I ought to be grateful. I told him to burn in Hades, slapped his face, and ordered him out of Nora's house. Then I went around to the Franklin home and accepted their offer of employment."

"Can anyone corroborate your story?" the constable asked.

She looked at him sharply. "Of course not. Nora has been dead over a year, and even if she weren't in her grave, she couldn't verify what I just told you. She wasn't home when it happened."

"What about the servants?"

"I think the housekeeper might have been there, but I don't think she was eavesdropping."

"Did you tell your cousin or anyone else about Bremmer's behavior?" Witherspoon asked.

"Absolutely not. Why would I? The whole episode was humiliating and disgusting. But when she came home that day, Nora knew something horrible had happened. She knew Bremmer was coming to the house; he'd claimed he wanted to sell me back one of my father's paintings. When I told her I was leaving, she didn't even try to get me to change my mind."

"Is it likely she would have mentioned anything to anyone?" Witherspoon pressed. He sensed she was telling the truth, and if that was the case, he didn't think it likely she'd have waited eight years to get vengeance. More likely, she'd do her best to avoid Bremmer rather than kill him.

Elise shrugged. "It's possible. Later, she may have mentioned something to James."

"James Pierce?" Witherspoon said.

"Yes, of course. She was his wife. They married a few months after I left."

CHAPTER 7

"Your cousin and James Pierce married after you left?" Barnes blurted.

Her expression hardened and a faint flush crept up her cheeks. "That's right."

"Mrs. Cory, how did your cousin die?" Barnes watched her closely.

She looked from one policeman to the other, her expression incredulous. "What on earth does Nora's death have to do with Stephen Bremmer's murder? She died over a year ago."

"While you were still in America," Barnes said. "Nonetheless, the lady, like Mr. Bremmer, is dead."

"Heart disease, Constable, she had a weak heart. She'd had it all her life. It finally killed her." Her eyes filled with tears. "I felt terrible that I was so far away when she passed. We were very close."

"You kept in touch after you left?" Witherspoon asked.

"Of course. Nora took me in and was very kind to me. I loved her very much. But she understood my need for independence."

"Did James Pierce understand it as well?"

She drew back. "I've no idea what you're talking about, Constable. Why should James have had any opinion on the matter?"

"Because we have it on good authority that you and he were practically engaged and then you suddenly up and left."

"That's an impertinent question and I refuse to answer it. What happened eight years ago has nothing to do with Bremmer's death." She shot to her feet. "Now, if you'll excuse me, I've an appointment."

Barnes didn't move until he saw Witherspoon get to his feet, then he followed suit.

"Thank you for your time, ma'am." The inspector bobbed his head politely. "I do assure you, we're not deliberately being disrespectful. We're trying to solve a murder and often that involves asking what appears to be insolent or personal questions."

Her expression softened. "Yes, I suppose you're only doing your job. Forgive me, I shouldn't have reacted so badly. Let's start again, shall we? I loathed Bremmer, but I don't approve of murder, Inspector. It's only right that *even* his killer is caught."

"Thank you, Mrs. Cory, I appreciate your willingness to help us. Were you and Mr. Pierce contemplating marriage?" Witherspoon sat back down.

"We had talked about it." She smiled. "James and I had been close for many years and people assumed we were going to marry. After my father passed away, James proposed to me."

"And what did you say?" Barnes took his seat as well.

"I asked him for time." She closed her eyes.

"Was he willing to give you the time you needed?" the inspector asked.

"It surprised him. I think he expected I'd agree immediately." She sighed. "I loved him very much, but there was something else I wanted in my life and I wasn't sure that it would fit well with his ambitions."

"What do you mean?" Witherspoon queried.

"I'm an artist, Inspector, and as I've said, my interest is portraits. That's where my talent lies."

"Like that one?" Witherspoon pointed to the portrait hanging opposite the fireplace.

She smiled. "That's my father. I painted it the year before he died. He was a wonderful man and a wonderful artist. He did that seascape." She nodded toward the mantelpiece. "It was the only one of his paintings that I took with me to America. I had to sell all the others."

"You didn't keep his portrait?" Witherspoon asked in surprise.

"I only kept the seascape. I had to sell the portrait. Luckily, I was able to buy it back. But that's neither here nor there, Inspector. You want to know why I didn't marry James Pierce. That's the reason right there. My work."

"I don't understand, Mrs. Cory." Barnes stared at her skeptically. "You've already told us that when your father died, you didn't have the desire to paint. You said it was several years before you could pick up a paintbrush again. So how could that be a problem between you and Mr. Pierce?"

"Because I knew that, one day, I'd stop mourning and want to paint again."

"Mr. Pierce objected to you being an artist?"

"Not at all, but he didn't need an artist for a wife." She put her hand on her throat. "He was working very hard. I barely saw him. He was consumed with expanding his business. Pierce and Son was no longer just a small company with three barges pulling cargo off the big lines. They were growing fast and James was determined to make Pierce and Son a force to be reckoned with in the business world. James is a very modern man and he'd never object to my doing what I loved doing, but I knew that his company had grown so much that he had to consider the social aspects of his decisions."

"In what way?"

"In every way, Constable. It was pointed out to me that James needed someone to act as a hostess and do the required entertaining. He didn't need a wife with paint smudges on her face."

"But a wife with paint smudges on her face who can produce a work like that"—Witherspoon nodded at the portrait as he spoke—"should make any man proud. You've made your father come alive; it's as if he is going to step out of the frame and into the room with us. You've an amazing talent, Mrs. Cory, and such talent should be shared with the world."

"Thank you, Inspector. You're very kind and you've touched upon the heart of my dilemma. James would never forbid my work from being shown and that's of course what every artist wants, but in this day and age it wouldn't do his business any good."

"I don't understand, Mrs. Cory." Witherspoon thought of his beloved Ruth and her tireless work for women's equality. "There are a number of women artists. Why shouldn't they be allowed to show their work? Why shouldn't they have the same opportunities as men do?"

"I agree, Inspector." She looked amused. "They should, but you've a very enlightened attitude. Despite women making progress in society, the prevailing attitude is that women should be in the home, not the world. Prejudices run deep, Inspector, and I didn't want James' business prospects harmed by my being an artist. It was as simple as that."

"Thank you so much for your help, Mrs. Guthrie." Betsy gave the middle-aged woman a grateful smile. "I've never been so confused before in my life. I was sure I was following the directions correctly." She'd arrived at Nicholas Parr's address just in time to see Constable Barnes and the Inspector going inside as this lady came out. She'd made Mrs. Guthrie's acquaintance by asking for directions.

Betsy knew she was good with people, especially servants; she could almost always get them talking about their households. But this woman was no housemaid or footman and Betsy was glad she'd worn her blue and gray tweed suit and matching hat. It was an elegant outfit she never wore to Upper Edmonton Gardens, but the expensive tailored clothes seemed to reassure Mrs. Guthrie. She insisted on accompanying her to Oxford Street. She hadn't needed much persuading to have a nice sit-down and a cup of tea.

"It was my pleasure, dear. London streets can be very puzzling and I was glad to help you." Adele Guthrie, housekeeper for the gentlemen lodgers at her Marylebone home, glanced around the crowded tea shop and then at the tray of pastries in the center of their table. She reached out a chubby hand, picked up a lemon tartlet, and put it on her plate. Her hair was more gray than brown, her face pleasant, and her eyes a dark blue. She wore a formfitting checked jacket over her short, plump frame. "Some of my gentlemen get lost when they first come to London. But I tell them not to worry, there's always someone who'll point you in the right direction."

"Your gentlemen?"

She took a bite of tartlet, chewed, and swallowed. "I have several gentlemen lodgers. When Mr. Guthrie passed away, I couldn't afford the upkeep on that big house so I turned to taking in lodgers. I know some people look askance at letting rooms in one's own home, but my gentlemen are properly scrutinized. I insist on two character references. The situation has worked quite well for me. I can keep my home and I have some very delightful company."

"How very clever of you." Betsy helped herself to a chocolate biscuit. "Your lodgers must be interesting people."

"Indeed they are. One of my lodgers, Mr. Parr, had the police come today to speak with him." She picked up the delicate white and green teacup and took a sip of Earl Grey.

Betsy's eyes widened. "Gracious, how very exciting. Why did they wish to speak to your lodger? I'm sorry, perhaps I shouldn't ask. My papa always told me I was far too inquisitive."

"Nonsense, if one doesn't ask questions, one never finds out anything." Mrs. Guthrie put her cup down and waved dismissively. "They came to speak to him about that murder at the Wrexley Hotel. Surely you've read about it, it's been in all the papers."

"I saw it this morning," she assured her. "Do go on. Was your Mr. Parr a witness, then?"

"Indeed he was. He was right there when the poor man died. He was sitting at the same table."

"Was he friends with the gentleman who was murdered?" Betsy took a sip of her tea.

Mrs. Guthrie shook her head. "Not at all. He and Stephen Bremmer, he's the one who was killed, were business acquaintances. The two of them were going to serve on the same board of directors for some company, it's a shipping firm I believe. Poor Mr. Parr was in a dreadful state when he came home."

"I'm sure he was. Seeing someone die in such a manner must have been awful."

"Luckily, I happened to be up when he got home. I don't usually stay up that late. If my tenants are going to be out past nine o'clock, I give them a key to the front door, but I had indigestion and so I got up to mix a bicarbonate of soda. The moment Mr. Parr walked into the kitchen, I could tell something was wrong. His face was as white as a sheet." She looked thoughtful. "I suppose it must have been the shock. They weren't friends. Mr. Parr was annoyed that the two of them were going to be on the same board of directors, but his company in America did a lot of business with this firm here and so he had no choice."

"Is Mr. Parr an American?"

She took another bite before she answered. "He is. He's a nice man, very kind and helpful. But he does find some of our habits strange."

"What do you mean? Aren't Americans very much like us? After all, we speak the same language."

"I don't mean to imply he thinks we're barbarians, but he does take exception to some of our culinary choices." She laughed. "Mr. Parr loves his coffee and simply cannot understand the English obsession with tea, which he dislikes intensely. It's become a bit of a joke in the household; at dinnertime he tells us about the lengths he goes to to avoid drinking it. But sometimes he simply gets trapped and has no choice. The afternoon of the murder, he was at a board meeting before the ball and, of course, after the meeting, tea was served. Mr. Parr thought he saw his chance when everyone started chatting and moving about the office, looking out the window and being sociable. He was going to pretend to take a sip and put the cup on the windowsill. But that didn't work because Stephen Bremmer had put his cup on the sill and one of the ladies picked it up and brought it to him. He didn't wish to call attention to the fact that he loathes one of our national drinks, so he waited until no one was looking and dumped the tea into a potted plant."

"He should have said he didn't like tea," Betsy commented.

"I asked him why he didn't and he said that he didn't feel he should." Mrs. Guthrie took another tartlet. "He said his relationship with the owner of the other firm was already a bit awkward and he didn't want to add to it."

Barnes finished paying the driver and joined the inspector on the pavement. They were at Pierce and Son. After leaving Elise Cory, they'd gone to the station and read through the statements made by the guests at the other top table. They'd made good time across town but the end of the workday was fast approaching. "I hope he is still in his office."

"Why wouldn't he be here? They're still doing business," the inspector said as he headed for the open side of the huge bay doors. A flat wagon was being loaded with boxes, barrels, and trunks.

"Because he's in the shipping business, sir, and according to his secretary's statement, Mr. Pierce is the sort of man who relies on his own eyes and ears rather than just listening to reports. He spends a lot of his time out of the office and keeping a close eye on his shipments. Not because he doesn't trust his employees, sir, but because he likes to know what's what."

"His secretary was most forthcoming about Mr. Pierce and the way he does business. It was a good idea for us to stop at the station and read their statements."

The two policemen were in luck, as James Pierce was in his office. "Inspector, Constable Barnes, I didn't expect to see you quite so soon. Come in and have a seat. Do you have news? Have you arrested the culprit?"

"I'm afraid not, sir," Witherspoon said as he and the constable sat down. "But we do have more questions for you, sir."

Pierce looked puzzled. "But I've already told you everything I know about what happened."

"You told us what you know about the night of the murder, sir, but we've some questions about the board of directors meeting you had earlier that day."

Pierce looked confused. "The board meeting? Surely you're not interested in my business terms. They're standard limited liability terms."

"No, Mr. Pierce, we'd like to know if anything unusual might have occurred?"

"We had the business part of the meeting and then I asked Phillip to bring in the tea, we drank our tea, and then"—he broke off with a laugh—"then Mrs. Mannion volunteered to wash up the tea things because I was letting the staff go early. It's a fair distance between the East End and the hotel. People needed time to go home and change their clothes."

"How long did the board members stay after the staff had gone?" Witherspoon asked.

He thought for a moment. "Not long, perhaps twenty minutes or half an hour. It doesn't take long to drink a cup of tea, Inspector."

"What was everyone doing?" Witherspoon asked.

"People chatted and milled about the office. Nicholas Parr showed us a set of photographs from the American West. Montague Pettigrew was looking at some old manifests—they're actually quite interesting—and Stephen was staring at one of the paintings on the wall. Camilla Houghton-Jones and Anne Bremmer had gone over to the window. I could see Camilla and Anne were amused by Louise offering to wash up the tea things and, truth be told, so was I. But she's tried very hard to help me with this event so don't think I'm not grateful to her. "

"I take it Mrs. Mannion isn't domestic," Barnes said.

"She was raised with servants." He folded his arms over his chest and sat back. "I don't see how the board meeting had anything to do with Stephen's murder. Why are you asking all these questions?"

"Background information is very important, Mr. Pierce," Witherspoon replied. "Additionally, I'd like to get some sense of everyone's movements and whereabouts on the afternoon of the murder."

Pierce relaxed. "I can't speak for anyone but myself, but I was here until five o'clock and then I went home to get ready for the ball. The meeting was over at about half past three and then, as I said, everyone stayed for tea. Most of them left about four. Except for Anne Bremmer and Louise; she went down the hall with the tea things and then came to say good-bye a few minutes later."

"What about Mrs. Bremmer?" Barnes asked.

"I kept her company while she waited for Louise and then they indicated they were going to share a hansom back to their homes. They live quite close to each other."

"You'd let the staff go so there is no one who can verify you were here until five that evening," Witherspoon commented.

"That's right, but I did stop and speak to Mr. Crawley on my way to the station. He runs the tobacconist stand across the road."

"Do you keep any poisons on the premises? Rat poisons, prussic acid, anything like that?" Barnes asked.

Witherspoon noticed the constable hadn't mentioned arsenic.

Pierce laughed. "No, we don't. My father never liked using poisons, he said they were too dangerous. We use cats. They're quite efficient and they not only keep the rats out of the warehouse, but they keep them from coming up here."

"Was this the first meeting of your board?" Witherspoon shifted in a bid to get comfortable.

"No, we had a preliminary meeting on January eighteenth."

"Was that the first time that Mr. Parr met Stephen Bremmer?"

Pierce's expression grew wary. "It was."

"On the eighteenth, Mr. Parr stayed behind to speak to you privately after the others had gone," Barnes commented. It was a statement, not a question.

"I think you already know the answer to that, Constable," Pierce retorted. "Nicholas told me that he had it on good authority that Stephen Bremmer was a blackmailer."

Witherspoon stared at him coldly. "Don't you think this is information you should have told us immediately? Blackmail could have been the reason Stephen Bremmer was murdered."

"I doubt that, Inspector." Pierce got up and walked to the window. "I struggled with whether or not to repeat what I'd heard. But I couldn't bring myself to do it. There was no proof, you see. I only had Nicholas Parr's word on the matter and he refused to say how he'd learned it. So I said nothing." He turned to face them.

"Was that because you didn't believe Mr. Parr?"

"I believed him; I knew it to be true."

"How did you know?"

"Because Stephen tried to blackmail me, Inspector." He sighed, went to his chair, and sat down. "But it was such a stupid, clumsy attempt I simply didn't take it seriously. Frankly, when Nicholas Parr made the accusation against Stephen, I assumed it was the same sort of ridiculous nonsense he'd tried with me."

"But you still asked him to be on your board of directors?" The constable met his gaze.

"That's right. As I just said, I didn't take him seriously. But what I did take seriously was my promise to my father." Pierce smiled wryly. "And I believe I've already told you about that."

"What information did the victim claim to have against you?"

"It was so idiotic, it was unbelievable; but then, Stephen was quite stupid."

"Tell us anyway," Barnes ordered.

"It happened about seven years ago. I don't recall the exact date. Stephen asked me to meet him for dinner. I thought it odd as we weren't friends and had nothing in common, but he insisted. We met at Carnack's on Oxford Street. He'd already ordered a bottle of wine and was well on his way to being drunk when I arrived. We ordered our dinner and chatted politely. Finally, as the coffee was being served, he told me he knew something about me, something that would ruin my reputation." Pierce broke off and smiled cynically. "He said he had it on good authority that Elise had gone to America because she was terrified of me. That he knew I had threatened to kill her and our unborn child."

"What did you say?" Witherspoon asked.

"I laughed in his face." Pierce leaned forward. "I'm sure by now you'll have discovered that at one time, Elise and I were very close." He looked away. "I'd hoped we would marry. But our relationship was not of a carnal nature nor was she ever involved with anyone else. She was certainly not pregnant when she left England."

"Then why did Bremmer think he could blackmail you?" Barnes stared at him curiously.

"He was desperate for money," Pierce replied. "Anne had cut him off that quarter and he was about to get tossed out of the only club that still allowed him in as a member."

"But surely, sir, he had to have known you'd not go along with his foolishness," Barnes argued. "The two of you have known each other for years. I've only met you a few times, but given what I've seen and heard about you, you'd be the last person I would think could be blackmailed."

Pierce gave a genuine laugh. "Thank you, Constable, I think you've either complimented me or let me know you think I'm lying. But I'm not. As I've said before, Bremmer was a fool. He thought everyone was like him: vile, stupid, and willing to do anything for money and status. He tried it on with me because he knew the firm had expanded and he was hoping I'd pay him off to avoid a scandal. It would have been bad for business. But I didn't. Instead, I laughed at him and invited him to my home to see all the letters that Elise had written to my wife, Nora."

"What did he do then?" Witherspoon asked.

"He shrugged, drained his coffee cup, stood up, and said, 'It was worth a try.' Then he left, sticking me with the bill."

Hatchet frowned at his host, Reginald Manley. "I've been here twice since Christmas, so you can't accuse me of only coming to see you when I need information."

"Don't take him so seriously. Reginald's just teasing you." Myra Manley cast a quick frown at her handsome husband. The three of them were sitting in Myra's comfortable morning room sipping tea. "Regardless of why you're here, we're delighted to see you."

Reginald put his teacup down. "Of course we are. I can't believe this case involves Elise Newcomb. She's a brilliant portrait artist. She's much better than I am."

Hatchet laughed. Reginald and Myra Manley were always wonderful to visit. He was black-haired, blue-eyed, and middle-aged, but still handsome enough to cause more than one matron to cast an envious glance at his wife, Myra. She was brown-haired, long-faced, and slightly bucktoothed. Her face wasn't conventionally beautiful, but it was compelling. Reginald was an artist but not one who'd found substantial success. Myra was from one of the richest families in London. They'd met, fallen in love, and married against the wishes of just about everyone in both their circles. Neither his bohemian artist friends nor her aristocratic ones could understand the bond between these two. But Hatchet could see it; they were devoted to each other.

They were also devoted to justice and had provided important information on other cases. Reginald had colleagues from the art world in both England and Europe while Myra had access to news and gossip from the wealthiest in London.

"Now, don't say that, darling," Myra chided. "You can't compare the two of you. Even if you both do portraits, you're still very different. Besides, you've only seen one of her paintings. Perhaps the others are dreadful."

"Where did you see her work?" Hatchet didn't recall anyone saying that Elise Cory—or Newcomb as she was then—had exhibited in London.

"At her father's funeral reception," Reginald replied. "I'd gone to pay my respects because I was acquainted with him and I admired his work. He painted seascapes and still lifes. He was quite successful. But like so many artists, he spent it as soon as he got it and left his poor daughter destitute."

"But you said she was a brilliant artist," Myra pointed out. "Why couldn't she sell her own work? People with money always want their portraits done."

"Yes, but Elise Newcomb was young and very, very beautiful, so I doubt that many wives would fancy her painting their husband's picture. Some women, especially rich ones, don't respect the idea that a woman can even be an artist."

"Surely that can't be true," she protested. "If her work was as good as you claim, even the stupidest of the rich would rather have their portraits done by a woman with talent than a mediocre man."

"There's the rub, my dear." Reginald smiled ruefully. "Very few people would have been able to see her work unless they'd gone to her father's funeral."

"But surely she could have had an exhibition. And galleries are always wanting fresh talent."

"They say that, but it isn't true. Art galleries are in business to make money, not give budding talent a showcase," he said. "Getting an exhibit is difficult even for an established male artist. For a young woman, it would have been nigh impossible."

"Perhaps that is why she left the country," Hatchet speculated. "Perhaps it's easier to be accepted as an artist in America."

"In the West, perhaps, but in the big Eastern cities like Boston or New York it's much the same as here." He stretched his shoulders. "But it is easier now than it would have been eight years ago, which I believe is when you said she left England. I'm not saying a woman artist couldn't be accepted, but it is ten times more difficult for them. Add to that she was so very young when her father died. I doubt anyone would have taken her work seriously."

"But you saw the portrait she did of him and you said it was brilliant." Myra sat up straighter.

"And it was, but that doesn't mean anything," he argued. "Creativity cannot be equated with commerce and galleries show what they think will make them money. Many wonderful artists never get their work recognized and she was a young woman with only a small body of work. Even if a gallery owner recognized the quality of her talent, they'd have been wary of giving her a chance."

"Humph, that's what's wrong with this world," Myra said. "Hard work and talent should be rewarded, not gender and prejudice."

"I agree, darling. On the bright side, I think we've made progress in the past eight years. Perhaps now that she's a rich widow, she'll buy a gallery and have her own show." He looked at Hatchet. "Who else might be a person of interest to your inspector?"

"Do either of you know or know anything about James Pierce or Nicholas Parr?"

"Sorry, no," Reginald said.

Myra gave a negative shake of her head. "I'm afraid not. Anyone else considered a suspect?"

"His wife, Anne Bremmer, she was sitting next to him and could easily have added poison to his glass. Add to that, we've heard she made him miserable."

Myra interrupted. "She did, but as you already know it, go on."

"Louise Lyndhurst Mannion was on his other side, but I can't see her murdering him. As far as we know, she had no reason to want him dead, and they grew up together."

"From the shipping family?" Myra asked.

He nodded. "Do you know her?"

"I've met her socially but we're of different generations so it was only the most superficial of acquaintances." Her brows drew together. "She's an odd one, though. Incredibly beautiful, but with such a perfect face, she's—"

"Boring," Reginald interrupted.

"Yes, I think so. At one time, she had every young man in society paying court to her. People were quite stunned when she married Osgood Mannion. He was rich but hardly a dashing, romantic figure. He drowned in a boating accident at their country house last year."

"And she's now a very rich widow," Hatchet mused. "As are several of our other suspects."

"Who else?" Reginald prodded.

"Camilla Houghton-Jones and her fiancé, Montague Pettigrew." He paused as they exchanged amused glances. "I think I know why you're smiling. We've already heard that Pettigrew was in love with an actor."

"It's common knowledge," Reginald stated. "What I can't understand is why she wants to marry him."

"Because he's going to inherit a fortune." Myra smiled wryly. "If he can keep his uncle in the dark."

"But she's rich herself," Reginald argued. "With her money, she should be able to do better than Pettigrew. The man's a silly fool, and I'm not saying that because of the actor fellow."

"Her family was rich," Myra corrected. "But all she has is that huge house and an allowance from a trust. Her father lost everything and that big house belonged to her mother, who left it to Camilla. She lives on the interest from the trust and is continuously short of money."

"How do you know that?" Reginald charged.

"The same way we know everything, darling: gossip. As far as I can see, she and Pettigrew are well suited to each other."

"So she needs Pettigrew's inheritance," Hatchet murmured.

"I imagine so," Myra said. "From what I've heard, Camilla Houghton-Jones is very ambitious socially."

"As is Anne Bremmer." Hatchet sipped his tea. "She wants to be presented at court."

"Ironic, isn't it." Myra put her cup down, her expression thoughtful. "Louise Mannion and Elise Newcomb Cory are the only two women involved in this affair that don't seem at all concerned about their social status."

"Louise Mannion is," Reginald said. "I remember her now; I saw her at the Barrington ball. She pranced in as if she owned the place. I doubt she'd allow anyone to sneer at her."

"True, but only because she always assumes she's better than everyone else," Myra declared. "She would have had an irrationally high opinion of herself even if she'd been born poor. Her character is very strong; she's never cared what people think of her."

"How do you know that?" Hatchet asked.

"Because she fell in love with a man from the working class, and despite it causing a minor scandal, she declared she'd never give him up. At one point her father almost disowned her. But they reconciled and her father agreed that if she went on a European tour for six months, when she returned, she could marry the man of her choice."

"So he gave in to his daughter's demands? Why? He was the one with the money." Reginald looked skeptical.

"Because she was all her father had left." Myra smiled triumphantly. "Her father wouldn't cut her off because her brother had died."

"But she agreed to leave the man she loved for six months," Hatchet pointed out.

"Yes, but perhaps she thought that it was worth leaving if she got to marry him when she returned."

"All right, I'll grant you that one, but why didn't she marry this pauper when she returned?" Reginald asked.

"Because by the time she got back from Europe he'd married someone else."

"Let me go first," Luty demanded when everyone, except Wiggins, had settled at the table. "I've got to get home so I can get ready to go to dinner tonight."

"Of course, Luty," Mrs. Jeffries said.

"But Wiggins isn't here yet," Phyllis protested. "Shouldn't we wait for him?"

"You can tell him later," Luty replied. "I spent most of the day with bankers and tryin' to get anything interestin' out of that tight-lipped bunch would take a miracle. But I got one. I found out somethin' good."

"Do tell, madam," Hatchet said.

"Camilla Houghton-Jones is desperate for money. She's got creditors chasin' her and she's been pestering Pettigrew to set the date for the wedding. The gossip is that Pettigrew's uncle is going to give the two of 'em a hefty settlement when they marry." Luty stood up. "That's all I found out; now I'm goin' to git home to change into my clothes for my dinner out. Hatchet, you listen sharp so you can tell me what everyone said later tonight."

"I'll probably have retired by the time you come home." He sniffed disapprovingly.

"You still have your nose out of joint because I'm lettin' Jon accompany me tonight instead of you," she accused. "I'm only doin' it so you can stay here and hear what's what. We can't both miss the meetin'. I'll see you at home tonight." She hurried off down the back corridor.

They heard the back door open well before Luty could have reached it. "It's about time you got here," Luty said. "The meetin' has started but I'm the only one who's talked yet, so you git on in there and have some tea. You look half frozen."

"As usual, Madam has the last word," Hatchet muttered.

"Sorry I'm late," Wiggins apologized as he slipped off his coat and hat. "Where was Luty goin' in such a hurry?" He hung up his garments and took his seat.

"To a dinner party. She's meetin' a source tonight." Mrs. Goodge reached for the teapot and poured a cup for the footman.

"At least she found out something useful today. I didn't learn anything."

"Neither did I," Smythe said. "No one in James Pierce's neighborhood knew anything about him. He's not lived there very long." He'd also gone to see Blimpey but he wasn't at the pub.

"I didn't find out much more than you did." Betsy shot her husband a quick grin. "I had morning tea with Nicholas Parr's landlady." She told them what she'd heard from Mrs. Guthrie.

Mrs. Goodge looked doubtful. "Why was Nicholas Parr so upset if he didn't like Bremmer?"

"Mrs. Guthrie thinks it was the shock of seeing someone die."

"That's possible, I suppose." The cook still didn't look convinced. "But it seems to me that we'll need to find out more about Nicholas Parr."

"You don't like him because he doesn't like tea," Betsy teased.

"I don't trust anyone who doesn't like tea. It's barbaric!"

"Can I go next?" Wiggins paused for a second, and when no one objected, he plunged ahead. He told them about meeting with Joey Finnigan. "Things are miserable for the workers. I felt sorry for poor Joey and the rest of 'em."

Mrs. Jeffries thought for a moment. "Wiggins, this Hilda Jackson, she said one of the champagne flutes was missing before the ball?"

"That's right, but Joey claimed she liked to exaggerate and make herself sound important."

"Nonetheless, I think you should speak to her," Mrs. Jeffries said. She realized his comment had sparked a thought, something much like the one that had flown into her head last night and then disappeared as fast. "Find out all you can about when she noticed the flute was gone."

"Alright, I'll see if I can find 'er tomorrow."

"The same thing happened to me today," Phyllis murmured. "I spoke to a maid from the Mannion house today. Her name was Marie Parker and she's miserable about her work as well." She told them about their conversation, taking care to ensure she didn't forget any of the details.

When she'd finished, Mrs. Goodge shook her head in disgust. "Why is it the rich are always so tight-fisted. You'd think Louise Mannion could afford to buy a serviette instead of tormenting that poor girl."

"She can, but I'm not sure it's in her character to want to," Hatchet said. "According to my source today, Mrs. Mannion has a highly exaggerated opinion of herself and an overly developed sense that she's entitled to anything and anyone she wants." He told them everything he'd heard from Reginald and Myra Manley. "So, there you have it. By the way, my source also told me about Camilla Houghton-Jones being desperate for money."

"Good, the more confirmation, the better." Mrs. Jeffries looked at Ruth. "Anything?"

"No, I'm sorry; I tried my best today but no one at either of my committee meetings knew anything. But I'm having tea with an old friend tomorrow and she might know something."

"Excellent. Goodness, it's getting late." Mrs. Jeffries started to get up but then sat back down. "I'm going to see Dr. Bosworth tomorrow."

"But why?" Phyllis stared at her curiously. "We already know Bremmer was poisoned."

"I know, but there's something bothering me, something that keeps prodding the back of my mind. I think I know what it is, but

I'm not certain," she explained. "Perhaps Dr. Bosworth can help me see it more clearly."

They broke up a few minutes later. Wiggins took Fred for a walk, Hatchet set off to find a hansom, and the others left to their own homes. Mrs. Jeffries went upstairs to tidy the drawing room while Phyllis and Mrs. Goodge attended to their supper.

Mrs. Jeffries lighted the lamp by the window and tested the tabletops for dust. She looked down at her finger, saw a few specks, and decided the room could wait a day or two before it needed a good clean. Walking to the window, she loosened the curtain ties and started to pull the heavy velvet drapes shut, when she saw a hansom pull up and the inspector step out.

She dropped the curtains, letting them fall together, and hurried into the foyer.

"Good evening, sir." She reached for his bowler. "We weren't expecting you this early. Usually when you have a murder, you're home late."

"It was a busy day, Mrs. Jeffries, and frankly, I didn't think my poor brain could cope with taking another statement."

"You know what that means, sir," she said cheerfully.

"Huh, er, no . . . What does it mean?"

"Oh, sir, now you're teasing me. It means your 'inner voice' needs to have a good, long think about the case." She meant every word. Over the years, she'd realized that though they helped with his cases, he was now quite a good detective in his own right. His skills had sharpened and his "inner voice," or policeman's instincts, had blossomed.

"I certainly hope that's true." He laughed as he unbuttoned his overcoat, slipped it off, and then hung it on the coat tree.

"It absolutely is true. This is your method, sir, the way you do things. It happens in every case and I, for one, am delighted it's happening now. It means you're getting closer to the truth. Would you like a sherry? Dinner isn't quite ready as yet."

He laughed as he started down the hall. "Not to worry, I'm in no hurry to eat. Let's have a nice glass of sherry. I've so much to tell you."

CHAPTER 8

Mrs. Jeffries followed the inspector into his study. She closed the heavy drapes, lighted the gas lamps, and then went to the liquor cabinet and poured their drinks. Outside, the weather had worsened as a storm rolled in from the west. The windows rattled and rain splattered hard against the panes.

"Have you had a successful day, sir?" She handed him his glass and took her own seat across from him.

He thought for a moment before he replied. "I'm not sure. We learned a number of facts but I don't see how any of them come together in any meaningful way." He took a sip.

"It's still early days yet, sir," she assured him. "And you generally don't see any sort of pattern until you've had time to think everything through and connect it all together. Now, sir, do tell me about today."

"We started off by interviewing Nicholas Parr. We'd left him till last because he seemed the one person to have had the least involvement with the victim, but our assumption was wrong."

"In what way, sir?"

"Let me rephrase my comment, I'm not saying it correctly. It wasn't that Mr. Parr had any prior involvement with Bremmer, at least none that we know of as yet, but he had information." Witherspoon took a sip and put the glass down on the table next to his chair. "He told us that Stephen Bremmer was a blackmailer."

"A blackmailer? If that is true, sir, it could well explain why Bremmer was poisoned." Mrs. Jeffries thought about Mrs. Goodge's comments after they'd heard Betsy's report on her chat with Parr's landlady. Perhaps the cook was right; perhaps Nicholas Parr should be examined more closely.

"It's true, Mrs. Jeffries. We verified it when we spoke with James Pierce. He admitted that seven years ago, Bremmer tried to blackmail him."

"Why didn't Pierce tell you this before?"

"He claims he had good reasons for keeping quiet, but I'm getting ahead of myself." Witherspoon wanted to take his time reciting the events of the day. His discussions with Mrs. Jeffries helped him to make sense of the information. It was folly to rush ahead with only the dramatic highlights.

"Why don't you start at the very beginning, sir," she suggested. "I do love hearing all the particulars."

"As I said, our first stop was with Nicholas Parr." He told her everything he could recall and then continued on with the interview with Elise Cory. The only way he could keep things straight in his mind was to go through his day in chronological order.

Mrs. Jeffries listened carefully, but the facts and details were piling up quickly and she was afraid she'd forget something important. She started to fret and then took a deep, quiet breath. Calmer, she sipped her sherry and reminded herself that come tomorrow, they could ask Constable Barnes anything she might miss tonight.

Witherspoon paused and took a quick sip.

"So Mrs. Cory admitted she genuinely loathed the victim and not just because of the way he'd treated her father," Mrs. Jeffries said.

"That's right, but the most shocking thing she told us was that her cousin had married James Pierce." The inspector's eyebrows rose. "This was the first time we'd heard this information."

Mrs. Jeffries went rigid. Ye gods, she thought, surely they'd not made this sort of mistake? They already knew about this. Wiggins had heard it from Ellen two days ago. She thought back to their meetings with the constable and her worst fears were realized. Both she and Mrs. Goodge had forgotten to mention it. This wouldn't do, it wouldn't do at all, but right now, she had to concentrate on what the inspector was saying. She'd deal with this matter later. "That is odd, sir. I wonder why it was never mentioned."

"Perhaps no one thought it important." He pushed his spectacles up his nose as he thought back to the interview. "Mrs. Cory seemed to think we already knew."

"And this came out after she'd admitted that Bremmer tried to force her into becoming his . . . uh . . . paramour?"

"Yes, that's the reason she took the job with the Franklin family and left London." He resumed his narrative, telling her about the remainder of the interview. "After we left Mrs. Cory, we were so close to the station it seemed foolish not to stop in and read the statements from the guests sitting at the table next to the victim. Mrs. Cory was sitting there as well as several members of James Pierce's family and some of the office staff."

"Did you learn anything new, sir?"

"None of them had seen or heard anything of significance when the lights went out but we found out more details about the board meeting they'd had that afternoon before the ball. Then we went to see James Pierce." He drained his glass and started to set it down. "Do we have time for another before dinner?"

"Of course, sir." She went to the liquor cabinet, refilled his glass, and topped hers up.

"What happened at Pierce and Son?" She handed him his sherry and sat down.

Witherspoon told her about their meeting. "His reasons for keeping silent about the blackmail attempt were because Nicholas Parr refused to tell him where he'd heard it and because Bremmer was so incompetent at it that he didn't take him seriously," he concluded.

"And his blackmail attempt was about seven years ago or thereabouts," Mrs. Jeffries asked.

"That's what he said." Witherspoon grimaced as another blast of wind rattled the windows.

"Blackmail is a compelling motive for murder." She took a sip and stared out at the rapidly darkening sky. "Bremmer may have been incompetent seven years ago, but you know the old saying: Practice makes perfect."

Witherspoon chuckled. "I had the same thought myself, Mrs. Jeffries."

* * *

Luty frowned as the wind slammed against the windows of John and Chloe Widdowes' Mayfair mansion. Her hosts sat across from her on a coral and green silk striped sofa. She dragged her gaze away from the burgeoning storm and took another, fast glance around the lovely room. The walls were painted a rich cream color and hung with some beautiful paintings of landscapes and still lifes. The decorative molding along the ceiling was white and bright, and colorful rugs covered the oak parquet floor. A huge mirror hung over the white marble fireplace, which was flanked by two brass urns containing peacock and ostrich feathers.

"Luty, you look worried. Is everything alright?" John Widdowes asked.

She caught herself. "I'm fine, just don't want Hatchet tyin' himself in knots because I'm out so late. But he knows that Jon is with me and Cecil—he's my coachman—is better at handlin' a team of horses than anyone I've ever seen."

"Good, we want you to enjoy yourself with us," Chloe Attwater Widdowes exclaimed.

Luty laughed. "I intend to. Now, what is this big news you've been hintin' at since I walked in your front door?"

"You won't believe it, but let me start by saying I had such fun tracking the woman down." She waved her wineglass in the air. "And I'm so glad I did, because as they say in California, I hit pay dirt." Chloe Widdowes was past the first flush of youth, but still very beautiful. Her dark brown hair was devoid of gray and her complexion unlined. Tonight she wore a formfitting teal evening dress that accentuated her still slender figure. But it was her character, not her appearance, that drew people to her. She was smart, fearless, fair, and most of all, kind.

"How'd ya do it?" Luty asked. "More important, how'd ya know who to track down? I've never heard of this Mabel Philpot."

"Neither had I until I started asking about James Pierce," Chloe explained. "That led me to his late wife, Nora, and then to Mabel Philpot, who was Nora's housekeeper before she married James Pierce."

"But why did you think she might have something useful to say?" John stared at his wife curiously.

"I didn't know if she could tell us anything or not, but I thought it might be worth my while. If you'll recall, I've been somewhat involved in two of the inspector's previous cases—once as a suspect and once as a witness."

"As have I," John said.

"You were never a suspect." His wife laughed. "I was, but that's not my point. In both of those two cases, the roots of the crime were in the victim's past. So I decided that the past might be a good place for me to start."

John looked doubtful. "But Nora Pierce wasn't the victim. Stephen Bremmer was. Nonetheless, you obviously learned something that you think might be useful. Come on, tell us what you heard before we get called in to dinner. You know how easily I'm distracted by good food."

"To start, I went back to the neighborhood where Nora and her cousin lived before Elise went to America and Nora married James Pierce." She broke off and took a quick drink of chardonnay.

"But why them in particular? There's half a dozen suspects in this case." Luty thought she knew the answer to the question, but she wanted to see if her thinking was right.

"Because the murder occurred within a few weeks of Elise Cory returning to England. All the other suspects have been here and in quite close contact with one another for years. The only circumstance that we know changed was her arrival." Chloe smiled brightly.

Luty was relieved, glad that her own ideas were being echoed. "I was thinkin' along those lines myself."

"I don't know that I agree." John put his whiskey glass on the table next to him. "You're both forgetting James Pierce. For the first time, he's bringing in investors to Pierce and Son. That could just as easily be a factor in Bremmer's murder."

Chloe didn't look convinced. "True, that could be what triggered the murder, but I don't think so. Now, let me tell you what I've found out. Elise Newcomb, as she was then, lived with her father the artist, Dounton Newcomb, in the house next door to the Pierce family. They all lived on Whalebone Lane in Dagenham. Nora, Elise's cousin, lived with her parents in Greenwich but she was often at the Newcomb home. She developed an attachment to James Pierce, but from what I've learned, he only had eyes for Elise. Everyone, and I mean everyone, was sure that James and Elise would marry. To put it simply, they were madly in love. Then Dounton Newcomb died and Elise had to sell their home and move in with her cousin, Nora."

"Who also had romantic dreams about Pierce," Luty clarified. "Nell's bells, he must be a handsome feller to have so many women moonin' over him."

Chloe laughed. "It wasn't just those two, either; the gossip I heard was that Louise Mannion was wild about him as well. Apparently, all of her friends were taking wagers on who Pierce would end up marrying. The odds-on favorite was Louise because she had a reputation for getting anything or anyone she wanted."

"But he ended up not marryin' either of 'em," Luty said.

"Let's not get distracted here," John interjected. "Tell us about Mable Philpot."

"I won't bore you with the details of my finding Miss Philpot; needless to say, I found her."

"You can tell me the details later." John's eyes narrowed.

"You just want to make sure I didn't do anything outrageous," Chloe charged.

"I want to make sure you didn't do anything *dangerous*," he shot back. "But do go on. Mabel Philpot was the housekeeper, right?"

She nodded. "Yes, and by this time, Nora's parents had passed away and she'd been left a decent-sized inheritance as well as her home. Elise moved in with her when her father died and she began giving drawing lessons to children."

"Private lessons?" Luty asked.

"That's right. According to Mabel Philpot, it was about this time when Stephen Bremmer began to make a nuisance of himself. He'd call at the house uninvited and apparently began to pester Elise with his attentions. Mabel claims she tried to get Elise to tell James about the harassment, but she was frightened that Pierce would get angry and thrash the fellow."

"I would have," John muttered. "Go on."

"One evening when Mabel was serving dinner, Elise told her cousin that James was going to propose as soon as the mourning year for her father ended, but that didn't happen. The next day, Elise was at the house alone and Stephen Bremmer practically forced his way inside. Mabel wasn't able to keep him out, but she did go to the kitchen and get a heavy cast-iron frying pan. She was afraid something was going to happen."

"She thought Bremmer was going to hurt the girl?"

"Yes, so she stood outside the drawing room door just in case. That's when she heard Bremmer tell Elise that James Pierce had impregnated Louise Lyndhurst and that the two of them were going to the Continent to get married."

"Why would Elise believe him?" John's expression was skeptical. "He was known to be a liar."

"I asked Miss Philpot and she said that James and Elise had quarreled over Louise more than once. Elise claimed that the woman had set her cap for James and he told her she was being absurd. Additionally, Pierce and Son were still very dependent on the Lyndhurst shipping line so he wasn't going to offend Louise by telling her to stay away from him. Plus James had left the day before on business and Louise had gone to Paris, so the story did make sense."

"So Bremmer shows up and tells Elise that James is elopin' with the Lyndhurst girl, right?" Luty wanted to get the sequence of events right in her own mind. "And then what happened?"

"Bremmer left a few minutes later. Miss Philpot put the skillet back in the kitchen, and before she had a chance to see if Elise was alright, she said she heard the front door slam. When she went into the parlor, Elise was gone. When she came back, she announced that she'd taken employment with the Franklin family as a governess and was going with them to San Francisco."

Luty frowned. "Didn't her cousin object?"

"Not really. Miss Philpot told me she was certain that Nora thought once Elise was gone, she might have a chance with James Pierce. By the time James got back to London, Elise was gone. A few months later, he married Nora."

"Was Bremmer lying? Was there something between James and Louise Lyndhurst?"

"It was a lie. Louise had simply gone to Europe to appease her father." Chloe sighed.

"Why did Bremmer do it, then?" Luty asked. "He didn't get anything out of it."

"Spite probably." Chloe looked disgusted. "He wanted Elise Newcomb to become his mistress, she refused, and this was his way of ruining her chance for happiness."

"That means she has a motive for murderin' Bremmer," Luty speculated.

"Are you certain of that?" John said. "It doesn't sound like she spent the rest of her days in mourning over what could have been. It appears she did very well in America. She got married to Cory."

"And from what Miss Philpot said, it was a good marriage."

"How did she know?" Luty asked.

"She and Nora wrote to each other regularly," Chloe said. "The only time the letters stopped was when Nora told her she and James had married. But a few months later, she wrote her cousin and all was apparently forgiven."

"But that lie changed the whole course of her life," Luty said thoughtfully "Maybe the way she sees it, Bremmer kept her from marryin' the man she really loved."

"I hope she doesn't turn out to be the killer." Chloe sighed.

"Her story is very much like mine was. I, too, went to America because I'd lost someone." She turned and smiled at her husband. "But I got very lucky and fate or circumstance or whatever one wants to call it gave me a great blessing. I found you."

John blushed. "I'm the lucky one, sweetheart, and if Elise Cory isn't the killer, perhaps she and James Pierce will have another chance."

Mrs. Jeffries grabbed her heavy winter cloak from the coat tree and tossed it around her shoulders. Their morning meeting was over and the kitchen was quiet. Mrs. Jeffries had told everyone what she'd heard from the inspector, and Luty had given a full report on the information she'd found out at her dinner party.

No one had been particularly shocked when they learned of Bremmer's disgusting behavior and they'd been split on whether or not Elise Cory might have nursed a grudge long enough to return to England after eight years to murder him. Wiggins, Hatchet, and Smythe seemed to think it unlikely, while Phyllis, Luty, and Betsy had argued vigorously that it was not only possible but probable.

Mrs. Jeffries had decided to reserve judgment on the matter and the cook hadn't said one way or the other. As soon as the meeting was finished, Phyllis murmured something about going to the Bremmer neighborhood, Wiggins volunteered to walk with her to the omnibus stop as he was going to have "another go" at finding out something about Nicholas Parr, and Betsy decided that Louise Mannion's neighborhood might be fruitful. Smythe announced he was meeting with a source this morning, Hatchet hadn't said where he was going, and Luty, who'd been out late the night before, had said she was going home to have a rest.

Mrs. Jeffries fastened her cloak and put on her hat. "I'll be going, then. If I leave now, I should get to St. Thomas' Hospital just after Dr. Bosworth has finished his morning round." Mrs. Goodge was still at the table staring glumly at the teapot. "Don't take it so hard, Mrs. Goodge, it was a simple mistake."

"But it's the sort of mistake we can't afford to make." She shook her head. "Not if we mean to do this properly and ensure that justice is done. I knew this was going to happen. I knew that there would come a time when I'd forget something important."

"You weren't the only one who forgot." Mrs. Jeffries moved to the table and sat down next to her friend. "I did, too, so stop being so hard on yourself. It's my fault as much as yours."

"No, it's not; you're the one who we rely on to solve the case, to think things through and see all the connections and bits that none of us can see. I'm the one who is supposed to remember the details that we need to tell the constable, and I forgot. This was an important bit as well. Nora Pierce was Elise's cousin and she married the man Elise loved because of what Stephen Bremmer did. If that's not a motive for murder, I don't know what is."

"Don't be silly. There's no evidence Elise Cory has spent the last eight years pining for James Pierce or plotting vengeance over her lost love. According to the information Luty found out, the Cory marriage was not only a happy one, but Elise kept up a regular correspondence with her cousin."

"Not when she first found out she'd married James Pierce," the cook pointed out.

"She probably was hurt and upset when she learned of the marriage," Mrs. Jeffries argued. "But she got over it."

Mrs. Goodge dragged in a long, harsh breath and sighed.

"You're probably right, Hepzibah. I just feel so guilty that I forgot something that may end up being important."

"I forgot it, too, and we've already decided that in the future, we'll both start writing things down. Now come on, we've got a case to solve and you sitting around with a long face instead of plying your sources with sweets and treats isn't going to help us find the killer."

"Constable, it seems to me that if it is true that our victim tried to blackmail James Pierce, then it's likely he also tried to blackmail others."

"I agree, sir," Barnes said as they turned the corner into Uxbridge Road. "We've heard he had a source of income that was unrelated to his wife's money. I'll bet my pension that blackmail is a good part of it. Especially since everyone who was at the table with him that night detested him." He raised his hand at a hansom that had just dropped a fare. "Maybe they didn't just hate him because he was obnoxious; maybe he knew something about all of them. You know, the sort of thing no one wants spread about London."

"Indeed, I was thinking along those lines myself. All of them are people with either social or business reputations they'd not want damaged."

"And he was chargin' them a pretty penny to keep his mouth shut. Where are we heading first, sir?"

They stopped as the cab pulled up next to the curb. Barnes grabbed the handle of the cab door, yanked it open, and stepped back so the inspector could enter. But Witherspoon hesitated. "Considering the gossip we've heard, Constable, I think we ought to speak with Montague Pettigrew. He would be the one who would be most seriously damaged if Bremmer were blackmailing him. But let's go to his home. It isn't the sort of conversation Miss Houghton-Jones should hear."

"Thank goodness you've come to see me." Dr. Bosworth held his office door open and motioned her inside. "If you hadn't, I was going to drop by Upper Edmonton Gardens."

"You're always welcome at Upper Edmonton Gardens and the others will be annoyed if they find out my coming here deprived them of seeing you." She took off her cloak and hung it on the coat tree. His office was much as she remembered it. The walls were the same gray green, the blind was up on the single window, and there were medical books, box files, and periodicals stacked everywhere.

"It's kind of you to say so, Mrs. Jeffries. I enjoy seeing the household and your friends. Perhaps at the end of this case we can all get together." He closed the door and then swept a stack of journals off the straight-backed chair in front of his desk. "Have a seat and get comfortable. Would you like tea? I can send the porter up to the kitchen."

She shook her head. "No, I'm fine and I promise not to take up too much of your time. You know why I've come?"

He sat down. "I do, and as I said, I'm glad you're here. As I'm certain you know already, the postmortem determined that it was arsenic poisoning that killed the victim."

"The report was certain it was arsenic and not some other poison," she clarified.

"Oh yes, but the situation isn't as straightforward as it might appear."

"What do you mean?"

"As you know, I spent some time in San Francisco after my medical training here."

"Of course. That's why you know so much about guns and the sort of holes—oh dear, that doesn't sound right." She laughed at herself. "You know what I'm saying. Because of all the bullet holes you saw in San Francisco, you're an expert on the type of wounds various weapons make when they impact and leave a human being."

He gave her a grateful smile. "True, but bullet wounds weren't my only interest. There was another aspect of my training in America that might have some bearing on this case. This is hard to admit, because Dr. Haley, my mentor in San Francisco, was such a good man. But I was young and back in those days I saw all of life as a competition. Oh Lord, aren't we stupid when we're young."

She laughed. "I think that's the nature of being young, sir."

He gave her a rueful smile. "So because he was an expert on the kind of entry and exit wounds guns made, I wanted to make my mark as well and, uh . . . well, I decided I needed to become a bit of an expert on something that didn't interest him in the least."

"Poisons?"

He nodded. "My reason for doing it was stupid, youthful vanity and pride, but once I began studying the subject, I became genuinely interested and wanted to know whether or not all human beings reacted to a poison with the same symptoms."

"And what did you find out?"

"What I learned was fascinating. Not everyone responds in precisely the same manner when they've been poisoned."

"Really?"

"Don't misunderstand; a lethal dose of a poison is precisely that: a lethal dose. But the point is, most murderers have no idea about how much to use in order to ensure their victim actually dies. For instance, one of the cases I examined was a wife who wanted to rid herself of a violent, drunken husband so she put an arsenic-based rat poison in his whiskey. Unfortunately for her, she didn't use enough to actually kill the fellow. The man lived and testified against her at her trial. On another case, a man used foxglove to poison his business partner. Foxglove, as I'm sure you're aware, is used to make digitalis. But the killer used a very small amount, not nearly enough to harm someone. Yet his victim died."

"Why would he die?"

"Because unbeknownst to anyone, the victim had an undiagnosed heart condition—he had an irregular heartbeat, so even a small amount of foxglove was enough to put the poor man six feet under. Foxglove is generally used to treat heart problems, but with some heart conditions, it can also kill." Bosworth shrugged. "My point is that poison, even though we've a number of tests that can detect its presence in the human body, can have different effects on different people."

"You mean, if someone already has a medical condition, the effect of the poison can either be exaggerated or even nullified? Is that what you're saying?"

"Not necessarily nullified; as I said, a fatal dose is a fatal dose. What I'm saying is most people have no idea about how much to shove in someone's food or drink. Additionally, we know very little about how poisons interact with other medications, and that's what worries me about this murder. The victim died far too quickly."

She realized the accounts she'd heard of Bremmer's death were what had been bothering her about this murder. She was no expert on poisons but she had read about them. "Yes, I agree, there's something odd about the sequence of events, don't you think? He shouldn't have died so fast."

His eyebrows rose in surprise. "You think so, too? Of course, I should have realized, you know more than the average layman when it comes to poison and murder." He leaned forward, putting his elbows on the desk. "It was definitely arsenic that killed him. But there's something strange about what was found in the contents of his stomach."

"In what way?"

"The police surgeon was surprised there were very few granules of arsenic in the victim's stomach. But a number of them in his mouth and throat."

"You're concerned about this?" Mrs. Jeffries was concerned about it as well. The last thing this case needed was complication about how the victim had actually met his demise.

"Of course, the arsenic was in the victim's champagne flute. We found both granules and dissolved traces on the glass. But the reason I'm worried is that the form of arsenic we found, which was ordinary run-of-the-mill vermin poison, isn't easily soluble in cold liquids, and champagne is a cold liquid."

"But you just said you found granules." Mrs. Jeffries was getting a bit confused.

"We did, and that was to be expected, but the trace arsenic we found smeared on the inside of the flute wasn't enough to have caused the symptoms Bremmer expressed before he died." Bosworth's brows drew together. "It's a very odd situation."

"So what are you saying? That Bremmer wasn't killed by arsenic after all?"

"No, he definitely was, but I think there might be other

mitigating circumstances about his death. The man had a number of ailments, some of which the police surgeon detailed in the post-mortem. Bremmer was taking at least three other medications. One was a digitalis pill for his heart and the other two medicines were for his gout and indigestion. That could certainly have changed his symptoms." He sighed heavily. "I'm not sure what to tell you, Mrs. Jeffries. All I know is that Stephen Bremmer shouldn't have dropped dead so quickly. According to my research, the fastest arsenic has ever killed someone is two hours after ingestion. Normally, it takes two to four days for death to occur but this man died within minutes. But then again, as I said, there is a lot about poison and individual reactions to it that we simply don't know."

Montague Pettigrew wasn't happy to see them. He lived in the bottom flat of a five-story redbrick building with a gray stone façade. They'd been let into the small sitting room by an elderly old man wearing a threadbare black butler's coat and a frayed white shirt. The walls of the room were covered in a pale lavender and gray striped paper, the faded purple drapes had seen better days, and the floor was covered with a frayed gold and blue Oriental carpet. Pettigrew, who'd been reading the *Times* in an overstuffed horsehair chair by the window, leapt to his feet as they entered. "What are you doing here?" He didn't wait for them to reply; instead he glared at his manservant. "Collins, why didn't you announce these people? I'm too busy to see anyone now. I've an appointment."

"Sorry, sir," Collins muttered as he shuffled out of the room, closing the door behind him with a definite bang.

"Well, what do you want?" Pettigrew tossed his paper onto the chair.

"We want to ask you some questions," Barnes replied. "We've learned some information that might be important, sir, and we'd like to speak with you about it."

Pettigrew's eyes widened and he swallowed nervously. "Alright, then, get on with it." He swept the paper off his chair and flopped back down, leaving the two policemen to stand.

"Mr. Pettigrew, are you aware that Stephen Bremmer was a blackmailer?" Witherspoon watched him carefully as he asked the question. He wasn't as adept at reading expressions as he'd like, but he was getting better at it. Pettigrew's face paled as the blood drained out.

"I've no idea what you're talking about. I know nothing about such a matter. Why would someone like me have any idea about whether or not Bremmer blackmailed people?"

"We were wondering if he'd tried to blackmail you, sir," Barnes asked softly.

Pettigrew's right eye began to twitch. "Certainly not. That's a ridiculous idea. What are you trying to imply? There's nothing in my life that anyone, even a blackguard like Stephen Bremmer, could possibly know about me that would constitute grounds for blackmail."

"Mr. Pettigrew." Witherspoon wasn't sure how to phrase the question, but in all fairness it had to be asked. "I'm sorry to say this, but we've heard that there is something in your life that could cause you great harm, both legally and socially."

Pettigrew drew back and took a deep breath. "I don't know what you could possibly mean. What's more, I'm going to contact my solicitor immediately."

"That might be a good idea," Witherspoon agreed, his expression sympathetic. "As the constable just said, what we've heard is not only socially unacceptable, but it is also illegal."

"Oh, dear God, I didn't kill the bastard." Pettigrew's eyes filled with tears. "Please, please, if this comes out I'll be ruined. He's been bleeding me dry for months now, ever since my engagement to Camilla was announced. You must believe me. I hated him, but I didn't murder the man."

"Why don't you tell us what happened?" Witherspoon said.

"Can we sit down, please?" Barnes asked. He nodded toward the ugly dun-colored horsehair sofa.

"Yes, of course. I'm sorry, I should have asked you sooner. Forgive me, please. I was just so upset when you walked into the room." He hung his head. "I should have known it would all come out. I thought he cared about me, but obviously, Andre isn't one to keep his mouth shut."

"I'm not sure who you're referring to," Witherspoon said as he sank into the thin cushions of the sofa, "but that's not who we spoke with."

"He didn't betray me, then." Pettigrew brightened. "That's some consolation, I suppose. Oh, dear God, what am I going to do?"

"The wisest course of action, sir, is to answer our questions honestly." The constable pulled out his notebook and pencil, flipped open the pages, and balanced it on his knee. "First of all, you admit that Stephen Bremmer was blackmailing you?"

Pettigrew nodded dully. "Yes, as I said, two days after our engagement was announced in the newspapers, Bremmer paid me a visit. I don't know how he'd done it, but he had some letters in his possession, letters I'd written to Andre Bellefleur, the actor. He said that if I didn't pay him, he'd show the letters to my uncle." He broke off and closed his eyes.

"I presume your uncle would have disapproved?" Witherspoon murmured.

"My uncle believes the Church of England is too liberal. He doesn't smoke, drink, gamble, or enjoy life in any way, shape, or form. What's more, he thinks that those of us that do enjoy life in any way, shape, or form ought to be punished accordingly."

"Why did it matter what your uncle thought?" Barnes already knew the answer, but he wanted Pettigrew to say it in front of the inspector.

He laughed cynically. "Or course it mattered. I'm his heir. He's a very rich man and I'm the only family he has left. But if he found out about my relationship with Andre, he'd cut me off without a penny and leave it all to the Great Awakening Bible Society."

Witherspoon nodded. "Is your uncle the only person who might be upset if they, er . . . uh . . . You're engaged to be married, Mr. Pettigrew. Does Miss Houghton-Jones know about your uh—"

"My past," Pettigrew interrupted. "She might or she might not. But even if she did, I doubt it would bother her greatly. She needs this inheritance as much as I do. We're not in love romantically but we do admire and respect each other. We get along well and we genuinely like each other. That's more than many couples have, and despite what people may think, I'm quite prepared to fulfill all of my obligations as a husband."

"I tell ya, that woman is in league with the devil." Norma Baumgarten picked up her tankard of ale and took a drink.

Phyllis nodded in agreement and took a sip of her beer. She

hated the taste, but she had no choice if she wanted the woman to keep talking. Her day had started out as they usually did when she was on the hunt; she'd gone to the shops near the Bremmer home and started asking what she hoped were very discreet questions. Apparently, she'd not been discreet enough because as she was leaving the baker's, she'd been accosted by one Norma Baumgarten, a red-haired, blue-eyed, pockmarked woman of late middle age who claimed she worked for Anne Bremmer. She'd insisted on the two of them coming to this pub, but now, after buying the woman a second tankard of ale, Phyllis was beginning to think she'd been tricked.

"You've said that several times." Phyllis put her beer mug down on the counter. "But you've not said anything specific. How do I know you even work for Mrs. Bremmer?"

Norma eyed her suspiciously. "I've told you who I work for. You're the one that isn't bein' honest. I heard you askin' all them questions at the baker's shop and tryin' to pretend you was lost and lookin' for the Bremmer house, but that's not true, is it?"

Phyllis studied her adversary for a few moments. Despite the alcohol she'd imbibed, Norma's eyes were crystal clear. "You're right, I'm not lost. I'm a private inquiry agent and I've been hired to look into the murder of Stephen Bremmer."

Norma's jaw dropped. "You a private inquiry agent? That's nonsense, you're a woman. Whoever heard of a woman doing such a job?"

She sat back, crossed her arms over her chest, and gave her opponent a slow, knowing smile. "Of course no one has heard of such a thing, that's why I'm so good at it. Now, why don't you tell me what it is you know? I've bought you two tankards, and if you're as clever as I think you are, you can tell me lots of things that may help me." She waited to see how Norma would react and was both pleased and surprised when Norma shrugged and took another drink of her ale.

Phyllis struggled to keep her expression calm. She couldn't believe she'd done it. This was like a scene from one of those wonderful plays she loved in the West End theaters. She was delighted by her own audacity. She was truly a heroine. She couldn't believe she'd had the courage not only to say such things but to actually use her smile and her body to convey the same message.

Norma slammed her tankard onto the tabletop. "Right, then, what do you want to know?"

"You said Mrs. Bremmer was in league with the devil. What did you mean?"

"What do ya think? She's a mean one, she is." Norma leaned across the small table. "She found out he didn't care anymore that she wasn't goin' to give him a settlement, he was goin' to leave her anyway. I overheard her talkin' to one of her friends and she said that if he left her, she'd never get presented at court and that's what the stupid woman lived for, can you believe it? She's got ten times more than any of us but the only thing the stupid woman wants is to meet the ruddy Queen."

"How did she know he was going to leave her?" Phyllis knew this was the most important question. "Had he told her that he was going?"

Norma shook her head. "He never told her nothing." She waved her empty tankard under Phyllis' nose. She took the hint and signaled to the barmaid for another. Neither of them said anything until the woman brought the ale.

Phyllis paid her and waited until Norma had taken a long swig. Then she said, "How did she know?"

"She overheard him braggin' to one of his mates that he had something in the works that was goin' to make him a lot of money, enough lolly so that he didn't need a settlement from her nibs."

Phyllis wasn't sure she believed the woman. "That was stupid of him. Where and when did this happen?"

Norma's eyes narrowed. "You think I'm lyin'? I'm not. He wasn't very smart and he was always trying to impress people. It happened less than two weeks ago. I remember because it was my afternoon out and I was tryin' to get the downstairs done so I could leave right after lunch."

"Who was he talking to?"

"One of them idiot friends of his from the only club that will still have him as a member. He'd invited the fellow for luncheon because Mrs. Bremmer was supposed to be out and gone to a fancy birthday do. I was out in the hall when it happened and I saw her standing by the drawing room door with her ear pressed to the wood. He thought she'd gone but she'd come back because she'd forgotten to take the gift she'd bought special for the hostess. Mr. Bremmer had a loud voice and you could hear him clear as the church bells on Sunday morning."

"What was he saying?"

"Exactly what I just told you. That it didn't matter if the cow—that's what he called her when she wasn't around—gave him any money or not. He had something big planned and it would give him enough so that he could do what he liked for the rest of his life."

CHAPTER 9

Camilla Houghton-Jones was as unhappy with their reappearance in her drawing room as her fiancé had been. She stopped in the doorway and glared at the two policemen. "Really, Inspector, how long must you keep intruding into our lives? This is getting most tiresome."

"I imagine Stephen Bremmer thought being poisoned was tiresome as well," Witherspoon replied. "Miss Houghton-Jones, we're not here to harass you, but we do have a murder to solve."

"I've already told you everything I know about it." She flounced into the room and sank down on the sofa.

"Have you, ma'am?" Barnes fixed her with a hard stare.

Her eyes widened in surprise. "Of course I have. Oh, do get on with it. Ask your wretched questions and then get out. I've an appointment with my dressmaker soon and I don't wish to keep her waiting. I'm being fitted for my wedding dress, and frankly, that is more important to me than worrying about who put arsenic in Stephen Bremmer's champagne."

Witherspoon glanced at Barnes. A thin, white line of pain circled the constable's mouth and he realized his knee was probably hurting. "This will go faster if we can sit down," he said. "The constable needs to be able to take notes."

She hesitated before finally giving a bare nod of assent. They each took a seat in one of the chairs catty-corner to the sofa. The inspector stayed silent while Barnes pulled out his pencil and notebook.

Witherspoon tried to think of a polite way to broach the subject he and the constable had discussed only this morning. Barnes had a large network of informants, and after their visit to Montague Pettigrew, he'd realized the constable's sources had been correct. It had been embarrassing enough to bring up the subject to Pettigrew; it was going to be dreadful to bring it up to a refined woman. But justice had to be served and the truth had to come out. He cleared his throat. "Miss Houghton-Jones, this is a very lovely house."

She drew back in surprise. "Yes, it's been in my family for generations. But I hardly see what my home has to do with Stephen Bremmer."

"It takes a lot of money to keep up a place like this, doesn't it," Barnes interjected.

"That's not your business," she snapped. "Look, if you've questions to ask me, get on with it."

"Did you know that Bremmer was blackmailing people?" Witherspoon blurted. He'd tried taking the long way around the issue, tried to soften what was going to be a blow by discussing the costs of living in her social set, but she was having none of it.

An ugly red flush crept up her cheeks. "I don't know what you're talking about and, what's more, it's disgraceful to say such awful things about a man who is no longer here to defend himself."

Witherspoon remained quiet, staring at her and hoping she'd keep talking.

"What you're implying is vile and disgusting"—she leapt to her feet—"and I won't have such things discussed in a decent home."

"Please sit down, Miss Houghton-Jones," the inspector said. "You'll be more comfortable answering our inquiries here than at the station. Mr. Pettigrew has already admitted that Bremmer was blackmailing him. Now the only question is, was he blackmailing you as well?"

She sat down, staring off into the distance as the blood drained out of her face and she turned a deathly white. "He was a horrible man and I'm glad someone poisoned him. I only wish he'd suffered even more than he did."

"You were sitting very close to him; did you put the poison in his glass?" Barnes asked. "You could have easily done it when the lights were out."

"I didn't kill him."

"Was he blackmailing you?" Witherspoon pressed.

She gave a harsh laugh. "Of course he was. He had his hand in everyone's pocket."

"When did it start?" Witherspoon asked.

"He came to see me the day after my engagement to Montague was announced in the newspapers. He pretended it was a social call but it soon became apparent he was after much more. He began dropping hints about how awful it would be if Montague didn't inherit from his uncle." She broke off and gave him a sharp look. "I presume you know about my fiancé's expectations?"

"We do, Miss Houghton-Jones, please go on."

"At first I couldn't fathom what he was going on about, but then I realized that all the rumors I'd heard about him were true, that he blackmailed members of his own set and he had set his sights on me."

"How much did he ask for?" Barnes asked.

"More than I could give," she admitted. "He wanted fifty pounds a month. I told him that was impossible, that my personal allowance couldn't stretch that far and he'd have to be content with fifteen. He didn't believe me; he kept arguing with me even when I explained that this house and the servants' wages and even my clothes were paid for out of a trust that I couldn't touch. He started yelling that my family had plenty of money and if I didn't give him what he asked, he'd show everyone Montague's letters to that actor." She closed her eyes and took a long, shuddering breath. "I got angry then and I slapped him across the face. I said if he did such a thing, I'd make sure he was a social pariah and he'd not be welcome in any decent home for the rest of his life."

"Did he believe you?"

"Not at first. He sneered at me and said that I wasn't the only one with influential friends. He claimed that Louise Mannion and the Bremmers would come to his defense." She looked at the inspector and smiled cynically. "But I held my ground. I may not have any money, but my family does, and if I was to be socially ruined, they'd make sure the man who did it was ruined as well."

"So he agreed to your terms?" Witherspoon pressed.

She nodded. "Reluctantly, but he saw that I wasn't going to relent. I wasn't going to let him ruin Montague's and my life."

"Did you mean it?" Barnes stared at her curiously. "Forgive my asking, ma'am, but you don't appear to be in love with Mr. Pettigrew, yet you'd risk social ruin for his sake."

"What makes you think I don't love my fiancé? I know exactly what he is, but that doesn't mean I don't care for him and I know he cares for me. We're good together and we bring each other a measure of genuine happiness. Why should our love, just because it's different, be any less important than any other?"

"I'm sorry, ma'am, I didn't mean to imply anything," Barnes said softly.

"I realize Montague and I are now suspects, but you'd be foolish just to focus your investigation on us." She got to her feet.

"Why is that, ma'am?" Witherspoon got up as well.

She smiled slowly. "Because the only person Bremmer wasn't blackmailing at the table that night was probably his wife, but he'd have done it to her if he could."

Mrs. Jeffries dug her feet into the floor as the omnibus jolted over a bump on the road. She stared out the window, past the matron sitting next to her, her mind so intent on her thoughts that the streets of London, generally something she enjoyed watching, barely registered. She went over and over everything she and Dr. Bosworth had discussed. There was no doubt the postmortem was done correctly and that Bremmer had indeed been poisoned, but she, like Dr. Bosworth, thought the sequence of events didn't make sense. But perhaps she was wrong. Even Dr. Bosworth, who knew a great deal more about poisons than she did, thought the current method of understanding arsenic wasn't foolproof; that a variety of other factors could possibly influence the length of time it took for a dose to be fatal. Frowning, she thought back to some of their previous cases and then realized that neither of the two poison cases she could recall involved arsenic. Think, Hepzibah, think, she told herself. You must know something about poisons. You've read about them in books and magazines, surely you can recall something that might be useful. But the trouble was, she had no way of knowing what was an old wives' tale from what was fact. Mrs. Vincent, who lived next door to her when she lived in Yorkshire, swore rat poison, or arsenic, could be used to polish silver. Her other neighbor, Mrs. Teasdale, insisted that she was wrong, that poison ruined metals. But as neither of them had so much as a silver spoon in their homes, no one ever knew the truth of it. Then there was Harriet Hockman, another Yorkshire neighbor who used arsenic because she thought it stopped wrinkles, and old Mrs. Lark, the village crone who girls seeking love charms and poor people who couldn't afford doctors went to for help; she prescribed it for everything from insomnia to food poisoning. But that was years ago; surely no one believed this nonsense now, and even if someone did, what could it possibly have to do with Bremmer's murder?

The vehicle plodded along, stopping at three-minute intervals to let passengers on and off. She sighed inwardly and gave up trying to make sense of the science of the murder. Taking a deep breath, she let her mind drift and flow of its own accord. Snippets of their meetings mingled with facts. "The lights didn't stay out for a full two minutes" intertwined with "Stephen Bremmer was only good at one thing: making enemies."

The woman by the window spoke, startling her out of her reverie. "Excuse me, ma'am, but I need to get out, my stop is next."

"Of course." Mrs. Jeffries rose and stood in the aisle for the lady to pass. She had a long way to go so she took the seat just vacated and once again gazed out at the city.

The evidence was beginning to show that the champagne flute must have been tampered with before the lights went out. But by who? The only person seen near the table before the ball started was Elise Cory and she claimed she was simply looking at the place cards. Mrs. Jeffries gasped. The place cards, of course. How could she have forgotten? She snapped to attention as the vehicle trundled slowly up Whitehall. Drat, they weren't even at Charing Cross yet. Right now, getting home was important. She debated getting off at the next stop and taking a hansom, but the traffic was so terrible it probably wouldn't be any faster. Double drat. She crossed her fingers, hoping she'd get home in time to have a quick word with Wiggins.

"I'm sorry, I can't allow that without Mrs. Bremmer's consent. Please wait here." Mrs. Martin disappeared, leaving Witherspoon and Barnes standing in the foyer.

"We can insist if we need to." The constable's gaze was fixed on the open drawing room door, where they could both hear the low murmur of voices.

"Let's hope she'll cooperate." Witherspoon smiled politely as Anne Bremmer stepped into the hallway and charged toward them. The housekeeper followed at a more sedate pace.

"What do you mean, you want to speak to my servants?" she demanded.

"That's normal procedure." The inspector shifted his bowler from his right hand to his left. "We can either do it here or we can ask your staff to come to the station. Additionally, I've more questions for you, Mrs. Bremmer."

"This is outrageous," she snapped.

Behind her, Barnes saw the housekeeper lower her head to hide a smile.

"Your superiors will hear about this." Mrs. Bremmer looked over her shoulder. "Mrs. Martin, go fetch the footman and then bring me my writing case. He can take my note directly to Chief Superintendent Barrows at Scotland Yard." She started to turn but was stopped by the inspector's next words.

"Mrs. Bremmer, we have it on good authority that your husband was blackmailing your friends and neighbors."

She flinched and stared at him with an expression of horror. "That's a lie. I don't know who is saying such things but it isn't true."

"It is true, Mrs. Bremmer," Barnes added. "We've confirmed it with three separate sources. You wouldn't be the first to complain to Chief Superintendent Barrows, but after he hears our evidence, it wouldn't do you any good."

Barrows wasn't immune to the machinations of the rich and powerful, but he was also a good policeman who had come up through the ranks and believed in following the law, so the constable was fairly certain he could pull off this bluff. Add to that, Witherspoon had his own supporters in the Home Office and senior officers were wary of interfering in ongoing investigations.

She stared at them for a long moment and then she seemed to collapse into herself. "Oh God, this is a nightmare. I thought when he died, I'd have some peace, but it's getting worse and worse." Her eyes glazed over, her skin had taken on a deathly pallor, and she seemed to be talking to herself. "Even now he's found a way to torment me. My father was right, Stephen was a devil. No matter how dead he is, he'll not stop until he destroys me."

Alarmed, Witherspoon looked at the housekeeper. "Can you bring tea, please, I think your mistress needs to sit down."

Mrs. Martin nodded and disappeared down the hall. Witherspoon jerked his chin toward the disappearing housekeeper, indicating that Barnes should follow her. Then he took Anne Bremmer's arm and led her into the drawing room.

"He's found a way to ruin me." She muttered it over and over as the inspector tugged her across the room and eased her gently onto the sofa.

Witherspoon sat down beside her and gazed at her sympathetically. She was staring at the floor and still murmuring something he couldn't quite catch under her breath. He had no wish to cause her further distress but he also knew his duty. "Mrs. Bremmer, I'm very sorry you're upset. Mrs. Martin is bringing tea."

"Tea? That's not going to do me any good." She raised her chin and pointed to a cabinet across the room. "If you want to help, get me a whiskey."

Downstairs, Barnes followed the housekeeper into the noisy kitchen. The room went silent as the cook, two maids, and a young man in a footman's livery caught sight of the constable.

"Devlin, get a pot of tea ready," Mrs. Martin ordered.

"We've just made a fresh pot," the cook said. She'd been rolling out pastry but she stopped, her rolling pin in her hand, and stared at Barnes.

The maids hurried to get the tea tray ready, and a few moments later Mrs. Martin picked it up. She hesitated. "Rankin, show the constable into the old butler's pantry. He needs to speak to all of you. Constable"—she started for the back stairs—"start questioning whoever you'd like."

"This way." Rankin, a lanky youth with a baby face and curly blond hair, waved him down the corridor and into a room with a long, narrow table and half a dozen rickety-looking chairs. Shelves filled with old crockery, pots and pans, and iron kitchen utensils lined one wall and opposite it was a line of locked cabinets.

Barnes pulled out a chair and sat down. "Don't go," he said as the footman started to leave. "I might as well start with you. Come and sit down."

Rankin, his mouth slightly agape, did as he was told.

"What's your name?" He opened his notebook.

"Lewis Rankin, I'm the footman here."

"How old are you?" The constable was hoping a few innocent questions might get the lad to relax a bit.

"Fifteen, sir." He swallowed nervously.

"How long have you worked here?"

"Just over a year."

"Do you like it here?"

Lewis blinked. "Uh, I don't know, I guess it's alright."

"Just alright," Barnes pressed. "Come on, lad, your master has been murdered. We already know he wasn't a very nice person, so just answer my questions honestly. There's no one here but you and me and I promise, I'll not repeat anything you've said to Mrs. Bremmer or the housekeeper."

Lewis smiled in relief. "Good. I don't like it here but it pays decent and I want to keep my job. Truth is, none of us like it here much. They was always arguin' upstairs and making life miserable for us down here."

"Did anything unusual happen on the day that Mr. Bremmer was murdered?"

"Not that I can remember," he said.

"How about in any of the days prior to his death. Anything odd occur?"

"Well, it weren't unusual, but the day before he died, they had one of their nasty rows." Lewis shrugged. "They was screamin' so loud I could hear them all the way down the hall."

"What were they shouting about?"

"Mrs. Bremmer was shoutin' that he was a monster and that one of these days he'd be punished for being so horrible. She told him he was goin' to end up dead and she'd not pay for his funeral."

"Do you know specifically what they were arguing about?"

"Not really, they argued a lot but this was a real nasty one." He brightened. "But the funny bit was he did end up dead and now she is havin' to pay for the funeral. I didn't hear any more because Lily came up and told me that Mrs. Martin wanted me to polish the brass fireplace sets. They're right fancy ones and take ages to do but the mistress wanted them cleaned for the fancy luncheon she was having that day. You might want to talk to Lily. She needed to clear the dining room so she might have heard more."

"Right, then, could you go fetch Lily for me?"

Lewis got up, but when he reached the door, he stopped. "Oh, there is one more thing. That was the day that Mrs. Martin sent me to the chemist's to buy rat poison."

* * *

Upstairs, Witherspoon handed Mrs. Bremmer a second shot of whiskey. She gulped it down. Mrs. Martin put the tea tray on a side table, gave her mistress an anxious glance, and then retreated, pulling the door closed behind her.

Anne Bremmer's color was better and her lips had stopped trembling. She put the glass down next to the tea tray and looked at him. "I suppose your constable is downstairs."

"That is correct, ma'am," the inspector replied. "We have a right to question any and all witnesses that may have pertinent information while investigating a murder."

"The only information they'll be able to tell you is what you already know; my husband and I loathed each other."

Witherspoon wasn't in the habit of sharing information with suspects, and she was most definitely a suspect, but in this case, he thought it might work to his advantage. "We have been told that your marriage wasn't a happy one."

"And you think that means I murdered him." She laughed. "Don't be absurd, Inspector, half of the women in London hate their spouses. Stephen was a dreadful husband and an even worse person, but I didn't kill him."

"No one has accused you of that, Mrs. Bremmer. As Constable Barnes said earlier, we do have confirmation that your husband was a blackmailer and that he was targeting his friends and acquaintances."

She closed her eyes briefly. "I suspected he might be doing something like that, but I didn't know for certain. The truth is, I didn't want to know."

"How long has it been going on?"

"I honestly don't know." She shook her head. "When we married, I gave him a generous allowance but it was never enough. Before we returned from our honeymoon I realized I'd made a terrible mistake by marrying him. From the very beginning, he rarely spent an evening at home and had no interest in me whatsoever. But he needed me, you see. Stephen had very expensive tastes. Only the best restaurants, the most expensive champagne, the finest clothing would do for him and he had no money of his own. We hadn't been wed six months before he started badgering me to raise his quarterly allowance, but I refused."

"What made you suspect he was blackmailing people?"

"He stopped harassing me constantly. He still wanted money, but it wasn't a continuous stream of lying or whining or complaining. At first I thought he was stealing from me, so I kept a close watch on all the valuables in the house. But he wasn't as stupid as I thought; he knew not to steal from me. Then I noticed some of my friends were very uncomfortable around Stephen; before they'd accept an invitation from me, they'd want to know if he was going to be present."

Witherspoon wasn't sure she'd be able to answer his next question, but he had to ask. "How did he get information on his victims?"

"I don't know, Inspector. It wasn't a subject we ever discussed. But he was always a cunning, sly sort of person. Before we were married, my father found him going through the desk drawers in our study and I know he eavesdropped on private conversations. Twice I've caught him listening at doors, once when we were at the Fellingham estate and once at the Mannion house."

* * *

"Sorry I wasn't here yesterday," Blimpey apologized as Smythe took the stool across from him. "But Nell's aunt had one of her fainting spells, and as she's her only living relative, we had to go and see she was alright."

"Is she?"

"She's fine now, it was just a bit of light-headedness. But you know women; Nell was frettin' so about her that I've hired a nurse to stay with the old girl for a few days," Blimpey replied. "I've got plenty to tell you, though, some of which I suspect you and your lot have already heard."

"Probably so, but go on."

"First, your victim is a blackmailer. That was his mysterious source of income—" He broke off. "But your lot already found that out, right?" Smythe nodded so he continued. "Second, your victim wasn't a very good blackmailer but he was smart enough not to try it on anyone who was outside his own social set, so none of the real toughs in town were after him and that's good news. That means no one from outside bribed a waiter or a maid to add a bit of arsenic to his champagne."

"We were already sure he was murdered by someone at one of the two tables in the front," Smythe agreed.

"Right, then, I'll get onto what we found out about that lot. There was only one person at the table next to where Bremmer was sitting who might have hated him enough to kill him and that was—"

Smythe interrupted, "Elise Cory. We already know about her. Go on."

"Now, the only person at Bremmer's table who wasn't one of his victims was the American man, Nicholas Parr. He's not been in England long enough for Bremmer to have the goods on him. Years ago, he'd tried to blackmail James Pierce but Pierce wouldn't play along. He had some really damaging information on Montague Pettigrew. Do you need me to tell you what it was?"

"No, we know."

"Right, then." Blimpey continued, "So he was blackmailin' Pettigrew and Camilla Houghton-Jones."

"Both of them?"

"That's right, Miss Houghton-Jones needs for her beloved to get his inheritance as soon as possible. Apparently, she's run up big bills all over town and her creditors are gettin' a tad impatient. Pettigrew's uncle finding out about his love affair with an actor could ruin both their prospects. There was also a rumor that he was blackmailing Louise Mannion."

"For what?" Smythe asked. This was definitely new information. "What did he 'ave on 'er?"

"My source wasn't sure but he thought it was something to do with Osgood Mannion's death. He was supposed to have accidentally drowned last spring in the lake at the Mannion estate when the skiff he was in overturned. But Osgood was a good swimmer and the local medical man found a wound on the back of his skull. Louise Mannion was the only witness to the accident. She claimed she was at the water's edge. She'd gone to call him in to tea, and just as she arrived, she saw the boat overturn. Osgood could swim, but as he went in, he hit his head on one of the oars."

"She didn't jump in to save him?"

Blimpey grinned. "She claims she can't swim, but my source

says that's a lie. Years earlier, her brother almost drowned, and after that, her father insisted both of them learn to swim."

"Wasn't there a coroner's inquest?"

"Of course, but Louise's godfather was the county magistrate, and oddly enough, the fact that Louise Mannion could swim wasn't mentioned during the inquest. The official verdict was death by accident. Which is understandable because all the estate servants testified that the Mannions had a happy marriage."

"So she'd have no reason to kill her husband, is that it?"

"That's what the servants said, but as we both know, servants that need their positions will say anything to keep a roof over their heads and food in their bellies."

"What about Anne Bremmer, was he blackmailin' 'er?" Smythe asked.

Blimpey thought for a moment. "I don't know if you could call it proper blackmail, but he had somethin' in the works that meant he could leave her, that he didn't need to stay around because she was the one with the money."

"And her ambition is to be presented at court." Smythe's heavy brows drew together. "Is bein' deserted considered as bad as bein' divorced?"

"Not by most people but I suspect the Queen and her courtiers might see it differently." He leaned toward Smythe and lowered his voice. "My sources tell me that in the years since Prince Albert has died, she's become even more obsessed about the sanctity of marriage. Any woman who can't hang on to her husband wouldn't stand a chance at being presented at her court. She doesn't even approve of widows remarrying."

"But she'd allow a widow to be presented?"

"That's what my source says, so if Anne Bremmer knew he was up and leavin', I'd say that whoever killed him did her a great service."

"It's nice of you to buy me a drink." Hilda Jackson smiled as Wiggins put a glass of gin on the table in front of her. "I don't usually go with men I don't know, but Joey said you're a reporter."

"That's right." Wiggins sat down. It hadn't been difficult making contact with the tall, ginger-haired girl. He'd met Joey outside the Wrexley as the boy was coming to work and the lad had not only described her for him, but had offered to vouch for "Albert Jones." But Hilda's shift didn't end until half past three so he'd spent the day trying to pick up a bit more information. He'd gone to James Pierce's neighborhood and found out nothing and then tried his luck near the Mannion house. But he'd not found anyone there to talk to, either. Hopefully, his luck would change and he'd learn something useful here.

"It's a nice pub, isn't it?" Wiggins glanced around the crowded room. Working men in plain shirts and flat caps sat along the side benches, and bread sellers, railway workers, and travelers in business suits crowded the length of the bar. "We were lucky to get a table." Luck had nothing to do with it; he'd bribed two lads who'd been sitting here to leave because he wanted her comfortable and chatting.

"I've been here before," she announced. She looked him up and down, her expression assessing, and then she smiled. "Joey says you're a reporter and you're wantin' to speak to me about the murder."

"Yeah, that's right." He wasn't sure he liked the way she was eyeing him up but then he realized he was being stupid. What was wrong with him? He was starting to imagine that every woman he met liked what she saw. That was daft.

"I don't know what I can tell you. I wasn't even there that night. I went home at five that day." She took a sip.

"That's what Joey said, but he also mentioned that you said one of the champagne flutes went missing that morning. Is it true?"

"It is and I don't care what Mr. Sherwood says. One of them ruddy flutes went missing that morning. He's just trying to lay the blame on me so the cost doesn't come out of his wages, but I told Edwina Corbin when she came in to clean the storage pantry that day that one of them had gone missing, and now Mr. Sherwood is pretendin' we're both lying."

Wiggins didn't really understand why Mrs. Jeffries wanted him to learn what he could about the missing flute, but he'd do the best he could. "Tell me a bit more."

"There's not much more to tell. I took the tray of flutes into the storage room and put them on the counter next to the cutlery, plates, and serviettes that were going to be used that evening."

"So it was specifically for the Lighterman's Ball," Wiggins clarified.

"That's right. Those flutes are so expensive we don't keep them sitting around on trays. They're kept in a locked cupboard along with all the different types of wineglasses. But Mr. Sherwood wanted everything set out nice and proper. He told us he was expecting someone from the Pierce party to come along and see that we were doing what they expected."

"You counted them before you took them in?"

"Mr. Sherwood told me to take ten of them in and that's what I did. Three hours later, when I'd finished in the kitchen and he'd finished with the lady, I went back inside and there were nine of them." She gulped the rest of her gin. "I know that Mr. Sherwood broke one and he's trying to put the blame on me."

"Why didn't you report it to Mr. Sherwood right away, then?"

"He'd already gone. He had an appointment in Kent with someone about having an anniversary party at the hotel. So I couldn't tell him, could I? Boris, he's the maître d', had gone up to have a nap before the evening shift and he'd not thank me for waking him up, would he. So I told Edwina and now Mr. Sherwood is acting like we're both lying. But it's the truth."

"The lady who came to see everything for the Lighterman's Ball, who was she?"

Hilda shrugged. "How should I know? No one introduces us to the customers."

"Do you know what she looked like?" Wiggins asked.

"I never saw her. I was in the kitchen cutting vegetables but I heard Timmy Earl say she was blonde and pretty."

Mrs. Jeffries hung up her hat and cloak. "Has Wiggins come in yet?"

"Not yet." Mrs. Goodge put the teapot down next to a plate of brown bread. "Why? Have you thought of something? Do you know who did it?"

"I wish I did." Mrs. Jeffries smiled. "But I did have an idea. Unfortunately, it means he'll have to go back to the Wrexley." She stopped speaking as they heard the back door slam and a moment later Phyllis hurried into the kitchen.

"It's freezing out there." She pulled off her gloves and stuffed them in her coat pocket before she hung it up. "Am I the first one back?"

"Mrs. Jeffries beat you by five minutes." The cook put a plate of mince tarts next to the bread.

Luty and Hatchet were the next to arrive, followed by Ruth, Smythe, and then Wiggins. Betsy was the last one into the kitchen and was met with harsh frowns from both Luty and the cook.

"Where's the little one?" the elderly American demanded.

"Home. My neighbor is looking after her; she's fussy and I think she might be coming down with the sniffles."

"Then I'm glad you left her inside. It's too cold out there for our baby." Mrs. Goodge patted Luty on the shoulder as she walked past her chair and took her own seat. "Don't fret, Luty, once this case is over, you and I will take the little one out for a nice treat."

"And we'll have her all to ourselves," Luty declared. "I might as well go first, I didn't learn much today. Just a few bits and pieces."

"What did you find out?" Mrs. Jeffries helped herself to a slice of brown bread and then reached for the butter pot.

"Mainly what we already know, but I did find out that Louise Mannion might be rich, but she doesn't have control of her fortune yet. Both her daddy and her late husband left her money in trusts that are administered by one of her father's banker friends. She only gets control of the money when she turns forty. Apparently, they both figured by then she'd be smart enough to see through any smooth-talking fortune hunter that came a callin'."

"That's ridiculous. She's an adult and she should be allowed to make her own decisions about her finances." Ruth sniffed disapprovingly. "Why do men of that social class think women are such mindless morons, that they'll hand over their money to any handsome bounder that appears on their doorstep? If it's her inheritance, it's her money."

"I can give you one reason," Hatchet said. "She had a previous attachment they both considered unsuitable. Perhaps they were afraid she'd do it again."

"Did we ever find out who that person was?" Betsy asked.

"I did." Phyllis put a tart on her plate. "That's one of the things I found out today. But I'll wait my turn."

"Go ahead, I'm finished," Luty said.

"I went back to the Mannion neighborhood," Phyllis said. "I wanted to see if I could find Marie Parker and have another chat with her. Don't ask me why, it just seemed like a good idea."

"Then I'm sure it was a good idea," Mrs. Jeffries told her. "Always trust your instincts." Phyllis was now a confident young woman, but the housekeeper knew she still had moments when she doubted herself and reverted back to the frightened, cowed girl she'd been when she first arrived at Upper Edmonton Gardens.

Phyllis gave her a grateful smile. "I wasn't sure I'd be able to make contact with her and I was almost ready to come home when she finally came out. Apparently, Mrs. Mannion is always changing her mind about the dinner menu and Marie is the one who gets stuck going to the shops on the coldest days. But that's neither here nor there. I caught up with her and pretended to have accidentally bumped into her. As we walked to the shops, I got her talking and she told me that the man Louise was in love with all those years ago was James Pierce."

That wasn't precisely how it had happened. Marie hadn't

believed Phyllis had accidentally bumped into her and had demanded to know why she was asking so many questions. Phyllis admitted it was deliberate and then told her she was a private inquiry agent hired to look into the Bremmer murder.

"I thought it might be him," Betsy murmured. "Pierce was the only young man she saw socially who might also be considered unsuitable."

"Clever lady." Smythe grinned at his wife.

"And I expect he was only accepted because he'd saved Leonard Lyndhurst from drowning," Hatchet said.

Phyllis took a quick sip of tea. "But the reason Marie knew it was Pierce was because of what she overheard when she first started working for the Mannions. Just before Osgood Mannion died, he and his wife had a terrible row about Pierce. She overheard him yelling that now that Pierce was a widower, she wasn't to get any ideas, that he'd not stand for the two of them making a fool of him. She fought back and screamed that he was being ridiculous and then she demanded to know who was putting such silly ideas in his head. About that time, Marie heard the housekeeper coming up the hallway, but just before she rushed away, she heard the name 'Stephen Bremmer.'"

"Did Marie know *when* this argument took place?" Mrs. Jeffries asked.

"Not exactly, but it was last year soon after she'd been hired, and she started working there in the middle of March."

"I wonder how Mrs. Mannion feels about Elise Cory being back in town." Luty chuckled. "I'll bet that put her nose out of joint."

"Did Marie ever find the missing serviette?" Betsy asked.

"She did. It was in the umbrella urn by the front door. She said it was a right old mess, all wadded up and sticky with strawberry jam and dirt."

"At least the poor girl won't have the cost of the item taken out of her wages," Hatchet said. "That's good. May I go next?"

"Of course," Mrs. Jeffries said.

"I'm not done yet," Phyllis said quickly. She'd saved the best for last and was determined to tell it properly. "I got real lucky today and I met up with a housemaid from the Bremmer house. She gave me an earful." She told them everything she'd heard from Norma Baumgarten, repeating it almost word for word. The only fact she omitted was that she'd taken the woman to a pub.

"You did have a good day," Betsy said. "I didn't find out anything."

"So Anne Bremmer knew he was planning on leaving her." Mrs. Jeffries frowned slightly, but facts were facts and they had to be examined.

"That would kill her chances at being presented at court," Ruth said.

"And that gives her a motive," Betsy added.

"Sounds to me like everyone's got a motive," the cook complained.

"Indeed," Mrs. Jeffries murmured as she glanced at Hatchet. "I believe you're next."

"I took an acquaintance of mine to luncheon today mainly because he was someone who was part of the victim's social circle," Hatchet said. "He didn't tell me much more than we already know. But he did mention that once when he was having a drink with old Mr. Lyndhurst, Louise's father, he confided something quite horrifying. He said that Leonard Lyndhurst was frightened of his sister, that she'd always been jealous of him and he was sure she was the one who'd pushed him into the water that time he'd almost drowned."

"He claims his own sister tried to kill him?" Mrs. Goodge exclaimed. "Did Mr. Lyndhurst believe his son?"

"My friend didn't know. He said that when Lyndhurst realized what he'd said, he tried to laugh it off as nothing more than silly brother-sister rivalry."

"When was this?" Mrs. Jeffries asked. "I mean, when did your friend have this conversation with Lyndhurst?"

"Years ago, while Leonard was in the Far East. My friend remembered because the conversation was so surprising. Lyndhurst wasn't a man to discuss personal matters. That's it for me."

"I'll have a go, then," Smythe volunteered. He told them what he'd found out from Blimpey. He didn't bother repeating what they already knew; he just gave them a fast, complete report on the new bits and pieces. "So we can add Louise Mannion to the list of people Bremmer was blackmailin'."

"Was your source sure?" Ruth asked. "I've heard just the opposite, that Louise Mannion was the only real friend Bremmer had."

"My source is generally reliable, but anyone can be wrong," Smythe replied. "That's it for me as well."

Mrs. Jeffries looked at Ruth. "You found something?"

"Only what I just mentioned," Ruth said. "I had a quick word with Mrs. Ross today; she's on the finance committee for my women's group. She's known both Louise Mannion and Camilla Houghton-Jones for years. She claims that Camilla's dislike of Bremmer isn't recent; she's loathed him for ages."

"Did Mrs. Ross say why?" Mrs. Jeffries asked.

"She didn't know but what she was sure of was that Louise Mannion was the one Bremmer turned to when he was in any sort of trouble. Apparently, there have been times in the past when Anne Bremmer has literally locked her husband out of the house and he'd go to the Mannion home for the night. People have disliked Bremmer for years and the only reason he wasn't a pariah even amongst his own class was because Louise Mannion insisted he be included."

"Maybe he's been blackmailin' her for years," Smythe suggested. "Her own brother claims she pushed him into the water. What if Bremmer was holdin' that over her 'ead?"

"It's never been said that Bremmer was even there when Leonard almost drowned and even if he'd told Bremmer what he suspected, he wasn't certain. That's hardly grounds for blackmail," Ruth pointed out.

"Or maybe she genuinely cares about him," Betsy argued. "We've all known mean people that have that one friend who takes their part."

"Can I go now?" Wiggins glanced at the clock on the sideboard. "It's gettin' late." He paused a second, and when no one objected, he plunged straight in, telling them about his encounter with Hilda Jackson. "I'm not sure what it means," he finished, "but she was certain one of them flutes was missin' before the ball that night."

"It's a coincidence," the cook declared. "This case has been full of them and the girl is probably right, that Mr. Sherwood or someone else broke one and they'll not own up to it."

"I think it is all coming down to the flutes," Mrs. Jeffries murmured. "But we'll have a devil of a time making sense of it." She looked at Wiggins. "I want you to go back to the Wrexley tomorrow. You may have to speak to a number of your contacts there. There's a very specific question you need to ask." Without waiting for a reply, she told them what she'd learned from Dr. Bosworth. When she'd finished, she looked at Mrs. Goodge. "There's also a specific question we've got to get Barnes to ask as well. My memory isn't as good as it used to be so tomorrow before he gets here, I want you to remind me to have him ask who decided how the champagne was to be served."

She turned her attention back to the footman. "You'll need to be careful tomorrow, Wiggins. If my idea is correct, Constable Barnes and our inspector will be at the hotel."

CHAPTER 10

Mrs. Jeffries was waiting at the door when the inspector arrived home. She hung up his coat and bowler and ushered him down the hall to his study, all the while keeping up a steady stream of chatter. "I was afraid you were going to have another one of those dreadfully tiring days, sir. I'm so glad you're home at a decent hour. Mrs. Goodge has a nice pork roast in the oven but it's not quite done." She went to the liquor cabinet as he settled into his chair.

"That's fine, Mrs. Jeffries, I need to relax a few minutes before I have my meal. Today has been quite extraordinary."

"In what way, sir?" She handed him his glass and sat down.

"We seem to be making progress"—he frowned as he ran his finger around the rim of his glass—"but I'm not sure anything we've learned is actually helping me determine who murdered Stephen Bremmer."

"Nonsense, sir, you'll do as you always do; you'll let the facts and the gossip churn and bubble in the back of your mind, and at the last moment, you'll catch the killer. Now, tell me about your day."

"We had another word with Montague Pettigrew," he said. "It was awkward at first; one doesn't like to ask such questions but it was necessary." He stared at his sherry while he told her about their visit to Pettigrew's flat. "But speaking with him wasn't the worst of it, Mrs. Jeffries. Then we needed to reinterview Camilla Houghton-Jones. Luckily, she herself provided the opening one needed to broach the subject. Constable Barnes was deliberately blunt, and that appeared to annoy her so much she admitted she hated Stephen Bremmer and was glad he was dead." He sipped his drink as he told her the rest of the details about their visit. "She claimed that Bremmer had his hand in 'everyone's pockets.' "

"Just as you thought, sir," Mrs. Jeffries said.

"After that, we went to the Bremmer household and spoke to the staff and Mrs. Bremmer."

"You interviewed all the servants?"

"No, one of them had her afternoon out so we didn't get to speak with her, but if need be, I'll send Constable Griffiths along tomorrow to take her statement." He told her everything that had transpired at the victim's home. "It was unnerving to see Mrs. Bremmer; I think she had a bit of a breakdown."

"Either that or she's a very good actress," Mrs. Jeffries suggested. She was more interested in what Barnes had found out from the servants. "What did you do then, sir?"

"We went to the station. Constable Barnes wanted to write up the statements as quickly as possible and I wanted to go over the ones we'd previously taken." He took another sip, his expression thoughtful. "You know, I do believe you're correct, this case might be starting to make sense. Perhaps by tomorrow morning my 'inner voice,' as you call it, will show me precisely what I need to do next."

Mrs. Jeffries was sitting at the table drinking tea when Mrs. Goodge and Samson came into the kitchen. She stopped by the archway.

"Goodness, you're up early." The cook yawned. "You've figured it out, haven't you?"

Mrs. Jeffries shrugged modestly. "I'm not certain. It'll very much depend on what happens today." She was fairly sure she'd done it, but she could still be wrong. That had happened before so she was always wary of being overconfident about her conclusions.

"Nonsense, you always say that," Mrs. Goodge said as she and the cat headed down the back hall to the wet larder. She was back a few moments later with a covered bowl of leftovers. Samson began meowing—screaming, really—as they crossed the kitchen to his food dish. Picking up his dish, she put it on the counter, yanked off the tea towel covering the leftovers, and scraped a generous helping into his dish. With a grunt, she bent down and Samson shoved his head into the food before the dish hit the floor. She joined Mrs. Jeffries at the table. "Now, what do we need to do today?"

The cook was curious, but she knew there was no point in badgering the housekeeper to identify the killer until she was ready. "By the way, here's your reminder. You wanted Constable Barnes to ask the hotel who determined how the champagne was to be served." Fearing she'd forget to remind Mrs. Jeffries, she'd written this down and put the note by her spectacles before going to bed last night.

"Thank you, and we also must tell the constable everything the others have found out."

"That's a lot to tell. Let's hope the constable gets here early."

Constable Barnes did indeed get there early. He listened carefully as they shared what they'd learned and then he added a detail or two from his own recollections.

When both sides had finished, Mrs. Jeffries took a deep breath. "Constable, there's two things I think might be helpful today. One, I suggest you interview Mr. Sherwood at the Wrexley and ask him two questions." She told him specifically what he needed to find out.

Barnes looked perplexed. "Alright, I think that might be possible. Is that all?"

She told him the last question he should ask the catering manager. "That should be it, Constable. By the way, Wiggins will be there today as well, so if by chance you happen to see him, can you do your best to ensure the inspector doesn't?"

"I'll try my best." Barnes drained his tea and got up. "Let's hope your questions help us get this one solved," he said as he headed for the back stairs.

The morning meeting was short. Mrs. Jeffries relayed the information she'd received from the inspector and Constable Barnes. When she'd finished, she paused for a moment, trying to think how to word the various requests she was about to make. She turned to Wiggins first. "I know I told you to go to the Wrexley today and I still want you to, but there's another errand I'd like you to do after that." She gave him his instructions for the hotel and then told him the rest of what she needed.

Wiggins looked doubtful. "It might not be possible to do both, Mrs. Jeffries. If our inspector and Constable Barnes are at the Wrexley, it might be ages before I can find someone who was even on duty that night. It's not like I can just go strollin' in and get one of the maids to chat."

"You have a point." She thought for a moment. "But I need someone to go to Pierce and Son. It's important we know what time that board meeting ended."

"But we already know that," the cook protested. "James Pierce said it ended at around four that afternoon."

"I know what he said, but I want to know what time the staff left. Specifically, were they all gone by the time the meeting was over?"

Wiggins still looked a bit wary, but he nodded. "Right, I'll do my best. I'll ask Ellen, she ought to know."

"Make certain she can confirm when all of them were gone." She looked at Luty. "Can we use Jon today? I know he's not part of this, but he has helped in other cases."

Luty narrowed her eyes. "Yup, but why can't I do whatever it is?"

"Because I need you to do something else and Jon's task requires discretion and the ability to move quickly if people in the Cory neighborhood start getting suspicious of a stranger hanging about. I want him to keep a watch on Elise Cory's home and to let us know immediately if anyone comes to visit her or if she leaves her home. Tell him to try to avoid being noticed by the neighbors. But it's a fairly busy area, so he ought to be alright."

"He's a clever one; he can do it," Luty said proudly. She'd taken him in years earlier and given him a job as a footman, but she made certain he wasn't going to be a servant all his life. "He's going to University College in Bristol to study medicine. That boy's goin' to make a fine doctor."

"I'm sure he is." Mrs. Jeffries added some additional directions and then turned to Phyllis. "You're going to have the most difficult time of it. It might not even be possible."

Her eyes widened and she licked her lips. "What is it?"

"I'm not sure I should ask you to do this . . . there might be another way." Mrs. Jeffries hated to see the fear that had flashed across Phyllis's face. What if she was wrong, what if she sent the poor girl over there and it all fell apart?

Phyllis sat up straighter. "Go on, tell me. I'm not the little scaredy-cat I used to be, I can do whatever is needed."

"You weren't ever a scaredy-cat," Betsy protested.

"Don't be daft. You've always done your part," Wiggins added, even though it wasn't true. When she first arrived she avoided doing anything, including helping with their cases for fear of losing her job.

"You're bein' too hard on yourself, lass," Smythe said softly.

Phyllis gave a nervous laugh. "You're all being very nice, but when I first arrived, I was too frightened to say boo to a goose in a barnyard."

"As well you should be," Luty said. "Geese are mean."

"But I'm not that girl anymore, and one of these days, I might really be a private inquiry agent. There's no law that says only men can have that job." She looked at Mrs. Jeffries. "Tell me the rest."

"Can you go back to the Mannion home? Only this time, don't

hang about in the front of the house. Go down the stairs and ask to see Marie Parker. You've already told her you're a private inquiry agent, so keep up the pretense with her but tell whoever answers the door that you've an urgent message from Marie's family and you must speak with her."

"What then?"

"Then I want you to convince her to give you the serviette Marie dug out of the umbrella stand."

Ezra Cutler, the day manager at the Wrexley Hotel, ushered the two policemen into his small, cluttered office and then shut the door. He was a short, stocky man with curly brown hair. "I do hope you are here to give us good news." He smiled hopefully as he went behind his desk. "Would you like me to get you some chairs?"

"No, that won't be necessary," Witherspoon said quickly. "We won't be taking much of your time."

"Excellent, then you've made an arrest."

"I'm afraid not. We're here to have a word with Mr. Sherwood."

Cutler's face fell. "The catering manager?"

"That's right, is he here now?"

"He is in the dining room with the head chef going over menus."

"Oh good, that sounds as if business is picking up," Barnes said.

"Not really. We had to cut our rate in half to get the business and they still haven't given us the deposit." He sighed and got up. "Come along, then. I'll take you in."

He took them into the dining room, introduced them to Elliot Sherwood, and then disappeared, muttering under his breath as he walked away.

The chef nodded politely, picked up his menus, and went to the kitchen.

Sherwood waved them into chairs. He appeared to be in his late twenties with black hair, brown eyes, and a huge mustache. "What can I do for you, gentlemen?"

"I'm sure you know why we're here," Witherspoon said.

Sherwood interrupted. "Would you like tea or perhaps coffee?"

"We're fine, thank you," the inspector continued. "As I was saying—"

"You're here about the murder," Sherwood interrupted again. "Of course, why else would you be here? But I was gone by the time the ball started."

"We know that." Witherspoon hoped the fellow would keep quiet for a few moments. "We're not concerned with what happened that evening; we'd like to ask you about the plans for the ball."

"Plans?" he repeated, his expression confused. "I don't understand."

"All you have to do is answer our questions, sir," Barnes said. "How long have you been a catering manager?"

"This is my second position. I worked for the Toplin Hotel in New York for three years. That's where I met the Wrexleys. Charming couple. They really were impressed with the way the Toplin used its facilities all the time, even when the hotel business was slow."

"So you've a lot of experience in planning large events," the constable continued. "Is that right?"

Sherwood nodded eagerly. "Absolutely."

"Is it usually the custom to have the champagne glasses on the table when there is going to be a toast?" Witherspoon asked.

"That depends on the size of the function." Sherwood stroked the top of his mustache. "For large parties, we generally like to bring the glasses in with the bottles on large trays, it's faster that way. There are usually two waiters per table, one to fill the glasses and one to hand them to the guests."

"But this time, the champagne flutes were already on the table, correct?" The inspector glanced around the huge dining room.

"That's right. I suggested that we bring the flutes in on trays but the host, Mr. Pierce, insisted we have them on the tables and the waiters go from guest to guest to fill the glasses. I explained to Mrs. Mannion—she's the one who conveyed Mr. Pierce's instructions—that it would be much faster doing it my way, but she said he was adamant they be on the table with the cutlery and the serviettes. The china was on the buffet table—odd, but that's the way they wanted it."

"On the day of the ball, I understand Mrs. Mannion came to ensure that everything was done as Mr. Pierce wanted, right?" Barnes put down his pencil.

"That's right. She was here about eleven o'clock that day and I showed her everything we'd be using that evening."

"Including the champagne flutes?" Witherspoon asked.

"Of course. I took her into the storage room and she examined the china, the cutlery, the linen tablecloths, and the flutes. She seemed quite pleased."

"At any time was she ever in there alone?"

He looked perplexed by the question. "Certainly not. I was with her the whole time. We don't allow guests to wander willy-nilly about the place. She examined a champagne flute and then asked me to show her where the two head tables would be placed. We went into the dining room and I pointed out where the tables and the musician's platform would be placed. She said that Mr. Pierce would be delighted with the arrangements and then she left."

Wiggins was so cold he couldn't feel his feet. He was in his usual spot across the mews so he could see if anyone came out the back door of the hotel. Hiding from the inspector hadn't been a problem—he'd come and gone hours ago—but if a waiter or a bellboy didn't show up soon, he'd not be able to get to Pierce and Son before they ruddy well closed for the day. He hoped Mrs. Jeffries knew what she was doing. To his way of thinking, she should have asked Constable Barnes to find out about the ruddy place cards.

The back door opened and Joey Finnigan rushed out and down the stairs. Once again, Wiggins raced across the road, catching up with the young man just as he came out of the mews. "Hello, remember me?"

Finnigan gave him a hard stare. "'Course I do, I saw you two days ago. What do ya want? I'm in a hurry. For once, they had me work late and I want to get home in time for a hot supper."

"Now don't be so mean. I bought ya a pint, the least you could do is answer a quick question. It's a right easy one as well."

They'd reached the corner. Finnigan stopped. "What is it?"

"The night of the ball, who put the place cards on the table?"

"How should I know? That kind don't introduce themselves to the staff."

"But you worked that night, right?"

"I told ya that already."

"Were you in the dining room when the place cards were put on the table? Did you see who did 'em?"

Joey stared at him doubtfully. "What kind of question is that? You said you're a reporter, why would your newspaper care about who put out the ruddy place cards?"

"I don't know why my guv wanted me to find it out." Wiggins was going to bluff it out. "Right, then, I'll tell ya the truth, sometimes my guv passes a few bits and pieces along to the police. You know, stuff we find out that the peelers don't know. In return, there's some detectives that owes him a favor, so they'll tip him off when there's been a murder or something important happening."

"That makes sense," Joey admitted grudgingly. "Explains why you show up so much faster than the rest of your lot."

"So did you see who did 'em?"

"I did. I'd just finished setting out the flutes and the cutlery. She was real polite, waited till I was done before she went to the table and set them out." He grinned. "I don't know her name, but she was a real pretty one."

Witherspoon stared out the window of the hansom cab as it made its way to the Ladbroke Road Police Station. "James Pierce strikes me as a very practical man, and that dining room is huge. Why on earth would he insist the glasses be on the table rather than coming out on trays, which, according to Mr. Sherwood, is a much faster and more efficient method, especially in such a large space?"

"I'm not sure it was Pierce who made that decision," Barnes said. "According to Sherwood it was Mrs. Mannion who claimed it was Pierce's idea. But he told us once he made the initial booking, he handed the arrangement of the details over to her."

"We must speak with Mrs. Mannion again," Witherspoon decided.

"Shouldn't we ask Mr. Pierce first?"

"We will, but I'd like to see what she has to say first. I want both of us to pay close attention to her reaction when we broach the subject. We'll go to Pierce and Son afterward."

"What are you thinking, sir?"

Witherspoon wasn't sure he could put it into words, but after talking to Mrs. Jeffries last night, he'd begun to sense that there was more to this case than just blackmail. "I think there's more to Bremmer's murder than we thought. Once we learned he was a blackmailer, we concentrated on that aspect."

"That's normal police procedure, sir. But I understand what you're saying; there's more to this than we know. There's something else, something ugly and mean just under the surface that we can't see yet."

"But we will," Witherspoon said confidently.

"Then let's hope we don't have to spend too long at the station," Barnes complained. "It's interruptin' this investigation just when things seem to be picking up a bit."

They'd been called back to the station to ensure the evidence and paperwork for the upcoming trial of a confidence trickster they had arrested were in order.

"Chief Inspector Barrows was adamant we do it today. Not to worry, though, it shouldn't take too long. Everything was done properly."

"True, and it'll give us a chance to have a word with Constable Griffiths. He was going to find out what he could about the deaths of Nora Pierce, Osgood Mannion, and even Bartholomew Cory."

"I thought we were going to speak to the mother about Mr. Cory?"

Barnes grinned. "I'm sure he did. He's clever and he was certain he could find a way to have a word with her when Mrs. Cory wasn't around."

"Are the others here yet?" Wiggins asked as he raced into the kitchen. "I've got news and it might be important."

"You're the first one back," Mrs. Jeffries replied. "What's happening?"

"I've just come back from the Pierce office and it's a good thing I got there when I did—they was gettin' ready to shut the whole place up. James Pierce let everybody go home early today because he and Elise Cory are getting married. They're takin' the night train to Glasgow Central from Euston Station."

"Married?" Mrs. Jeffries repeated. She said nothing as her mind frantically worked to assess the situation.

"What does this mean?" Mrs. Goodge demanded as she looked at the housekeeper.

But Mrs. Jeffries didn't answer her. She looked at Wiggins, her expression worried. "What did you find out at the Wrexley today?"

"What you wanted me to find out, the name of the person who put out the place cards. It was Louise Mannion, not one of the hotel staff. What's more, Joey Finnigan said that she took her sweet time doin' it. He noticed because he'd just put the flutes, the cutlery, and the serviettes on the table but he'd forgotten the saltcellar. He was hangin' about, tryin' to put the ruddy thing out when she turned and asked him what he was doin', and when he said he needed to put something on the table, she told him he could do it later."

"Oh dear." Mrs. Jeffries turned to Mrs. Goodge. "How long ago did Phyllis leave?"

"She's there by now. It was fifteen minutes ago and the Mannion home is only a ten-minute walk from here. Why? Is something wrong?"

"What do ya mean? What are you talkin' about? Didn't Phyllis go out this morning?" Alarmed, Wiggins looked first at the housekeeper and then at the cook.

"She didn't. We realized that she'd have a much easier time getting to Marie Parker when the kitchen was busy and both the cook and the housekeeper were occupied with dinner," Mrs. Jeffries replied.

Wiggins looked stricken with worry. "Cor blimey, Mrs. Jeffries, Phyllis might be walkin' into a serpent's den. There's somethin' wrong with that lady. Joey Finnigan claimed the way Louise Mannion looked at him scared him to death."

"Let's not jump to conclusions or anticipate the worst. Louise Mannion is only a threat to Elise Cory and James Pierce. We don't know that Phyllis is in any danger."

But she knew as soon as she said the words that they were wrong. She'd miscalculated and now an innocent young woman might find herself in harm's way. "Oh dear Lord, go and bring her back, Wiggins. Hurry, I'll never forgive myself if anything happens to her."

Phyllis stood on the corner, far enough away from the Mannion house not to be noticed but close enough so that she could see it clearly. A telegraph boy stood on the door stoop; he'd just handed a housemaid a telegram. The door closed and the lad turned and hurried off.

She wondered if she ought to wait a few moments before going ahead with their plan. Telegrams often brought news, sometimes good, sometimes bad, and for their idea to work, the household servants should be doing their normal routines. But telegrams were so common these days that it probably wasn't anything important. Besides, she told herself, you don't have all day. Get it done so you can get back in time for the meeting. She crossed the road, moving slowly and keeping her spine ramrod straight. You're a private inquiry agent, she told herself, and you're investigating a terrible crime. In one sense, it was true she was sort of a private detective, only she didn't get paid for it. Not yet anyway. But one day she would. She could see it now: She'd have her own office and dozens and dozens of clients lining up for her services. Her confidence soared as the image of a sign reading PHYLLIS THOMPSON, PRIVATE AND DISCREET INQUIRIES popped into her head.

She was now opposite the walkway. But she didn't want to let go of her fantasy, so she took a few moments to let the images drift through her mind. Her office would be lovely, with a huge rosewood desk and original paintings done by grateful clients on the walls. Her secretary, a woman, would be in the outer reception office, typing up reports and invoices and making tea for distraught women seeking to find missing children. Oh, she could see it now. She'd be doing good for the world as well as making money. The clatter of horses' hooves shattered her reverie as a hansom came racing around the corner. She started to step off the pavement but stopped when the cab pulled up in front of the Mannion house. She moved back against the trunk of a tree. Phyllis jumped in surprise as several loud bangs blasted the quiet street.

Then the screaming started.

Someone grabbed her arm and jerked her behind the trunk. "It's the inspector and Constable Barnes," Wiggins hissed in her ear.

Then everything began to happen at once. The front door of the house and the door of the cab opened simultaneously. Inspector Witherspoon and Constable Barnes poured out of the cab just as a housemaid ran out the front door. "Help, help," she screamed as two policemen charged up the walkway. "She's shot Mrs. Tingley!" The girl pointed to the house. "Hurry, hurry, she's shot Mrs. Tingley!"

Barnes and Witherspoon ran into the house.

"That's Marie," Phyllis whispered. "Let's see if we can find out what happened." She started to move, but Wiggins jerked her back. "Don't be daft. We can't be seen here."

Marie screamed again as Louise Mannion came up the servants' steps, shoved the housemaid out of her way, and then walked calmly to the cab. The driver stared at her, his expression confused, but she gave him a sweet smile and said, "Liverpool Street Station." She stepped inside and closed the door. Wiggins and Phyllis watched in horror as the cab pulled away.

"You get back to the house and tell 'em what's going on," Wiggins said. "I'll see if I can suss out what's 'appened 'ere."

"Be careful," she warned.

"I will," he promised. She sounded calm but he could see the panic in her eyes. He didn't like sending her off on her own, but he had no choice. "But you hurry now, get right to the house as fast as you can."

As soon as she was out of sight, he turned his attention to Marie Parker. She'd wandered out onto the pavement, her expression one of stunned surprise. Wiggins knew he was taking a risk, but he needed to know what happened. Stepping out from the shelter of the tree, he crossed the road, silently praying that the inspector would be occupied inside.

"Excuse me, miss." He kept his voice low and soft. "You look like you've had a fright. Are you alright?"

She looked at him. "Oh dear, yes, I'm fine. Oh my Lord, it's been awful, she shot Mrs. Tingley. The police are here, I don't know why they came, but thank goodness they did. Poor Mrs. Tingley wasn't doing anything, she simply wanted to show Mrs. Mannion the serviette, the one I found in the umbrella stand. But Mrs. Mannion was upset. It was the telegram, you see. She'd been looking forward to going to the director's luncheon tomorrow, she'd bought a new dress and everything, then she got the telegram saying it was canceled and that Mr. Pierce was going to Scotland with someone else."

Wiggins cast a quick look at the front door of the house and saw that it was partially open but no one was coming outside. That was good. "Who is Mr. Pierce?"

"The man Mrs. Mannion is sweet on. Mrs. Porter, she's the cook, told Beulah, she's the scullery maid, that Mrs. Mannion set her cap for Mr. Pierce years ago, but he married someone else." She giggled. "I shouldn't be saying all this to you, you're a complete stranger, but you've the kindest face. I'm a bit light-headed." She took several deep breaths. "Don't look so worried, I'm fine now."

Inside the house, Barnes found a housemaid that wasn't hysterical and sent her off to fetch a doctor. "You there"—he pointed at another maid, who was gaping at the wounded housekeeper—"bring me some clean linens." She just stood there. "Get me some clean linen before your housekeeper bleeds to death," he yelled.

She jumped, shocked into action by the harshness of his voice. "Yes, sir."

Witherspoon knelt down next to the housekeeper. She was propped against the drawing room door. The top of her black bombazine dress was soaked with blood. "Don't move, ma'am," Witherspoon instructed. "Constable Barnes has sent someone for a doctor. He'll be here any moment."

"I'm not dying, Inspector, Mrs. Mannion is a dreadful shot. She fired three times before she actually hit me." Mrs. Tingley smiled slightly. Her topknot was askew and her legs splayed out. "The bullet went through my shoulder. There's a lot of blood but I don't think this is fatal."

"What happened, ma'am?" Barnes asked as he knelt down on the other side of her.

"Mrs. Mannion shot me." She shook her head in disbelief. "I showed her the serviette and I told her I was going to have it laundered. I started to take it downstairs to the basket, when I heard her say, 'Give it to me now.' I thought she didn't understand what I'd just said. You see, the serviette has been missing since the day she had tea with Mr. Bremmer and she's been haranguing the household to find it ever since. I turned to her and I said, 'But you'll not want this, ma'am, it's filthy. I'll just have it properly cleaned. It'll be fine, ma'am, it's not ruined. I'll take it to the laundry basket.' I saw her lift her arm and then I realized she was holding Mr. Mannion's revolver. He kept it in his study. I didn't even know it was still in the house. I couldn't believe my eyes. She shot me."

"She shot you over a serviette?" Witherspoon asked.

Mrs. Tingley shook her head and the movement sent another spurt of blood out of her wound and onto the front of her dress.

“Where’s those linens?” Barnes bellowed.

“Here, sir, here, sir,” the maid cried as she ran into the room with an armload of white towels, stumbling as she reached the three of them.

The constable snatched one and placed it directly against the open wound. “I’m going to press down now and it’ll hurt, but we’ve got to try and stop the bleeding.”

“Go ahead,” she whispered.

“Mrs. Tingley, why would Mrs. Mannion shoot you over a serviette?” Witherspoon really didn’t understand.

“It weren’t just the serviette, sir,” the maid said. “She got upset when she saw the telegram that come.”

“What telegram?” Barnes demanded.

“The one that come a few minutes before she started shooting.” She got to her feet. “She took it into the study. I’ll see if it’s there.”

She disappeared down the hall and returned a few seconds later holding the telegram. “Should I give it to him?” She pointed at Witherspoon.

“Thank you.” The inspector grabbed the paper, read it, and then read it again. He looked at the constable. “It’s from James Pierce. I’ll read it to you.”

Must cancel our luncheon for tomorrow.
Elise and I are going to Scotland tonight.
We’re finally getting our chance.

“Where’s the serviette now?” Witherspoon glanced around the room, but didn’t see it.

"She took it with her," the maid said. "I saw her stuff it into her coat pocket. She put the gun there, too."

"Coat pocket? What does that mean?" Witherspoon looked at Mrs. Tingley. "Where is Mrs. Mannion now?"

"She's gone." Marie Parker stepped into the room. "She got into the cab and told the driver to take her to Liverpool Street Station."

"Liverpool Street Station," the inspector repeated. "Gracious, she's making a run for it."

Mrs. Tingley closed her eyes and moaned softly.

"Where's that ruddy doctor?" Barnes eased up on the pressure and was relieved when the wound didn't immediately spurt more blood.

They heard a commotion at the door as two constables followed by a man carrying a medical bag hurried into the room.

Mrs. Tingley opened her eyes and looked directly at Witherspoon. "She said something right after she shot me. She said, 'I'm not letting her have what's mine. Not this time.' "

"She's not making a run for it," Witherspoon said as Barnes got to his feet to make room for the doctor. "She's going to James Pierce's office."

The others were all there when Phyllis raced into the kitchen. "Louise Mannion just shot her housekeeper," she announced. "Wiggins is still there and he's going to try and find out what happened."

There was a stunned silence. Ruth, who was closest to Phyllis, saw that her face was pale and her lips trembled. She got up and put her arm around Phyllis' shoulder. "Sit down and tell us what happened."

"I need a cup of tea." Phyllis felt tears flood her eyes and she blinked hard to keep them back. "It was a bit shocking, hearing those gunshots."

"You need a drink," Luty said. "People shootin' each other ain't ever nice and it ain't ever something anyone needs to get used to hearin'. Whatever happened will keep a few minutes; you knock back some of Mrs. Jeffries' nice brandy and then you can tell us what's what."

Mrs. Jeffries had already gone to the sideboard and pulled out the bottle she kept in the bottom drawer. She grabbed a glass out of the top cupboard and poured a healthy shot. "Drink this," she ordered as she handed it to Phyllis.

Just then, they heard the back door open and a lanky, dark-haired lad raced into the kitchen. He skidded to a halt, his gaze fastened on Luty. "Sorry, ma'am, I didn't mean to come bursting in without so much as a by-your-leave, but you told me to get here lickety-split if Mrs. Cory did something and she did."

"Come on in, Jon." Luty motioned him closer. "You know everyone here, so let's not waste time; things are heatin' up. What happened?"

"I was standin' watch, just like you told me, and then a housemaid came out and went down the road. She brought back a hansom cab, told him to wait, and then went back inside. A few minutes later, the maid and another lady—I'm sure it was Mrs. Cory because you said she was supposed to be real pretty and this lady was one of the prettiest I've ever seen—came out. The maid was carrying a carpetbag. Mrs. Cory got into the cab and the maid told the driver to take her to Liverpool Street Station."

"Why Liverpool Street Station?" Ruth murmured.

"She's going to see James Pierce," Mrs. Jeffries explained. "The Pierce and Son business is just across the road from the station. If my suspicions are correct, I think the two of them are going to elope to Scotland. From Liverpool Street they can take a local train to Euston and get the night coach to Glasgow."

"I'm better now." Phyllis smiled self-consciously and put her glass down. She told them exactly what had happened at the Mannion house. "I wanted to talk with Marie, to find out what happened inside the house, but Wiggins said I needed to let everyone know about the shooting and that he'd try to have a word with Constable Barnes and then he'd come home."

"I wonder why the inspector and Constable Barnes showed up?" Betsy asked.

Mrs. Jeffries thought about it for a moment and then she shook her head. "I expect we'll have to wait until Wiggins gets here."

"Should Smythe and I go to the Pierce office?" Hatchet asked.

"Not yet." Mrs. Jeffries looked at the clock. "Let's give Wiggins a few more minutes to get back."

"Uh, Mrs. Crookshank, can I sit down? I've been on my feet most of the day." Jon looked at the empty chairs.

"Have a seat and help yourself to some food." She gestured at yesterday's leftover mince tarts and the plate of bread slices.

"Have some tea as well. We've plenty." Mrs. Goodge poured him a cup as he took the vacant seat next to his mistress.

"We might as well finish our meeting," Mrs. Jeffries announced. She looked at Smythe. "Did you have any luck?"

She'd asked both Smythe and Hatchet to find out the same piece of information.

"Sorry, I tried a couple of sources but couldn't find it out." He cast a quick, worried frown at the clock. "What's takin' Wiggins so long?"

"He'll be here soon, I'm sure," Mrs. Jeffries said quickly. "Hatchet?"

"Sorry, none of my sources knew, either."

"Why is it so important to know who was with Leonard Lyndhurst when he died?" Ruth asked.

"Because Mrs. Jeffries thinks that Louise murdered him." Betsy looked at the housekeeper. "Don't you?"

"I do, I think she tried to kill him when he almost drowned," she said.

"But she was just a child herself," Ruth exclaimed. "Leonard was older than she was and he was, what, twelve or thirteen when he almost died . . ." Her voice trailed off as they heard a knock on the back door.

Betsy leapt up and ran to the back door. "Davey, what are you doing here?"

"Wiggins sent me, Miss Betsy." Davey's thin, reedy voice could be heard in the kitchen.

"Come along, then." Betsy ushered him in.

Davey was now about ten or possibly eleven years old. He was a street lad who hung around the local railway stations picking up a few coins carrying packages for shoppers or taking messages to and fro. He'd liked coming to the Witherspoon household; they always gave him something to eat. Today was no exception and his thin face lighted up as he saw Mrs. Goodge loading a plate with mince tarts and brown bread. Even better, if he didn't eat everything they put in front of him, they wrapped it up so he could take it home for his sister's supper.

"Come in and have a quick bite to eat, Davey." The cook pointed to a spot next to Jon. "Lads your age are always hungry."

"Ta, Mrs. Goodge." Davey pulled out the chair and sat down.

"But before you eat, why don't you give us Wiggins' message?"

He surveyed the faces around the table and grinned, not in the least put off by being among so many adults. "Wiggins told me to say the housekeeper was shot because of the serviette and that Mrs. Mannion has gone to the Pierce office. He's going there now and he wants Smythe and Hatchet to come as well, but he told me to tell 'em to be very careful. She's still got her gun."

CHAPTER 11

Phillip opened the door to James Pierce's office and stuck his head inside. "Mrs. Cory is here, sir," he announced.

James pushed the ledger to one side, got up from his chair, and came around his desk. "You're finally here," he exclaimed as Elise Cory stepped into the room. "I was beginning to think you'd changed your mind."

"I haven't." She smiled and went to him, holding out her gloved hands toward him. "But are you sure? This is a big step for both of us and it's so sudden. What will people think? James, I don't want to do anything that might hurt your business, and you know how conservative people can be."

He clasped her hands and pulled her close. "Don't be silly, you're more important to me than anything. Neither of us will concern ourselves with what other people think. Life is too short to deny ourselves a chance at happiness."

Phillip cleared his throat. "Uh, excuse me, sir, but I'll leave Mrs. Cory's carpetbag out here behind my desk. Everyone else has gone. Are you sure you don't want me to stay and sign in the Hansen shipment? It should be here soon."

"That won't be necessary." James laughed. "I'll see to the Hansen shipment. Just make certain to leave the lights on downstairs. We don't want Hansen's driver stumbling around in the dark."

"The bay doors are open, too, sir," he reminded him.

"Good. Now you go along home and have a wonderful evening. Make sure you take the spare set of keys with you when you leave. You'll be in charge for the next few days."

"Do you know when you'll be returning, sir?"

"I'm not certain. We want a few days to ourselves before we come back to London. You needn't worry, you'll do fine while I'm gone. Mr. Bingham can deal with any payment problems and Bobby Blankenship can handle anything that comes up in the warehouse."

"Yes, sir." Phillip started to close the door and then paused. "Congratulations to both of you, sir. The whole staff is delighted you're getting married."

"They're just happy I let everyone go early today," he teased.

Phillip laughed. "That, too, sir."

"Thank you, Phillip. I'll see you in a few days."

The secretary closed the door and picked up Mrs. Cory's carpetbag. Putting it behind his desk, he opened the top drawer and took out the spare brass ring holding the keys to the offices and the double bay doors. It wasn't dark as yet, but he left the two office lamps burning. Yet despite the illumination, the corridor was so dim he didn't see the figure standing just inside the office across the hall.

Louise Mannion waited till he'd disappeared down the stairs before she stepped out of her hiding spot. She stood in the doorway, staring at James' closed office door for a moment.

This was going to end tonight. He had to come to his senses. He had to understand that he belonged to her, she was entitled to him. She pulled the gun out of the inside pocket of her mantle and studied it intently. How many shots had she fired at Mrs. Tingley? She couldn't remember. How many bullets were in the gun? She didn't know that, either. But there was a bullet left for the arrogant Elise Cory.

"Darling, don't be such a worrier." James held the door open so Elise could go out first. "We've been parted for years and I'll not wait any longer to make you my wife. I know it's sudden but what we're doing is right. We belong together. We always have."

"You're right, of course, darl—" She stopped as she saw Louise. "What are you doing here?"

Louise held up the gun. "That's odd, I ought to be asking you that question. What are you doing here with my fiancé?"

"Fiancé?" Elise repeated. "Have you gone mad?"

"You're the one who is mad. He's mine. I've waited long enough, much longer than you have, and this time I'm keeping what's mine."

James kept his eyes locked on the weapon she held. "My Lord, Louise, what are you doing?"

"I'm getting rid of a problem," she replied calmly. "I usually drown my problems or use poison, but if need be, a gun will do as well."

"What does that mean?" James moved slowly, hoping to use his body as a shield.

But she was having none of it. "Stop. Don't move another step or I'll shoot."

"Louise, I don't know what you think, but you've made a mistake." He swallowed and tried to keep his voice steady. "We're not engaged. We never have been."

"Don't be absurd," she snapped. "You're mine. You have been for years. We've had a few obstacles along the way." She narrowed her eyes at Elise. "But you're mine and I'll not have her turning up to ruin things now, not when you finally realized how much you love me. Now, I don't want to do this here." She frowned thoughtfully. "But we're close to the river. Yes, that way I won't have to shoot. It made a terrible racket when I shot Mrs. Tingley."

Outside the office, Witherspoon grimaced and eased up another step. Barnes and Constable Evans were on the stairs behind him. They had heard her, too, and were already quietly moving back down to the warehouse.

"Louise, please," James pleaded. "I'll do as you ask. You're right, I do belong to you. Just let Elise go. There's no need for a gun."

"And then you and I will take the train to Scotland? We'll get married?"

"Yes, of course, that's exactly what we'll do."

Witherspoon could hear the desperation in Pierce's voice. He hoped Constable Griffiths would get here fast with more men. He glanced behind him and saw that Barnes and Evans had reached the bottom and were waiting for him. He eased down another step, then another.

She laughed, but there was no real mirth in the sound. It was a harsh cackle of a lunatic and it sent chills down the inspector's spine.

"Do you think I'm a fool, James? You'll only want me once she's dead, that's always the way it's been. She's bewitched you just as she did eight years ago, but I took care of her then and I'll take care of her now."

"You put Bremmer up to it, didn't you?" Elise charged forward but James blocked her with his arm. "You had him tell me those awful lies about James."

"Of course, but the best part was that you believed them." She shrugged. "It was so easy. I knew you'd leave. I knew you'd been offered that post as a governess. I didn't tell Stephen that part; he just wanted you to be his mistress. It didn't even cost much money, he did it for twenty pounds. I had to make sure you disappeared. Father had promised that if I went to Europe for six months, he'd let me marry James."

"What did Bremmer do?" James demanded.

"Don't concern yourself with him. He's dead and it's all in the past. Now come along, let's get on with it."

Witherspoon reached the bottom as they heard the movement of footsteps coming their way. The three policemen hastened into the warehouse. The inspector blinked to get his eyes to adjust to the light and surveyed the huge space, hoping to see a spot that might give them an advantage.

But he realized they were running out of time. The warehouse was full but there was no place big enough to conceal all three of them. He pointed to a stack of tea chests on the outbound side of the aisle. "Get behind them and be at the ready," he whispered to Constable Evans.

Evans moved fast and ducked behind the wooden boxes. He dropped to his knees, trying to make himself as small as possible.

Witherspoon looked at Barnes, who nodded in understanding. The two men moved to the bottom of the staircase and flattened themselves against the warehouse wall. If they were lucky, Louise Mannion would be so focused on her captives, they might have a chance to disarm her.

Outside, Wiggins had met up with Smythe and Hatchet. The three of them were crammed into a narrow passageway across the road from the open bay doors.

"I got here just in time to see Mrs. Cory go inside," Wiggins said. "A few minutes later, Pierce's secretary came out but I've not seen 'ide nor 'air of Pierce. The staff has been gone since this afternoon."

"Did you see Louise Mannion go in?" Smythe turned and saw a wagon come around the corner.

"No, but I've got a feelin' she's in there. I saw the inspector, Constable Barnes, and another constable go inside, but I've not heard a peep."

"Why is the electric lighting still on if everyone's gone?" Hatchet murmured.

"We've got to get closer. We've got to see what's goin' on in there. That woman has a gun." Smythe shoved away from the brick wall he'd been leaning against. Just then the wagon pulled into the spot in front of the open bay door. The driver and another man jumped down, walked around to the back of the vehicle, and started untying the ropes holding their cargo.

"Cor blimey, this is getting worse and worse. Now those blokes are goin' to be in danger," Wiggins hissed.

Inside the warehouse, James and Elise had reached the warehouse floor. Louise, still holding the gun pointed at Elise's heart, stood on the bottom step. Elise stumbled backward, eyes widening as she spotted the two policemen, but she quickly shifted her gaze back to the gun.

Louise sighed. "It's too bad this place isn't right on the water, that would have been very convenient. Well, we'll just have to go for a little stroll." She stepped onto the floor. "Walk in front of me," she ordered. But just then she caught sight of the inspector and Constable Barnes. "What are you two doing here?"

"We're here to stop you from committing another murder." Witherspoon hoped to keep her talking long enough to think of a way to get that wretched firearm out of her hand. She was still standing with her back to the staircase. James Pierce and Elise Cory were in front of her, both of them mere inches away from the muzzle. Even if Constable Griffiths arrived with a whole horde of police, it might not stop a bloodbath. "Mrs. Mannion, why are you doing this?"

"Why?" She looked at him as if he were a half-wit. "I don't need to explain myself to you. You're no one important."

"Was Stephen Bremmer not important? I thought he was your friend." He'd come up with a plan. If he could focus her attention on him she might lower her guard long enough for them to stop her from pulling the trigger. As plans went, it wasn't particularly good, but it was the best he could do.

"He wasn't anyone's friend." She laughed again. "The idiot thought he could blackmail me. Me, can you believe it? He said he was going to tell James that I'd murdered Osgood. He was there that day and he said he had proof."

"Did he?" Witherspoon asked.

"Possibly, but that wasn't the point. I couldn't have him telling James I murdered my husband."

"You didn't want Mr. Pierce thinking you were a criminal?"

She snorted. "Don't be ridiculous, petty laws don't apply to people like me. We're above them. I just didn't want Stephen saying such horrible things about me. It makes me look common."

"So you poisoned Stephen Bremmer to keep him quiet."

"Yes. As I said, he wasn't important."

"I take it you think you are?" Witherspoon shot back. "You're not, you know."

Surprised, she gaped at him. "How dare you speak to me like that."

"You've just admitted you committed murder, Mrs. Mannion." Witherspoon noticed that Pierce was moving back an inch at a time and pulling Elise Cory with him. "That means you're nothing more than a common criminal and I shall speak to you accordingly. It's no wonder that Mr. Pierce has gone to great lengths to avoid you."

"I'm Louise Lyndhurst Mannion and this man"—she jerked her chin toward Pierce—"is lucky that someone such as myself would even consider him for a husband."

"But he doesn't wish to be your husband," the inspector pressed. She was now looking at him, their gazes locked on each other. "If he wanted you, you wouldn't have had to come here with a gun to try and force him to love you."

"He does love me." She took a step forward, waving the weapon as she moved. Pierce moved back farther, yanking Elise away from the madwoman, but not far enough for safety.

"Does he?" Barnes interjected. He'd realized what the inspector was up to, and though it was risky, there wasn't much choice in the matter. "If he loves you, why was he going off to marry someone else?"

She turned her fury on the constable, stepping close and shoving the barrel into his stomach. "He wasn't going to marry her. He was only pretending so he could have his way with her. Tell him, James, tell him you weren't really going to marry that little nobody."

James pulled Elise back another step. "I don't love you, Louise. I never did."

"That's a lie, a lie I tell you. You do love me, you're mine. I'm entitled to have you. I've waited long enough."

The driver of the wagon backed into the warehouse pulling a handcart stacked with two tea chests. "Oy, where do you want these?" he called. His back was to them so he couldn't see what was happening, but he had heard voices.

Just then, Constable Evans jumped up from his hiding place and hurled his nightstick, which crashed into the wall with a loud bang.

Startled, Louise gasped and turned first one way and then another, taking the gun with her and away from the constable's belly. Pierce shoved Elise to one side. "Run, Elise, run," he shouted as he leapt upon Louise, his hand grabbing for the gun. Barnes jumped into the fray as well, pulling on her arm as hard as he could. Witherspoon seized Louise's other arm, yanking her to the ground.

But she wasn't giving up without a fight. Screaming obscenities, she kicked and tried to get her teeth into Barnes' shoulder. The driver let go of the handcart and the tea chests crashed to the ground. One of them burst open, spilling its cargo of kitchen utensils onto the concrete floor. Constable Evans blew his police whistle and half a dozen policemen suddenly appeared. Barnes got his fingers around the gun barrel and, using all his strength, he wrestled it out of her hand but it slipped onto the floor.

Elise Cory kicked it to one side out of harm's way. She reached down and pulled James away from the thrashing woman. He stumbled backward but regained his feet. Two other constables rushed in and helped wrestle Louise Mannion away from the inspector and Barnes.

She sat on the floor breathing hard. Her mantle was torn, her elegant hat was flattened, and there was a huge smudge of dirt on her nose. But she wasn't in the least subdued. She turned and glared at Elise Cory. "This isn't over. He's mine."

Witherspoon got up and then extended a hand to Barnes, who was on his knees and struggling to stand. "Are you alright, Constable?"

"I am, sir. You?"

He nodded and said to the two constables holding her arms, "Get her on her feet, please."

They pulled her up and stood her in front of the inspector. "Louise Mannion, you're under arrest for the murder of Stephen Bremmer and the attempted murder of James Pierce and Elise Cory."

She started laughing. "You can arrest me, little man, but I assure you, people like me don't go to prison. I've got too much money and too many friends in high places."

"You're not the only one with rich, powerful friends," James Pierce snapped. "And if I have to, I'll spend every penny I have making sure you pay for your crimes."

She looked at him, her expression one of disbelief. "You can't mean that. You love me. I know it. I'm entitled to your love, it's mine."

"My God, you're a monster." He pulled Elise closer. "How the hell have you managed to hide it all these years? The only thing you're entitled to, Louise, is the hangman's noose." He looked at her with contempt. "And I'm going to ensure that you get it."

Betsy came back to Upper Edmonton Gardens and slipped in the back door. "It's only me," she called as she hurried up the corridor and into the kitchen. "I couldn't stand it, so I asked our neighbor to stay with Amanda."

"What if Smythe goes straight home instead of stopping here?" Phyllis asked.

"He won't and if he does, he'll find out I'm here." She sat down next to Ruth. "So, we've heard nothing then?"

"Not yet," Mrs. Jeffries said. "But it's not too late. It's just gone eight." She looked at the window over the kitchen sink. "Luty, I think that's your carriage that's just pulled up outside."

Betsy got up and raced across the room. "It's them, they're back."

"Should I make tea?" Phyllis asked.

"No, get out glasses instead," Mrs. Jeffries ordered as she headed for the back stairs. "I've a feeling that tonight we could all use a drink."

A few minutes later, Smythe, Wiggins, and Hatchet had joined the ladies and Mrs. Jeffries had handed out sherry or brandy to those who preferred it.

"Now that we're settled"—Betsy looked at the three men—"tell us what happened."

"We'll tell you what we know, but keep in mind, we don't know too many of the details because we couldn't see inside the warehouse," Hatchet explained. "But after some sort of altercation inside, Inspector Witherspoon and Constable Barnes escorted Louise Mannion out of the warehouse. She appeared to be under arrest."

"Don't be so stingy with the story," Wiggins chided the older man. "You 'eard what them poor deliverymen said. There was a bit of fisticuffs goin' on in the warehouse and the Mannion woman was fighting and shoutin' like a fishwife. But they got the gun away from her and put 'er under arrest."

"Now, Wiggins, we can't take anything that driver told us too seriously. He was only inside the place for a few seconds."

"Yeah, but we've got ears and we 'eard the commotion ourselves," Smythe interjected.

"What happened?" Luty demanded. "Give us the details."

"The details might need to wait till later," Smythe said. "We only overheard part of what 'appened tonight."

"Tell us what you do know before the inspector gets home," Luty warned.

Smythe and Hatchet reported what they'd seen and heard outside the warehouse while Wiggins relayed what had happened at the Mannion house after Phyllis had left.

When they'd finished, Wiggins looked at Mrs. Jeffries. "It's your turn now. How'd you figure out it was Louise Mannion who poisoned Bremmer?"

"She wasn't a suspect at first; as a matter of fact, at one point in the investigation, she appeared to be Stephen Bremmer's only real friend. But appearances can be deceptive." Mrs. Jeffries took a sip of sherry. "What led me to consider her was the time. It was all wrong. I'm no expert on poisons, especially arsenic, but I have done some reading on the subject."

"What do you mean, the timing was wrong?" Phyllis asked. She needed to understand.

"He shouldn't have died so fast," she explained. "Bremmer drank his champagne and within just a few minutes he was dead. Arsenic doesn't work that quickly; according to Dr. Bosworth, the fastest death that has ever occurred with an arsenic victim is two hours. But the postmortem showed that Bremmer died of arsenic poisoning. The only logical conclusion was Bremmer must have been poisoned prior to the ball as well." She took another sip of sherry. "Once we learned he was a blackmailer, the motive was obvious."

"Which means most of 'em at that table could 'ave done it," Wiggins said.

"True, so then I set about thinking of where he could have been poisoned. At first I thought it might have happened at his home. Anne Bremmer certainly loathed him and if, as we found out, she knew he was planning on leaving her, she'd never be presented at court."

"Still, that seems like a flimsy motive, doesn't it?" Phyllis said, her expression doubtful. "Taking a human life just so she could meet the Queen?"

"People have killed for less," Betsy said quickly. "Why did you decide it wasn't his wife?" she asked Mrs. Jeffries.

"When the evidence began to point to someone else, mainly Louise Mannion. Nothing we learned about Bremmer's movements in the days before he died indicated he'd had food or drink with any of the other suspects. But he'd gone to tea at Louise Mannion's and she'd also been present at the board meeting."

"Anne Bremmer could have poisoned him at home," Phyllis said.

"She could have, but the inspector specifically said that Mrs. Bremmer had no idea of his movements on the day he died. If she'd poisoned him, she'd have been certain to watch him ingest it. Furthermore, it was what you found out from Marie Parker that tipped the scales toward Mrs. Mannion."

"The serviette?"

"That's right. Her obsession with it went far beyond a penny-pinching mistress making her staff pay for breaking or losing household items. When I put that together with the other things Marie told you, Louise Mannion had to be the killer."

"What other things?" Luty asked. "Come on, tell us in detail. I want to know what I missed and you understood."

"Me, too," Phyllis added.

"It was what Louise Mannion did when she had Bremmer to tea the day before the murder. First of all, she sent Marie downstairs to change the silver jam pot for a china one. Some people believe that arsenic tarnishes silver."

"Is it true?" Ruth asked.

"I've no idea, it might be just an old wives' tale. But there was a woman in my village in Yorkshire who believed it, so it was possible that Mrs. Mannion did as well. Second, she split the scones before they were served to Bremmer. Marie claimed it was because she was cheap and she didn't want him eating all her expensive food, but I think she did it because she wanted him to eat as much as possible as quickly as possible. By spreading the cream on herself, it gave him ample time to slather them with strawberry jam and eat to his heart's content."

"That's where she put the arsenic," Phyllis cried. "Of course, that's why she wanted the serviette back. She used the serviette to scrape the uneaten portion of jam out of the pot. You'd not want leftover jam with arsenic in it going down to the kitchen; the servants would eat it. No one lets good food go to waste, especially when you work for a mistress who's stingy."

"That's right." Mrs. Jeffries nodded approvingly.

"If she scraped the jam into the serviette, why didn't she know what had happened to it?" Hatchet asked.

"Because Marie also told Phyllis that just before she was going to clear up the tea things, James Pierce unexpectedly arrived at the Mannion house."

"That's right." Phyllis nodded eagerly. "Marie said something like, 'She shoved me and the serving cart out of the drawing room so she could entertain him. But the serviette wasn't on the serving cart. Louise Mannion had it.' "

"He's her obsession," Mrs. Jeffries explained. "The moment he walked through her door, she couldn't think of anything else."

"But how did it get into the umbrella stand?" Betsy asked. "Aren't they usually by the front door?"

"I imagine she wadded the serviette up and shoved it into her pocket. Perhaps when she was seeing him out, she absentmindedly tossed it in the umbrella stand without realizing what she'd done."

"So the jam was Bremmer's first dose of arsenic?" the cook asked.

Mrs. Jeffries nodded. "That's right. She gave him his second dose the day of the ball at the directors' meeting." She glanced at Betsy. "Your chat with Mrs. Guthrie, Nicholas Parr's landlady, put me on that particular path."

"I don't see how?"

"Parr hated tea. He told Mrs. Guthrie that he'd planned on

putting his cup down on a windowsill and leaving it there. But Bremmer had already put his cup down and someone, a woman, picked it up and brought it to him. I'm sure it was Louise Mannion and I'm equally certain that cup contained arsenic. Poor Mr. Parr ended up dumping his tea in a potted plant because he was scared that if he put it down, she'd do the same to him. Not poison him, of course, but bring him his cup. What's more, she offered to clean up the tea things, an act that was completely out of character for her, so that Phillip, Pierce's secretary could leave early. But she only did it to make certain she cleaned out Bremmer's cup. It contained the arsenic. Remember, Ellen told Wiggins that Phillip was in a foul mood the day after the murder because he thought the teapot had been properly cleaned when it hadn't been and he ended up spilling cold tea on himself."

"How did she manage to poison him at the Lighterman's Ball?" Ruth sipped her brandy.

"She arranged it so that the glasses were on the table when everyone sat down. But earlier that day, she stole a champagne flute from the hotel when she was there that morning to ensure that everything was in order. Inspector Witherspoon reported that the catering manager was with her the entire time she was in the storage room, where the flutes were kept, but he could have easily turned his back for a moment, giving her the chance to snatch the glass. Once she got it home, she treated it with arsenic, and when she arrived at the ball, when she was putting out the place cards, she switched the treated glass for the one that was at Bremmer's place setting. She didn't even need the lights to go out in order to kill him."

"That's why she got so nasty with Joey Finnigan and told him to come back later with the saltcellar. She didn't want him hovering close by and seein' what she was up to," Wiggins added.

"What did she do with the glass that had been sitting in Bremmer's place?" Hatchet asked. "She had to put it somewhere."

"She probably put it down on a tray or a table or even the buffet table. Remember, she was in charge so it was to be expected that she'd be moving about, checking the tables and making certain everything was arranged as she'd instructed."

"I wonder why she shot Mrs. Tingley," Phyllis murmured.

"We'll find out once the inspector gets home," Mrs. Jeffries assured them.

"Speaking of which, we'd best get home to our little one," Betsy said as she and Smythe both got to their feet. "But we'll be here for our morning meeting to find out the rest of it."

"We'll be here as well." Hatchet helped Luty to her feet. "Come along, madam, it's late and you need your rest."

"If you don't mind, I'd like to stay until Gerald comes home," Ruth said after everyone else had gone.

"Of course, but he might be quite late," Mrs. Jeffries warned.

"No 'e won't." Wiggins put down the empty milk jug he'd taken to the sink. " 'E's just got out of a hansom."

Mrs. Jeffries hurried upstairs, and a few minutes later, the two of them returned.

"Wonderful news," she announced. "Inspector Witherspoon has solved the case."

"I didn't do it all on my own." He shrugged modestly. "Constable Barnes and a number of other officers did their part." He sat down beside Ruth. "How nice to see you. I'm so glad you're here."

Ruth knew precisely what to do. "I came by to invite you to

supper tomorrow night but when I heard you weren't home and it was so very late, I insisted on staying. I was a bit worried, Gerald. You do such a dangerous job and I wanted to know you were safe. Your household has been lovely, we've even had a glass of sherry."

"Would you like one, sir?" Mrs. Jeffries had already taken a glass out of the sideboard and pulled the stopper out of the bottle.

"I'd love one."

She kept chatting as she poured. "You do look tired, sir, but if it's not too much effort, can you tell us what happened tonight? You know all of us are so interested in your cases, especially this one."

"Yes, please do, Gerald, I'd like to hear as well," Ruth beseeched him. "Who killed Stephen Bremmer?"

"It was Louise Mannion." He nodded his thanks as Mrs. Jeffries handed him his drink and took her seat. "Luckily, we managed to keep her from murdering James Pierce and Elise Cory as well, but we didn't get to her home in time to stop her from shooting her housekeeper, Mrs. Tingley."

"Why would she shoot her housekeeper?" Mrs. Goodge exclaimed. She, too, knew what needed to be done.

Witherspoon took a sip and leaned back in his chair, both happy to be surrounded by the ones he now considered his family and enjoying the attention. "Let me start at the beginning." He told them about the interview with the catering manager. "It occurred to both Constable Barnes and myself that Pierce is a practical sort of fellow, so why would he want the champagne toast, a toast that was very important to him, served in such an inefficient manner? So we decided to have another word with Mrs. Mannion, just to clarify who precisely had made that decision," he continued. "Now, we'd received a message that we had to return to the station, so we were delayed getting to the Mannion home." He paused, his expression thoughtful. "Unfortunately, the interruption resulted in Mrs. Tingley being shot, but it also led to us catching the murderer."

"Another coincidence," Mrs. Goodge murmured. "Do go on, sir. This is like one of them stories by Mr. Doyle."

He told them everything that happened at the Mannion house. "Of course, we couldn't just leave Mrs. Tingley bleeding on the drawing room floor while we pursued Mrs. Mannion, so we were delayed again getting to the Pierce and Son warehouse. But I am happy to report that Mrs. Tingley's wound was minor and she'll be fine. When we arrived at the warehouse, I sent Constable Griffiths to Liverpool Street Station—there are always constables on duty there—and by this time, I'd realized how very dangerous Louise Mannion was and decided we needed more men. I was right, too, because she was getting ready to either shoot or drown Elise Cory."

"She couldn't make up 'er mind?" Wiggins asked.

"According to James Pierce's statement, she threatened to do both. But we only saw Mrs. Mannion threatening with the gun." He told them the rest of it, taking his time and sipping his sherry as he spoke. "But we managed to get the weapon away from her," he concluded, "and no more blood was shed."

"Gerald, Louise Mannion might have killed you. She's mad." Ruth was genuinely distressed.

Witherspoon patted her hand. "I was in very little danger, I assure you. She was more intent on killing Elise Cory."

"She hated her, didn't she?" Mrs. Jeffries said.

"Indeed. At the station she said that if Elise Cory hadn't existed, James Pierce would have loved her."

"Unrequited love has much to answer for." Ruth shook her head in disbelief.

"I don't think she loved James Pierce, I think she felt entitled to him. She felt entitled to anything she wanted. She actually said that Pierce ought to be grateful that someone like her would have him for a husband," Witherspoon said.

"Is she genuinely mad?" Wiggins asked. "I mean, they don't 'ang mad people, so maybe they'll just put her in one of them insane asylums."

"And she's rich, too," Phyllis added. "She'll have half a dozen solicitors working on her defense to make sure she escapes the hangman's noose."

"Yes, and after a few years, they'll quietly let her out so her family can put her in one of those fancy Swiss clinics where the rich keep their lunatics." Mrs. Goodge looked disgusted. "It's not fair. She ought to pay for her crimes."

"But one can pay for their crimes without losing their life," Ruth said. She wasn't sure how she felt about hanging people. Last month, she'd attended a lecture that questioned the morality and effectiveness of the death penalty.

"But it says in the Bible, 'An eye for an eye and a tooth for a tooth,' " the cook quoted as she crossed her arms over her chest.

"That's the Old Testament," Ruth argued, "not the New Testament. Nowhere in the Gospel does Jesus encourage personal or state vengeance. Besides, insanity is really a sickness, isn't it? Only of the mind, not the body."

"I don't think she's insane, at least not by the standards the courts use to determine sentencing." The inspector toyed with his glass, his expression pensive. "She'll also have the best legal help money can buy. But I'm not so sure she'll escape justice. James Pierce is also a rich man and he was so furious, he vowed that he'd make sure she hanged."

"I'm confused, sir." Phyllis looked at the inspector. "Why did Mrs. Mannion shoot the housekeeper?"

"She said that the 'stupid woman didn't move fast enough when she told her to give her the serviette,'" Witherspoon replied. "We found it in her pocket and took it into evidence. She poisoned Bremmer three times, that's why he died so quickly when he got the third dose in his champagne glass."

They discussed the case for a bit longer, all of them asking questions. Mrs. Jeffries noticed that both Phyllis and Ruth asked the inspector about matters they already knew and understood. She was grateful to them; it did help to mask the fact they'd all been working on the case as well.

Their morning meeting started the moment the inspector and Barnes went out the front door.

"Right, then." Smythe sat Amanda on Luty's lap and took his seat. "We're all ears, Mrs. Jeffries. Tell us what happened."

The housekeeper told them some of what they'd heard from the inspector, stopping to allow Phyllis, Mrs. Goodge, and Wiggins to add to the narrative. When she'd finished, she looked around the table. "Any questions?"

"I wonder if Bremmer was right and she had murdered her husband," Betsy asked.

"The inspector said she practically confessed to it," Mrs. Jeffries said. "But it was odd in the sense that the woman was more concerned with Bremmer spreading common gossip about her rather than having evidence she'd killed someone."

"I think she did it, and I think he did have evidence against her," Phyllis said. "I think she tried to murder her brother, too. As Luty would say, I'll bet she was madder than a wet hen when James Pierce pulled him out of the water."

"She was probably getting ready to spit nails, too." Luty grinned. "The woman seems to have had a real temper. But I don't think she was crazy, leastways not in the way any of us recognize. Nell's bells, she fooled people for years. But what I don't understand is why James Pierce up and married Nora, Elise's cousin."

"I can answer that." Betsy gave Smythe a quick grin. "He was hurt and angry. The woman he loved hadn't trusted him. She'd believed Bremmer's lies and disappeared out of his life." That very same scenario had once almost kept Betsy and her beloved husband apart.

"Furthermore, Nora supposedly resembled Elise, and by all accounts, he was a good husband to her," Mrs. Jeffries commented.

"Mrs. Jeffries." Phyllis looked at her curiously. "How did you know that James Pierce and Elise Cory might be eloping?"

"I didn't know for certain, but according to the inspector, Pierce was very protective of Mrs. Cory. If he thought she was involved in Bremmer's death, he might marry her to keep her from having to testify in court."

"And he was in love with her," Betsy added. "Maybe deep down he suspected Louise Mannion was insane and he wanted to protect Mrs. Cory from her. Sometimes we know things about people, but we're afraid to admit them to ourselves."

"Mrs. Mannion was good at fooling people," Hatchet murmured.

Mrs. Goodge sighed. "But you know the strangest thing about this case isn't that Louise Mannion was crazy enough to fool people, it was all the coincidences. Makes you wonder, doesn't it?"

Everyone looked at the cook. Finally, Mrs. Jeffries said, "Wonder what?"

"Those coincidences helped get this case solved. It makes you think that there's more to life than we know, that maybe, for all our bein' smart and clever, maybe there's something else guiding us."

"You mean like the hand of God," Ruth suggested.

Mrs. Goodge shook her head. "God's too busy to bother with coincidences, I think. No, sometimes I think there's other forces out there, things we can't understand that just occasionally lend us a helping hand."

Wiggins shrugged. "Well, whatever it is, this time, it 'elped us deliver the goods, didn't it?"

ABOUT THE AUTHOR

Emily Brightwell is the *New York Times* bestselling author of thirty-seven Inspector Witherspoon and Mrs. Jeffries books. Visit her website at emilybrightwell.com.